Barclay blinked away the stinging blood in his eyes . . .

. . . and struggled to sit ⟨...⟩ one in the circle of stat⟨...⟩ chair was either dead o⟨...⟩ outer circle of auxiliary ⟨...⟩ a panic, he crawled across the deck, under the smoke, looking for Melora.

"Data! What happened?" shouted Deanna Troi, staggering to her feet.

The android's fingers were a blur as he worked his console. "An unknown singularity has disrupted all of our systems and is pulling us into a rift. I am attempting to compensate."

They were jolted again, and Barclay was pitched forward onto his face. With relief, he found himself staring eye to eye with Melora. She appeared to be pinned to the deck. "I don't know what's happening!" she said with a groan. "My anti-grav suit isn't working."

"Not much else is working either," said Reg.

"You're bleeding," she said, reaching with difficulty for his face.

STAR TREK
THE NEXT GENERATION®
GEMWORLD

BOOK ONE OF TWO

JOHN VORNHOLT

POCKET BOOKS
New York   London   Toronto   Sydney   Singapore

An *Original* Publication of POCKET BOOKS

POCKET BOOKS, a division of Simon & Schuster Inc.
1230 Avenue of the Americas, New York, NY 10020

ISBN: 0-671-04270-X

First Pocket Books printing February 2000

10 9 8 7 6 5 4 3 2 1

POCKET and colophon are registered trademarks of
Simon & Schuster Inc.

Printed in the U.S.A.

For Dennis and Mel

STAR TREK
THE NEXT GENERATION®
GEMWORLD

Chapter One

MAMMOTH PRISMS AND SPINDLY SPIRES stretched across the pale blue sky, catching the sun in a ripple of rainbow shimmers. Stairlike forms seemed to stretch forever, crossing and weaving in an endless dance of structure and light. From a distance, the crystalline fingers and branches looked fragile, like coral growing in a fish tank. But at close range, the giant prisms were as solid as marble columns, and as smooth and dazzling as diamonds.

Dwarfed by the towering crystals were five young humanoids; they soared among the spires like birds flying through a forest. Sails billowed from their arms and legs to catch the convection currents, but the fliers mostly depended upon graceful acrobatics to propel themselves. Tandra, the team leader of the five youths, glided to a thick green monolith, tagged up like a swimmer making a lap turn, then bounded off in an altered direction.

Two young Elaysians followed her lead, bouncing off the same crystal and racing after her. The other two members of the science team took different angles at the big monolith and soared off in parallel trajectories. One of the boys rolled into a midair somersault, just having fun. This close to the core of the planet, crystals grew in profusion, so there were plenty of smooth surfaces for pushing off.

Tandra frowned, deepening the crease around her V-shaped forehead ridges. Once they reached the hollow core, she knew they would have to be more careful with their flight patterns. She glanced over her shoulder to make sure the robotic hover-platform was following them. At a discreet distance, the meter-long disc floated along, its small thrusters making minute course changes. Once they reached the core, Tandra knew they might need the platform, for a push-off or a roost.

Laughing and chatting, the five students soared from one spidery, crystalline structure to another, plunging deeper into the center of the unique planet. To the few visitors who came here, Gemworld looked more like the intricate skeleton of a planet, or a giant snowflake made of prisms. For the Elaysians, it was a crystalline aviary. For the other sentient races, Gemworld was what they made of it. All of the inhabitants knew it was a special place, even if very few of them had ever seen a conventional planet for comparison.

As Tandra flew through a stand of rainbow-hued prisms—old growth before the natural geometry had been improved by fractal models—she gaped at the exquisite beauty. She thought angrily about the outsiders who claimed that Gemworld wasn't a real planet. They pointed to its forcefields and lack of mass, thinking that such a place had to be artificial, despite its immense size. They simply didn't understand.

Although the crystals looked cold and foreboding, even with their uncanny beauty, they sheltered a surprising variety of life. What could an outsider know about that? Outsiders couldn't stay long enough to really appreciate Gemworld because the low gravity was harmful to most gravity-dependent species. Although humans' muscles were a dozen times more developed, they could never soar between the sparkling archways like Elaysians born and raised in this gossamer cage.

A clearing loomed on the far side of a thicket of crystals, and Tandra realized they were getting close to the core of Gemworld. At one time, it had been a molten, metallic mass like a conventional planetary core, but the Ancients had sacrificed it to fuel the crystal. Now the inhabitants were slowly rebuilding the core with new crystal growth, which was the reason for the students' outing today.

Despite the fact it was empty—or because of it—Tandra found the core of Gemworld an eerie place to travel. Since it was hollow and equidistant from the massive crystal constructs surrounding it, the core was the most weightless part of the planet. Only trace gravity was measurable here.

As they flew farther into the ancient heart of the planet and the old-growth crystal, the light became more refracted and eerie, as if the ancient ocean were still there. Tandra felt the weight of ages, how many ages nobody knew, except perhaps the Lipuls. And even they had gaps in their history. The sparkling hues of the upper levels had given way to rust, olive, and sage colors, and the weathered facets were striated from elements that hadn't assaulted them for millions of years.

Tandra could well imagine the great oceans that pummeled these prisms eons ago, when even the Lipuls and the Gendlii were single-celled animals. Gemworld had been young then. Now it was old. But it was still a planet, thought Tandra, despite its low gravity.

Glancing around, she noted that her friends gave little regard to their solemn surroundings as they soared and tumbled through a swooping archway. They were just a flock of young people on a field trip, thought Tandra, and she shouldn't judge them too harshly. Hovering so close to the birthplace of the planet always gave her a sense of history—and a chill—but today it seemed more eerie than usual.

"We'll hold up at the purple prism!" Tandra shouted to her comrades.

"Oh, we can make it across!" scoffed one of the boys, soaring past her.

"We'll hold up!" she shouted back. "I'm the team leader."

Tandra knew she couldn't do much if the others

disobeyed, but none of them wanted to get stuck out here in the wilderness. They wanted to measure the new stand, see if the fractal modeling program was working as expected, and get out of here. It was too lovely a day to be plodding through kilometer after kilometer of empty air. Although the outing had been fun so far, it had also been long, and the young Elaysians were impatient to return to their research base about four hundred prisms above them.

One by one, the students alighted softly on the ancient purple spire at the edge of the clearing. Tandra gazed into the hollow marrow of the crystal and could see its pulsing gel center. It was a sight she always found reassuring, because it meant that Lipuls probably lived within the marrow. Before the students lay a wide expanse of nothingness, broken up by little islands of discarded equipment, dust, and debris, all of it floating uselessly. In the distance, the edge of the crystal growth shimmered like a mirage.

"How much farther?" asked Lucio, the cutest of the boys, with his slight frame and rare dark hair.

"I'll find out." From her backpack, Tandra took a small handheld device and turned it on. She waited a few seconds until the positioning device communicated with the shell that circled the planet and fixed their current position. As the students hovered around her, Tandra punched in the coordinates of their destination.

"About two hundred prisms." Tandra took a bit of ground crystal from her pocket and tossed it into the air to check the air currents. Now she knew what kind of arc to take to stay on course. "We can cover it in an hour if we get good jumps. Everyone, take a drink, because there won't be time to stop."

Taking her advice, the young Elaysians pulled out sip tubes and sipped from water bladders built into their backpacks. One by one, they used the hovercraft to crouch on the rough-hewn monolith then bound off into the wide-open wilderness. Strung out like a line of migrant birds, the Elaysians soared gracefully across the hollow core of Gemworld.

Tandra realized she would have to rely heavily on the positioning device, so she took it out of her backpack and slipped the strap around her neck, letting it float behind her. A quick glance assured her that the rest of the team and the hover-platform were following dutifully behind, then she double-checked to make sure they were on course. Finally satisfied that they would reach their destination in due time, the team leader spread her sails to catch the prevailing air currents.

It didn't take long for her to realize that something was wrong. Clumps of old mining equipment, which she used for landmarks, never materialized. Tandra checked the device hanging from her neck and discovered that they were considerably off course. That was odd. Tandra had always been the best flier in her class, as demonstrated by her promotion to team leader. Flying on course came naturally to her, but not today. Not down here in the bowels of the planet.

The dimness was more disturbing than usual, as if something were cutting off what little sunshine filtered down to the core. It was almost as dark as twilight, which was the closest they ever came to having a night on Gemworld. The air smelled dry, chalky, hotter than usual. Tandra felt a nervous prickling on her white skin, and her triangular forehead ridges deepened.

"Lucio!" she called. "We're going to stop, and I want you to check the tricorder."

"Why stop?" he responded. "We're making great time!"

"We're off course," she answered. "I want to know why."

A laugh came from Honroj, who was flying closely behind Lucio. "Could it be that our team leader is fallible?"

"Could be," she answered. "I hope it's that simple."

Lenora, who looked enough like Tandra to be her sister, caught a gust in her sails and swooped over Tandra's head. "If we stop," she complained, "we'll never get up to this pace again."

Several of the others shouted in agreement, but Tandra had her mind made up. And she wasn't in a mood to argue.

"Aid me," she ordered the hover-platform. Thrusters kicked on, and the small disc-shaped drone cruised to her side, letting her grab ahold of its low handles. She worked the control panel and stopped the platform, also stopping herself. The other students cruised ahead for some distance, but they soon unfurled backsails and began to float. Tandra noted how long it took for them to slow down, and she also saw something in the distance, something that shouldn't have been there.

She fumbled in her backpack for a pair of lenses, which she pulled over her eyes. At once, the empty distances evaporated, and she could see the apparition ahead of them. It appeared to be a cluster of crystals, where none should be, growing in unruly profusion. Even more disturbing was the color of the new growth: dark and cancerous.

It has to be a mistake, thought Tandra, *a trick of the dim light.* Things looked funny down here, where distance couldn't be judged by the ubiquitous crystals. Gripping the hover-platform, the young Elaysian put the conveyance into forward and cruised toward her friends. "Link up!" she shouted. "We're checking something out!"

"What?" came one response.

"Says who?" asked another.

She ignored the questions and kept cruising toward her friends, letting the platform do all the work. In a maneuver which they had performed since infancy, the Elaysians drifted together and linked hands. They were still grumbling about the unplanned stop when Tandra snagged Lenora's hand and towed the others behind her like a chain of paper dolls.

When she was certain the link was solid, Tandra increased speed until they were clipping along briskly. She had no spare hand to hold lenses to her eyes, but she could see the cluster of dingy crystals looming ahead of them. *It must be huge.* The others could see it, too, and they had stopped grousing. In fact, a worried hush had fallen over the team because none of them had ever seen a stand of crystals that looked anything like this one.

"What is it?" breathed Lenora.

"I don't know," admitted Tandra. Normally they would have released hands by now to fly individually, but there was an urgency to their mission. In the face of this unknown threat, it felt safer to hold onto each other.

As they drew closer, Tandra could see the nourishment strands hanging like spiderwebs around the ragged cluster. The strands stretched into the vastness, connected to distant relays. But who would feed this monstrosity?

"Is somebody growing *that?*" asked Lucio, voicing the thought on everyone's mind. "Is it an experiment?"

"It's not in the logs," answered Tandra. "Nor on any chart I've ever seen."

"Who would claim it?" asked Honroj. No one could answer his question, and the students fell back into an uneasy silence as they soared in unison through the deepening gloom.

With every passing moment, the mass of stunted, deformed crystals loomed larger and more foreboding—like an icy meteorite with spikes. Tandra almost ordered the group to turn around and flee from the anomaly; but they were training to be scientists, and scientists didn't run from the unknown. They would find a logical explanation for this aberration, she told herself. It had to be a failed experiment or a terrible accident. The young Elaysian didn't want to think about what it really looked like—a part of Gemworld's heart that was rotting from within.

Tandra cut the power on the hover-platform, and the students glided slowly into the shadows of the jagged cluster. Seen up close, the crystals were even more alarming than seen from a distance; they were twisted, broken, and streaked with imperfections. There were no fractal modeling programs at work here, no careful stimulation and feeding of the crystal—there were only rampant, obscene growth. Tandra shuddered, thinking that no power on Gemworld was capable of mutating the crystal to such a degree.

As soon as they stopped drifting, Lucio pulled a tricorder from his pack and began to take readings. A look of horror flashed across his handsome face.

"What is it?" she asked.

"Thoron radiation," he answered. "Enough to cause some damage. We've got to get out of here!"

"Not until we've taken a sample of it," said Tandra with determination. From her pack, she removed a small hammer and chisel. Even without being told about the radiation, she could sense danger permeating the dark growth.

Pushing off from the platform, Tandra drifted toward one of the largest, most deformed prisms. It looked like a blackened tree, burned in some monstrous fire. Tandra felt the odd sensation of gravity, and she wondered if these mutant crystals were somehow more dense than the typical variety. Her friends hung back. They obviously wanted to help, but were paralyzed with fear and indecision, and she couldn't really blame them. They needed a cutting for the professors, for the laboratory, Tandra doggedly told herself.

Without giving it a thought, she uncurled her legs to land on a dark facet of the prism. The moment her toes touched, she realized what a terrible mistake that had been—the murky crystal shattered at contact, and Tandra was engulfed in jagged shards and sooty powder. It burned her skin like an acid bath, and she coughed uncontrollably as she plunged into the crumbling morass. She couldn't stop her momentum! The deformed monolith broke in two, and the upper half closed on top of the young Elaysian like a clamshell.

"Tandra!" shouted Lucio. He and the others started to fly to her aid, but a black cloud spewed outward, forcing all of them back. They closed their eyes and shielded their faces, but even the diluted debris was noxious.

For several seconds, Lucio fell victim to a wracking cough. When he recovered, he realized that he had dropped his tricorder. Braving the venomous debris, he opened his eyes and spotted the device floating only an arm's length away. He quickly snagged the tricorder and checked to see if it was still working.

Lucio heard the others shouting at one another as they crowded around the hover-platform, but he tuned them out. There was only one thing he wanted to see—the lifesign display on the tricorder. He aimed the device toward the dark cluster and adjusted its field. Trying to ignore the disturbing data he was picking up, he concentrated on the lifesign scan. *Tandra has to be alive. She just has to be!*

When the first pass was negative, he tried again. And again.

"Lucio!" shouted Honroj, waving to him from the platform. "Link up with us! We've got to rescue Tandra!"

"No, we don't," answered the young Elaysian grimly. "She's dead."

"Shouldn't we look . . . for her body?"

"No. The thoron radiation is at dangerous levels. If we don't get out of here now, they'll be looking for *all* of our bodies."

Clenching his jaw to fight back the tears, Honroj piloted the disc to Lucio's side and grabbed his hand. One by one, he picked up the other students until he had collected a dispirited chain, linked by hands. With worried glances and stifled sobs, the young Elaysians pulled away from the dull, spiny mass of malformed crystals growing at the heart of their world.

Chapter Two

A CHIME SOUNDED INSIDE Captain Picard's ready room, and the distinguished commander of the *Enterprise* looked up from his desk. "Come."

The door slid open, and Commander William Riker stepped into the room. With his broad shoulders and commanding presence, Will Riker seemed to fill up the small office. He approached the captain and held out a padd. "Here's the new personnel. We've picked up twenty new crewmembers in the last forty-eight hours."

"Good," said Picard, taking the proffered device. It was a relief to be at peace after the Dominion War, when the harried crew of the *Enterprise* had been shorthanded and burned-out . . . on a good day. Now they were gaining crew, and even the most routine science mission seemed like a vacation.

The captain took a moment to politely glance at the data on the padd. They were nearly up to a full complement again, although they still hadn't assembled a community of families and civilians as they'd had aboard the *Enterprise-D*. Starfleet was depleted and in a state of shock after almost six years of war, starting with the Maquis and going through the Borg, Cardassians, and the Dominion. The altruism and idealism were still there, but tempered by hard-earned cynicism. These days, fewer families volunteered for active duty.

"Is there something wrong, Captain?" asked Riker, attuned as usual to his commander's moods.

Picard mustered a smile. "No, Number One. It's just that . . . I never thought I'd say this, but I miss them sometimes."

"Who?"

"The children. The families we used to have in the old days." He pointed to the padd. "This seems to be the usual mixture of career officers and new graduates."

Riker shrugged good-naturedly. "We're lucky to get them."

"I know," answered the captain. His voice took on a businesslike tone. "Any potential problems in this group?"

"Most of the ensigns are inexperienced, but I'll whip them into shape," bragged Riker with his usual bravado. Then the first officer frowned and pointed at the padd. "There is one officer with special needs: Lieutenant Melora Pazlar. She's Elaysian."

"Elaysian?" asked the captain in surprise. "That's rather unusual, isn't it?"

"Well, she's the only Elaysian in Starfleet," answered Riker, "but she comes highly recommended. She's on temporary assignment, for the low-gravity study on Primus IV."

"Mission specialist, shuttlecraft pilot, and stellar cartographer," said Picard, reading her dossier. "Decorated for valor after saving her ship and a hundred and ninety-two lives during the Dominion War."

Riker smiled. "She's a handy one to have around when the artificial gravity goes out. Then she's in her element."

"But in normal gravity?"

"Normal gravity is another story," said the first officer. "Her body just isn't geared for it. She has a special anti-gravity suit which works fairly well with the *Enterprise*'s gravity systems. At least she can get around. When she was on Deep Space Nine, she was confined to a wheelchair and special harnesses because they couldn't adapt the Cardassian design of the station to her needs. Even here, she'll need a cane and her suit to walk."

"Surprising that she's put up with this for so many years," said Picard, scanning through Melora Pazlar's illustrious record. "Couldn't Starfleet do anything to make her life easier?"

"Well, she was a candidate for an experimental treatment called neuromuscular adaptation. Dr. Bashir on Deep Space Nine was all set to do the procedure, but she backed out at the last minute. I guess it was irreversible, and she didn't want to take such a big step."

"But she's remained in Starfleet for almost a decade," said Picard with admiration, "despite being at an extreme disadvantage. Do what you can to make her feel at home, Number One."

"I will, sir. If she were here for an extended period, we could reconfigure our systems to turn off the gravity in her quarters. But she's going to be on Primus IV in a few days. For her, that will probably be like a vacation."

"I'm sure you're right," said the captain with a smile. The two old comrades knew instinctively when their business was over, and Will Riker started for the door. He paused to look back.

"Next time, Captain, I'll see if I can requisition some children for you."

Picard smiled. "Not too young. Toddlers are untidy, and I like my ship neat."

Riker chuckled and strode out of the ready room. After the door slid shut behind him, Captain Picard tapped his chin thoughtfully. Melora Pazlar was one crewmember he really wanted to meet, and he knew she wasn't going to be under his command for very long. The *Enterprise* was doing little on the Primus mission except to offer transportation and logistical support.

"Computer," he said, "give me the location and status of Lieutenant Melora Pazlar."

After taking a moment to consider the question, an efficient female voice answered, "Lieutenant Melora

Pazlar is in her quarters, cabin one-four-dash-six-three-one. Ambient readings would indicate that she is asleep."

"Asleep," echoed Picard. "I'll contact her later. No message."

"Acknowledged," said the computer.

The captain stood up, straightened his uniform top, and walked to the food replicator. "Tea, Earl Grey, hot."

He took his cup and saucer from the slot and returned to his desk. After taking a few thoughtful sips, Picard swiveled his computer screen and punched up progress reports for all of their current missions, plus recent Starfleet dispatches. After reading and sipping for a while, he decided that things were going smoothly. Very smoothly indeed. There was not a single crisis or emergency either on the ship or anywhere in the Federation.

It always made him nervous when that happened.

Melora Pazlar writhed uncomfortably in her bunk, her straight blond hair sticking to the V-shaped ridges on her forehead. Her face and body felt clammy from contact with the pillow and mattress, and her joints ached. Despite years of sleeping in gravity, she could never get used to it. *How can people sleep when they aren't floating? It's cooler, more comfortable, and more natural to float.*

At one time, she would have demanded that her quarters be in a natural state, gravity-free. But she had stopped doing that because it often created problems and resentment. Many ships and bases couldn't accommodate her, even if they wanted to. Of course, the *Enterprise* was a mighty starship—they could probably turn off the artificial gravity in a single room—but she wouldn't push for it. *Go along to get along* was her motto.

Over the years, Melora had found plenty of ways to get away from gravity, such as piloting long-haul shuttlecraft and volunteering for low-gravity assignments. She couldn't wait to get to Primus IV, which probably accounted for her restlessness. Melora had found that escaping into space was a lot easier than fighting the system everywhere she went; mapping, exploration, and science experiments fed her hunger for adventure. As long as the Elaysian was surrounded by the blackness of space—with its miniscule gravity—she felt at home.

When she felt sorry for herself, she recalled how dependent most species were on gravity. She had seen tadpoles from Earth that had been raised in weightless environments, with legs sprouting from their heads and tails growing from their stomachs. Without gravity, their genetic code simply didn't know where to put things; it couldn't get oriented. Other species needed gravity much more than she needed to be without it.

After she realized that she had been awake for forty hours straight, exhaustion finally conquered discomfort. Melora drifted into an uneasy sleep. As happened so often lately, she dreamt of home ... and flying. She could see herself soaring through the intricate archways and monoliths of Gemworld. The shifting light was filtered through a million glistening prisms, and the wind caressed her body and whipped her hair. She was home, and nothing was ever going to take her away again.

In her dream, she landed on an icy blue spire, one of the old-growth crystals in the former ocean. She remembered this crystal from years ago, when her family had picnicked on this very spot. Melora marveled that she had been able to find it again, but how could she forget it? Hovering over this spire, she had seen a Lipul for the first time in her life.

Just as she had done thirty years ago, Melora pressed her face against the weathered blue facet. It felt cool, solid, and aged. Light refracted through the crystal in a hundred different directions, giving the inner gel an ethereal glow. In the marrow of the crystal, bubbles and glints of light danced to unheard music—a miniature version of the sunlight dancing among the spires and monoliths above her.

Then *it* came into view, just as it had all those years ago . . . an amorphous creature moving with pulsing motions through the dense liquid. At an aquarium in San Francisco, Melora had seen a terran creature which looked something like a Lipul. It had been called a jellyfish, and the name fit both of them. Shy and retiring, Lipuls seldom revealed themselves to Elaysians, even though they were the two oldest sentient species on Gemworld.

In her childhood encounter, the Lipul had kept moving in its jerky fashion, taking little notice of the child floating above it. In this new encounter, the

Lipul actually stopped and confronted her from the other side of the crystal barrier. Although it had no eyes, the creature seemed to be gazing at her as intently as she stared at it.

This was unheard of. Melora tried to calm her thumping heart. She was certain that the Lipul knew of her presence—they were telepathic, after all—but what did it want? Was she supposed to do something, other than gape like a child?

Gradually the Lipul began to darken in color. It changed from a rough imitation of the color of the crystal into a much darker purple shade. Fascinated, the Elaysian pressed closer to see more. Before her horrified eyes, the filmy creature turned a ghastly shade of brown, flecked with black and yellow spots. A few seconds later, the Lipul was even more discolored, and the gel around it turned black, as if shot through with ink. Trapped within the murky depths, the poor creature began to writhe in its death throes.

Melora had no idea how she knew it was dying, but she *knew!* She screamed and beat her fists on the icy blue facet. It crumbled and began to turn black and brittle, and Pazlar froze in shock. Inside the diseased marrow, the Lipul continued to thrash about in its death. Melora sobbed pitifully, because it seemed as if the entire planet was dying. The elegant spire, which had shimmered like a rainbow only a few seconds ago, was now disintegrating into shards and soot. The dead Lipul floated in the debris, all dark and shriveled.

Melora recoiled from the grisly sight, an action

20

which had the strange effect of causing her to sit up. The sensation of gravity was her first inkling that she had been dreaming and was now awake. She certainly wasn't on Gemworld, not the way she was pinned to this bed. The Elaysian looked around at the dim, unfamiliar surroundings and wondered where she was. Then she remembered that she had shipped out on the *Enterprise* only that day. These were her new quarters.

Oddly, this knowledge was not reassuring. It was terrifying! Her dream had been so vivid and full of disturbing images that she was certain it *wasn't* a dream, even if it was. Melora rubbed her eyes, trying to make sense of it all. Her dream had replayed an old memory, but she knew instinctively that it was more than the mental gymnastics of her subconscious mind. The dream had been a cry for help from her homeworld, she was sure of it.

What made it so troubling was that Melora considered herself the most unlikely person to be called for help. She was physically removed from Gemworld, light-years away in the service of the Federation. Her desire to travel and see other worlds was a rare trait among her reticent people.

Perhaps, thought Melora, *that's the reason they contacted me.* She was one of the few natives of Gemworld who lived elsewhere, who was in daily contact with the Federation. When they contacted her aboard the *Enterprise,* they were contacting the Federation itself.

With a start, Melora realized who *they* were. The Lipuls had traveled the vast distances of space in order to deliver a desperate message to *her.* She knew about the Lipuls' dreamships, and the telepathic explorations that had brought them into contact with the Federation and numerous other races; but she had never experienced such contact firsthand. She was honored, humbled, and frightened by the encounter.

If only I knew what it meant! thought Pazlar with frustration. There was little she could do but get back to Gemworld as quickly as possible and hope she was in time.

The Elaysian rolled painfully out of bed and grabbed her gnarled wooden cane, which had been resting against the nightstand. The rustic cane helped her feel rooted to the ground—or the deck—and steadied her if her leg muscles weakened. *In this world,* she reminded herself, *I'm a tree, not a breeze.*

Already weary from these minor exertions, Melora took a few deep breaths and prepared to don her antigrav suit. It didn't make her movements that much easier, but the suit fooled her body into thinking that she was in her native low gravity. The pains and aches were relieved, side effects eliminated, and she had better muscle control.

Still she felt like one of those tadpoles with a leg growing out of her head.

Lieutenant Reginald Barclay strode briskly down the corridor on his way to the turbolift. The tall, sandy-haired man wasn't exactly late to his shift in engineering, but he would only be five minutes early if he kept up his current pace. He straightened his cuffs and made sure his tunic was hanging properly on his gangly frame. Then he brushed his hair back with his hand, wishing it wasn't thinning quite so quickly. Should he go with the captain's look and cut it short? Or would that make him look too aggressive?

Reg was checking the shine on his shoes as he rounded a corner and plowed into a blond-haired woman. He instinctively threw out his hands to catch her, and he was quite surprised when his hands closed around a black environmental suit. A moment later, he was shocked when the woman's cane clattered to the deck.

"I'm . . . I'm sorry," he stammered. "Are you all right?"

"Why don't you look where you're going?" grumbled the woman, shaking off his hands. He realized with a start that she was rather attractive, and not human, although he couldn't place her species.

She looked around for her cane, and he immediately bent down to retrieve it. This gave Barclay an opportunity to study her suit in detail, from toe to top. It wasn't an environmental suit, as he first thought, because it was open at the neck and head. It looked more like an emergency, full-body medical cast. He had seen some in sickbay. The only thing wrong with that theory was that the person within was vibrantly alive and apparently healthy.

"Are you looking for something?" she asked as his face neared her chest.

"Uh, no! Not at all," said Reg, straightening to his full height.

"Then may I have my cane?"

He remembered the wooden staff in his hand and gave it to her with a sheepish smile. "I'm . . . I'm really sorry I bumped into you. I shouldn't be in such a hurry. I'm Reginald Barclay."

"Melora Pazlar," she said curtly. She didn't offer him a hand in return because she was too busy clutching her cane with both hands. He noticed that the cane wasn't just an affectation—the way she leaned on it, she really needed it to stand up.

"Are you . . . injured?" he asked hesitantly.

"No, I'm not," she answered. "No thanks to you." She shuffled past him in the corridor, and he had no difficulty keeping up. He noticed the lieutenant's pips on the outside of her customized suit, and he realized that it was also her uniform.

"You're going to stare at me until I tell you about this suit, aren't you?" she asked irritably.

"Uh, well . . . yes. You see, I'm an engineer, and I'm always fascinated by gadgets. This suit isn't standard issue."

"No, it's an anti-gravity suit. Unfortunately, that doesn't mean that I can fly around. It just means that my body thinks I'm in low gravity."

"Elaysian!" blurted Barclay, snapping his fingers with delight. "Melora Pazlar, you are an Elaysian!"

"Thanks, but I figured that out some time ago." She stopped to take several deep breaths. "What I can't figure out sometimes is what I'm doing *here.*"

"Well, I can't figure that out sometimes either," said Reg with a shy smile.

For the first time, the attractive Elaysian really

looked at him. "Do you feel . . . out of your element sometimes, too?"

Barclay stuck his chin out, wondering how to answer that. "Let's just say, I'm willing to admit that I'm not perfect. For example, I don't find it easy to talk to people."

"But you're talking to me."

"Yes," he answered brightly. "You must be the exception that proves the rule."

For the first time, a slight smile crossed the Elaysian's face. "Lieutenant—?"

"Barclay. Reginald Barclay. But when we're off-duty, you could call me Reg . . . if you wanted to."

"Lieutenant Barclay, I've just arrived on the *Enterprise,* but I desperately need a special favor. I was going to talk to the captain, although I know that might be difficult—"

"Oh no, Captain Picard is very approachable," said Barclay, rising to his skipper's defense.

"Then we need to approach him, right now."

Barclay gulped, realizing that he had just gotten involved in some kind of strange personal crisis. But he had offered to help, hadn't he?

"W-Why do you have to see the captain?"

The Elaysian fixed him with icy but gorgeous blue eyes. "I'm only going to explain it once, and that will be to the captain."

Reg licked his lips and came to a decision. He tapped his combadge. "Barclay to engineering."

"What is it, Reg?" came the friendly but hurried voice of Geordi La Forge.

25

"I'll be a little late reporting for duty," he said. "I have to assist a new crewmember."

"I guess we can run the ship without you for a while," answered the chief engineer. "Report back if you're going to be longer than an hour."

"Yes, sir. Thank you, sir." With a relieved sigh, he looked down at the Elaysian.

"Now the captain," she insisted.

"Right." He tapped his combadge again and swallowed nervously. "Barclay to Captain Picard."

"Picard here," came the curt response.

"Yes, sir, this . . . this is Barclay."

"You said that."

"Right, Captain." Barclay took a deep breath and blurted it out. "I've met a new crewmember, Lieutenant Melora Pazlar, who's Elaysian. She urgently wants to speak to you."

Reg winced, waiting to be chewed out. Instead came the cheery response, "I'd be happy to meet Lieutenant Pazlar. Is now convenient?"

"Now?" echoed Reg in shock. He looked at Pazlar, and she nodded vigorously.

"Let's meet on the forward observation deck," said Picard. "In five minutes?"

"Yes, sir!" snapped Reg with relief. "Barclay out."

Melora Pazlar regarded him with increased respect. "You were right, he is approachable. Either that, or you have some special influence over him."

"It's not that," Barclay assured her. He gingerly touched her elbow as if to help her. "Shall we be going? We don't want to be late."

Shaking off his hand, Pazlar hobbled down the corridor. "Believe me, I can move fast when I have to."

Reg cleared his throat. "Uh, why are you here, if it's so difficult?"

"I've got the Starfleet bug," she grumbled. "Wanderlust. Even though the species on my homeworld don't get out much, I've always had this yen to see beyond the next star. Sometimes I doubt my sanity for choosing this life . . . and this is one of those moments. Is that the turbolift?"

"Yes!" Barclay hurried ahead of her and made sure the door opened, then he unnecessarily fidgeted by the door until she entered.

"Hurry!" she barked at him.

Elegant in its simplicity, the forward observation lounge consisted of a polished teak handrail and a convex window offering a panoramic view of the glittering starscape beyond. As the forward part of the saucer section, it was the only area of the ship that offered a view of space undiluted by nacelles, weaponry, and communication arrays. Captain Jean-Luc Picard gripped the handrail and gazed at the void, thinking it looked like a great jeweler's case—a swath of black velvet sprinkled with glittering diamonds.

No matter how many times he regarded this magnificent sight, it never ceased to awe him. Although it was dangerous and alien, space was the one constant in his life—it was the ocean in which he swam and the soil in which he grew. He ought to feel as comfortable here as he felt in the bistros of Paris, but that wasn't the case. In this environment, he would always be the outsider, dependent upon the strength of his protective cocoon.

Sounds of conversation and tinkling silverware floated from the nearby dining room, and a group of his shipmates passed by on their way to dinner. They nodded politely, and he returned the gesture. No one spoke because no one wanted to interrupt a captain in his quiet contemplation of the stars. Perhaps they thought he divined some special knowledge from his ruminations with the void. Picard supposed it had been that way since the days of the sailing ships, when a skipper could gaze for hours at the endless sea without rebuke. Call it a captain's prerogative.

He saw them emerge from the turbolift together, and he noted with some surprise that Lieutenant Barclay and Lieutenant Pazlar made a striking pair. They were both fair-skinned, fair-haired, and slim. Barclay, who was sometimes a bit flighty, seemed to be on his best behavior. Lieutenant Pazlar's anti-grav suit looked no more bulky than a flight suit, and she walked well, albeit with a limp and the help of a cane.

The last person Picard had seen carry a cane was the new Grand Nagus of the Ferengi, Rom. He was young and hardly needed a cane, yet it was a wonderful prop to impart stature and majesty. The Elaysian's wooden cane lent her a serious demeanor far beyond her years. Picard wondered if she was really as tough as she looked.

He applied his most gracious smile. "Welcome aboard the *Enterprise*, Lieutenant Pazlar."

"Thank you," she said. The ridges on her forehead creased. She didn't look very thankful.

Barclay fidgeted nervously. "It's good to see you, Captain. I . . . I suppose I should get back to duty."

"Can you stay, Lieutenant?" asked the Elaysian. "I may require a witness."

"A witness?" asked the captain with surprise. He glanced at Barclay, but the engineer looked just as puzzled as he was.

"Yes, there may be an inquiry later." Melora Pazlar squared her shoulders, stared frankly at the captain, and declared, "I need to leave the *Enterprise* immediately and return home. I'll give up my commission, if I have to. In fact, we must contact the Lipuls."

Picard tried to keep the edge out of his voice as he pointed to a sofa in the corner. "Let's sit down, Lieutenant, and you can explain yourself. Mr. Barclay, you're welcome to stay."

"Yes, sir . . . thank you, sir," stammered the engineer. He gazed at the young Elaysian with great concern as he escorted her to the sofa.

Chapter Three

CAPTAIN PICARD LEANED BACK in his seat and tried not to show his disappointment. He was not impressed by Melora Pazlar's reasoning. "So you've made this decision . . . based on a dream? Have you ever had this dream before?"

The young Elaysian bristled. "Sir, I've had hundreds of dreams, but never one like this. I'm absolutely certain that the Lipuls were trying to contact me using one of their dreamships."

"You mean those are real?" asked Reginald Barclay, leaning forward eagerly.

Picard shot him a glare, and Barclay withered back into his seat. The captain looked sternly at Melora Pazlar. "Lieutenant, may I remind you that you are here on a mission. You can request a leave through regular channels, and I'll do what I can to rush it through, *after* the mission is completed."

With considerable effort, Pazlar rose to her feet. "With all due respect, sir, you don't understand. I've got to go home now. Something there is terribly wrong." The Elaysian took a deep breath and seemed to compose herself.

"No one was looking forward to the low-gravity experiment more than I," she said evenly. "It would be like shore leave for me. But I'm needed more at home. If you can't divert the ship, can you at least loan me a shuttlecraft?"

"Can't we contact your homeworld?" asked Barclay.

"If you go through a special protocol, you can contact my people, the Elaysians, and maybe the Alpusta." Melora shook her head impatiently. "But there's no subspace contact directly with the Lipuls. They're not humanoids, and that's not their way."

"Nonetheless, let's try to contact them before we do anything else," said Picard with finality. He rose to his feet, anxious to resolve this problem. "Mr. Barclay, take the lieutenant to the bridge, and try to contact her planet. I'm sure Data will be of help. Lieutenant Pazlar, you'll be getting a call from our ship's counselor, Deanna Troi. I suggest you see her at your earliest convenience."

Pazlar glowered at him. "I don't need counseling, Captain. You can look at my record. I know this request is unusual, but I've never done anything like this before."

"You'll see Counselor Troi, or I'll have you confined to quarters. Is that clear?" Picard said in what he hoped was an understated, but firm, tone.

Melora shivered and clutched the handle of her cane. "Yes, sir. But about the shuttlecraft . . ."

"Out of the question until you see the counselor." He gave her a sympathetic smile. "And I wouldn't try to steal one—we've tightened up security since the war."

The Elaysian bowed her head and looked as downcast as anyone Picard had ever seen. She certainly wore her emotions on her tunic, making him wonder how she had garnered such glowing evaluations from her previous commanding officers. Then again, he wasn't seeing Melora Pazlar at her best.

The captain cleared his throat. "At a later date, I'll take you on a tour of the ship, as I intended."

Melora granted him the wisp of a smile, but it was clear her mind was elsewhere. "I would like that, sir. May we be dismissed?"

"Yes." He nodded to Barclay, and the engineer took the Elaysion under his watchful eye.

Tight-lipped, the captain tapped his combadge. "Picard to Commander Troi."

"I don't understand how it can be this difficult to contact a Federation planet," complained Commander William Riker, looming over Reg Barclay's shoulder. Data peered with interest over his other shoulder, and Melora Pazlar was practically in his lap. That was the only part of the arrangement that Reg wouldn't complain about. On the bridge of the *Enterprise,* the mightiest ship in Starfleet, half of the command staff was gathered around an auxiliary console on the back bulkhead.

"It can be very difficult, if they don't wish to be contacted," answered Pazlar somberly. "The Elaysians keep a subspace hot line open with the Federation, in case of emergencies, but it's not used for day-to-day chitchat. Access isn't automatic."

Barclay took his eyes off the auxiliary panel long enough to glance from Pazlar to Riker, who was slowly stewing. Barclay wanted to jump in and protect his new shipmate, but she was much better at verbal sparring than he was, especially with commanding officers.

Data had been surprisingly quiet until now. Reg attributed that to the fact that he hadn't yet made any mistakes in his laborious attempts to contact Gemworld. Commander Riker had come in late, annoyed that the process was taking so long on his watch, and Barclay felt a need to explain.

"W-We're waiting for the approval of the protocols from the subspace relay in sector six-ninety-one." Reg cleared his throat, glad to have gotten that much out. He was very relieved when Data jumped in.

"There is little need for regular subspace communications," said the android. "Due to gravity concerns, few inhabitants of Gemworld ever leave, and few outsiders ever visit. Although the planet has six sentient species, only the Elaysians have shown interest in regular contact. The other species are unusual, even by

Federation standards. For example, our first contact with their planet was telepathic, through the dreamships of the Lipuls."

Melora nodded impatiently. "I've been trying to tell everybody that the dreamships are real."

"The last contact with a dreamship was two hundred and four years ago," added Data. "Humanoids have short memories."

"Time doesn't mean the same to the Lipuls as it does to us," said Melora. "We've shared a planet with them for millions of years, and *we* don't even know how long they live."

Riker scowled and took a step back. "All right, it sounds like a place where people like their privacy. As for me, I like a minimal amount of distraction on the bridge. So do what you can to wrap this up."

"Yes, sir," answered Barclay quickly, never taking his eyes off his instruments. Finally new data began to appear. "I think I'm getting a response now."

He gaped in disbelief at the message which scrolled across the board. Captain Picard and Melora were not going to be happy about this.

Peering over his shoulder, Data read the message aloud: "Subspace contact with Gemworld suspended at this time, due to subspace warping and interference in sector six-ninety-one. Cause unknown."

"Exactly as I thought," said Melora with a mixture of vindication and worry. "Now the captain is going to have to give me a shuttlecraft. We should go right now and investigate!"

Data cocked his head. "Interruption of one subspace channel on a single relay is not normally cause for concern. There are many possible explanations."

Melora scowled and banged the tip of her cane on the deck. "What will it take? Do we all have to *die!* Can't you just take my word for it?"

"We do not know you very well," answered Data helpfully. "And your actions appear irrational."

While Melora seethed and nobody else knew what to say, the combadge on her anti-gravity suit suddenly beeped. She slapped it angrily. "Pazlar here."

"This is Counselor Troi," said a lilting voice. "I hope I haven't interrupted you at a bad time. The captain suggested we meet."

Melora grit her teeth, and Reg thought she was going to explode. Instead she replied very evenly, "Would now be convenient?"

"Cetainly. If you don't know how to get to my office, I'm sure—"

"Lieutenant Barclay will show me. In fact, I'd like him to sit in with us."

There was a pause before Troi answered, "That's highly unusual."

Pazlar took a deep breath and said calmly. "I don't know anybody on this ship, and Lieutenant Barclay has been very kind and understanding. I would just feel more comfortable." She patted Reg on the arm. "That is, if you don't mind."

"No, no! Not at all." Reg tried not to express his happiness at being indispensable, but he wished it could be under different circumstances. He recalled that Melora had also wanted a witness when she was talking to Captain Picard. She was no dummy. She knew that her actions might lead to an inquiry, or even a court-martial. Melora was convinced there was an emergency, and that she was in the right; so she wanted an impartial observer to back her up. That was probably all she wanted from him.

"We're coming now," said the Elaysian. "Pazlar out."

"We'll put our long-range scanners on it and see what we can find," said Commander Riker, giving Pazlar a sympathetic smile. "And we'll also keep trying to raise them on subspace."

"Thank you, sir," answered Melora, now sounding obedient and contrite. Maybe she realized it would be no simple feat to commandeer this great starship and take it home. She was biding her time while she built her case.

Barclay rose to his feet and motioned to the turbolift door. "After you."

"Thank you." As Melora shuffled off, he followed dutifully behind her. "I hope you don't mind helping me out," said the Elaysian.

"No, no. This beats a regular shift in engineering. I'm sorry we couldn't contact your homeworld."

Pazlar shrugged. "I didn't expect us to be successful."

As the turbolift doors closed on the two of them, Barclay said, "Deck nine." They began to move, and he tapped his combadge. "Barclay to engineering."

"La Forge here," came the familiar voice. "It's

okay, Reg, the captain told me you were on special duty. Report when you can."

"Thank you, sir. Barclay out."

Melora snorted a derisive laugh. "So I'm 'special duty.' I have to tell you, I don't usually cause a commotion when I arrive at a new post. Why did they have to contact *me?* I'm a stupid choice."

The door opened, and they stepped out of the turbolift onto deck nine. This was a public deck, with offices, classrooms, libraries, theaters, and similar facilities. They strolled slowly down the corridor, eliciting a few curious glances from passing crewmembers.

"I'm used to that," whispered Melora. "Either they're trying to place my species, or they're wondering why I need the suit and the cane. Since the war, there have been a lot more people with canes and crutches. Eventually all of them will get prosthetics. But I'll still have the cane."

Barclay cleared his throat, struggling to find the right words. "How . . . how do you know the dream wasn't just your mind . . . telling you it wants to go home?"

"Do you mean, how do I know I haven't finally flipped out after ten years in Starfleet? Am I pathetically homesick? Maybe. But I wasn't feeling any grouchier than usual before the dream. No, the only reason I want to go home is that they *need* me. If only there were other Elaysians in Starfleet, I could contact them . . . I could see if *they* had the same dream. But I'm alone here."

Pazlar straightened her shoulders with resolve and pounded her cane. "If I've got to convince everybody on this ship, one by one, I will."

"We're here," said Reg, stopping in front of a door which bore a small plaque reading "Ship's Counselor." He pressed the door chime.

"Come in," answered a voice, and the door slid open.

Counselor Deanna Troi rose from her desk to greet them. As usual, Reg was a bit awed by her sultry beauty. He had once harbored considerable fantasies about Counselor Troi. He had even brought a few to life on the holodeck. Familiarity and the pasage of time had tempered his feelings toward the dark-haired Betazoid, but he was still often tongue-tied in her presence.

"Counselor Troi, this is Lieutenant Melora Pazlar," he managed to blurt out.

"I'm pleased to meet you," said Deanna Troi at her most charming. She motioned to a small sofa. "Won't you sit down, Lieutenant. Make yourself comfortable."

"Thank you," answered Melora. She looked anything but comfortable as she made her way across the room and gingerly eased herself onto the sofa. "It's curious how people always want you to sit down to begin a meeting."

"Would you prefer to stand?" asked Troi.

"Actually, standing and sitting are both alien to me. I would prefer to be floating or flying, but that's not possible." Pazlar rested her cane on the arm of the sofa and folded her hands in her lap.

Troi turned to Barclay. "Where would you like to sit, Lieutenant?"

"Anywhere is fine." Barclay backed awkwardly into a corner and bumped into a chair. "I'll sit over here . . . out of the way."

"Would anybody like a refreshment?" asked the counselor pleasantly.

That was when Melora's studied patience evaporated. "Counselor Troi, can we please dispense with the niceties and get down to business? There's something wrong on my home planet, Gemworld, and I've got to get back there. Immediately! The captain won't release me or take me there until *you* give me a clean bill of health. So what do I have to do?"

"First you should remember that you're a Starfleet officer," answered Troi calmly. She sat across from the Elaysian on a small love seat. "Your life stopped being your own when you joined the Academy."

"Please, I don't need a lecture," said Pazlar. "I've served Starfleet to the best of my ability, but now it's time to serve my homeworld. This is a bona fide emergency. Tell her, Lieutenant Barclay, how we couldn't raise Gemworld on subspace."

Reg sat up at attention. "That's true."

Deanna held up her hand. "When I'm in this office, it's not my job to determine what's an emergency. That's for the bridge crew. My only concern is your well-being. I've never met anyone from your race before, but I'm a quick learner. Captain Picard said this all started with a dream?"

Reg could see the color drain from Melora's face as

she considered the impossible task of explaining her dream all over again. Nevertheless, she dove right in, describing Gemworld, the giant crystals, and the strange creatures which lived within them. Troi was very interested in her description of the Lipuls and their dreamships, and she made notes on her padd. She didn't interrupt or say anything until she was certain that Melora was finished with her tale.

"I can tell that you fully believe this," said Troi simply.

Pazlar blinked at her. "That's right . . . Betazoids are telepathic, aren't they?"

"To a limited degree. I'm only half-Betazoid, and the only person I'm fully telepathic with is my mother. But I can usually sense emotions and intentions, and I can tell that your feelings are genuine."

"Then you'll tell the captain to help me?"

Deanna frowned and looked away from the Elaysian's intent gaze. "You know Starfleet—I think you understand the captain's dilemma. He would have to suspend several ongoing missions and take the *Enterprise* a considerable distance off course. He needs some sort of independent verification about this problem, whatever it is."

"More than a dream," muttered Melora, sounding defeated. "I've never had a dream like this before. It was real, Counselor, you've got to believe me."

"I can put you in for a medical leave," said Troi, "effective immediately. That will get you off active duty."

"But it won't take me home," said Pazlar bitterly.

"Maybe in a week or a month we'll find a transport headed in that direction, and I'll get an indefinite leave. That will be fine, if I'm wrong. But if I'm right, I'll be too late." She rose slowly to her feet.

"You don't have to go yet," said Troi. "I'd like the chance just to chat . . . to get to know you better."

"I'm sorry," said Melora, "but I don't feel like chatting. And I won't be on this ship long enough for anyone to get to know me."

When she started for the door, Barclay bolted to his feet. "Where are you going?"

"Back to the lab to prepare for the mission on Primus IV. It's obvious that I've failed. The Lipuls have failed. Whatever message they wanted to impart, no one will get it."

Pazlar looked intently at Counselor Troi. "Someone the captain believes . . . someone like *you.* That would have been better." She turned and limped out the door.

"Should I go with you?" asked Barclay helpfully.

The Elaysian shook her mane of silky blond hair. "You've wasted enough time on me. Go back to your duties. But thank you, anyway." She exited, and the door slid shut behind her.

Reg sighed and flapped his arms helplessly. "I wish . . . I wish I could do something for her."

"So do I, but this is Starfleet. There are procedures. How far would *you* get if you had a bad dream about Earth, then wanted Captain Picard to turn the ship around and take you there?"

The engineer smiled, despite his forlorn mood. "Not far."

"Then we'll have to find some other way to help her." The counselor strode to her desk and punched up her screen. "I'm going to read up on everything we have in the computer about Elaysians. There may be a clue in there about what's really bothering her. This could be a recognized neurosis among Elaysians, for all I know. Was it really impossible to contact her planet?"

"Yes, but they're not in regular contact with Starfleet. There's a single relay and special protocols." Barclay glanced wistfully at the door. "She's very unusual . . . Lieutenant Pazlar."

Deanna smiled. "Keep in contact with her, Reg. She looks like she could use a friend."

He nodded, realizing that it had been unrealistic for Melora to think that an entire starship would stop what it was doing in order to investigate a dream. Even so, he had a feeling that she wasn't finished making her case.

Melora Pazlar went straight back to her utilitarian quarters, but she didn't open the files on the Primus IV experiment. Instead she lay down in her bunk still wearing her anti-grav suit, thinking it might help attune her mind and body to Gemworld. Since she hadn't slept more than a couple of hours in the last forty, she didn't think she would have any trouble falling asleep.

And she was going to dream. Not of Gemworld but of the woman she had just met . . . Deanna Troi.

Chapter Four

DEANNA TROI LEANED BACK in her chair and yawned. She blinked wearily at her computer screen and finally flicked it off. Even after reading a dozen essays, reports, and abstracts on Elaysians and Gemworld, complete with improbable pictures, she still couldn't imagine what it was like. A weightless planet with breathable atmosphere, giant crystals instead of soil, half a dozen sentient races, most of them not remotely humanoid. One essay had suggested that Gemworld was one of the oldest continuously inhabited planets in the Alpha Quadrant. Another had said it wasn't a planet at all, just an artificial construct; a third called it the curious remains of a planet. Even people who had been there couldn't agree on what it was.

One thing was certain, Melora Pazlar came from

there at considerable hardship. Compared to the other races on Gemworld, the Elaysians were extroverts, but by Federation standards they were still secretive and reserved. They were technologically capable of space travel, but apparently uninterested. Except for the redoubtable Lieutenant Pazlar. Maybe if you lived on such a remarkable planet—and could fly unaided like a bird—you were content to stay at home.

No doubt about it, Melora Pazlar was a true pioneer—the kind of woman who would be written about in history books, if she were human. Troi had known other pioneers in Starfleet—Worf was a good example. But Worf came from a spacefaring race—two of them, counting his human upbringing. Data was also unique in Starfleet, but Data had been designed to live among the stars. Both Data and Worf had struggled to fit in without losing their unique identities, and they had finally succeeded. Without knowing her better, it was hard to tell if Melora Pazlar had succeeded or not.

Some serious problem was bothering the Elaysian, that much was certain, and it had taken the form of a dream. But what did the dream represent?

With another yawn, Troi realized that she was not going to solve this riddle immediately, and the answer was not going to be found in a dry computer text. She rose to her feet and checked the time. Darn it! She had missed dinner with Riker. Of course, he knew she was working on the Melora Pazlar problem, per the captain's request, so he wouldn't have reminded her about it. Men either reached you when you wanted to be left alone, or they left you alone when you wanted to be reached.

She was really more tired than hungry, and she surveyed the empty couches in her office with more interest than usual. Maybe she could steal a moment's rest to recharge her brain cells, then she might try to contact other counselors who had served with Melora Pazlar. Maybe one of them could shed some light on her situation.

Before she could even debate the proposition, Troi's body had sunk onto the full-size sofa. Her legs stretched out all by themselves, and her head alighted on a throw pillow. It felt as if she were floating. "Computer," she said softly, "dim lights to one third and suppress door chime."

"Acknowledged," said a disembodied voice. The lights dimmed to a soothing, tasteful level, and Deanna had a sudden image of a broad purple ocean, with the sun hiding behind salmon-colored clouds. "Computer," she said, "may I have a background sound—ocean waves on the beach."

The office filled with the slow, cleansing sound of waves breaking on a distant shore, far from the cares of Starfleet, Melora Pazlar, or anyone else. Golden pink clouds billowed over the dark ocean, and Troi could see the waves rushing up the shore and fleeing again, wiping the sand clean. The effect was so serene and joyful that tears welled in the corners of her eyes, and her body floated on the gentle surf.

Without realizing she was asleep and dreaming, Deanna let the warm, dark water wash over her. She felt herself sinking, but this was no cause for panic, because her body was filmy and amorphous, accustomed to this world. Although the water seemed thicker than she expected, she found she could move up and down by opening and closing her limbs. When she wanted to move sideways, she merely floated on the favorable currents, which changed with every passing wave.

Under the water were murky pillars and encrusted monoliths, which she could dart under and use for cover. There were predators in these waters, and she realized it was a primordial time, when life was short and exciting. This was a memory, she realized, in which her dream logic was perfectly acceptable. Dreams often replayed true memories.

Without warning, her vision blurred, and she suddenly began to see through entirely different eyes. These weren't even eyes, but more like an inner vision of the mind, which Troi accepted as another memory. The dark ocean seemed to evaporate, leaving the monoliths and pillars behind like the bones of a departed animal. As the blazing sun and acidic rain bleached these stark monuments, dehydrating them, a remarkable transformation occurred: they turned into sparkling jewels! Giant prisms, clusters of gems, magical spires, and sweeping archways reached for the sky.

She saw this in a watery vision, and she knew that she was *inside* one of the great crystals. Eons of playing among them had led to playing inside them. A lucky few adapted and learned to synthesize sunlight and consume microscopic animals, and they survived inside the crystals when the oceans receded. That was a tragic time, Deanna knew, but it was a necessary step in their evolution to a higher level of intelligence. Trapped inside scattered crystals, they learned to communicate telepathically, or die of loneliness.

Epochs seemed to wash through her dream like the waves breaking on the shore. They still lived in the thick liquid, among the dancing lights and shifting rainbows, but they were no longer alone. There was a large community of beings drawn together by the unique qualities of this world. Some were as simple as children, but others were aged and possessed great wisdom. Before Troi could sort this out, she felt herself moving among the stars. She was racing at the speed of thought—looking for a receptive mind.

She was not alone in this massive exploration. There was a great armada surrounding her. Their silky bodies blossomed outward, and they filled the vast starscape like a million sailing ships catching the wind at once. She could see them coming . . . filling the sky! The sight was so magnificent that it again brought tears to her eyes.

As so often happens in dreams, there came a moment when she realized that she was dreaming. This epic drama wasn't happening to her—she was a privileged observer, not the star. But she was a part of it, Troi was certain. She had been brought in for a reason: to play a crucial role in a saga that had been unfolding since the universe was new. These events had not happened to her, but they *had* happened. She felt them as keenly as she felt her love for Will, her pride in her work, her loyalty to Captain Picard and her mother, and all the other absolutes in her life.

In a vivid farewell, the armada of dreamships turned gracefully in unison, caught the stardust in their sails, and melted into the night sky.

Deanna opened her eyes and sat up. Her heart was racing and her mouth was dry. *Did I really see what I thought I saw?* Maybe she had read too much about Gemworld, and her imagination had taken over. It was just a dream, after all.

She jumped off the couch and busied herself doing several small chores around her office. She knew that if this were a typical dream, she would forget the details quickly in the mundane pursuits of writing logs, filing reports, and working on her schedule.

After an hour, the images would not go away. They seemed as fresh as if they had happened to her personally just a few minutes ago. Athough not a word had been spoken, her interpretations were as clear now as during the dream—she knew exactly what she had seen. The fear, loneliness, struggles, and triumphs were just as vivid as any emotions in her own life. Like it or not, the Lipuls' collective memories had become her own.

And like it or not, she was about to become Melora Pazlar's staunchest defender. With a sense of duty but also a sense of awe, Deanna Troi straightened her uniform and set off for the bridge.

In the captain's ready room, Data cocked his head. "You would be the first member of the Federation in two hundred and four years to be contacted in this manner."

Troi nodded vigorously and looked from Will Riker to Captain Picard. She could sense their irritation, their reluctance to interrupt the current mission. "I know," she muttered. "And there's no video log I can show you, and no communications record, but the original first contact was well documented. In fact, the Lipuls led a Starfleet ship on a twenty-year mission to reach them. Believe me, it wasn't a regular dream—I can remember every detail vividly. Our two dreams have to be related."

"I see." Captain Picard scowled and turned to Riker. "What have we gotten off our long-range scans?"

"Nothing conclusive. There is a surprising amount of subspace interference in the region, but nothing our sensors can identify as the cause. We haven't been able to get through on subspace either."

"Let's find out if there are any ships in the area who can investigate."

Riker nodded and started for the door. He paused long enough to smile at Deanna. "You wouldn't be trying to get us shoreleave, would you?"

"I wouldn't mind seeing Gemworld," she admitted. That was just like Will, thought Deanna, trying to cover his discomfort with a joke.

After he left, she turned to face Captain Picard and Data. "Is there anything else you'd like to know?"

"When I talked to you after you met Lieutenant

Pazlar," said the captain, "you didn't seem to believe her story."

"I believed that she was truthful in her concern," answered Troi. "Did I believe it was something we should all be concerned about? I didn't then, but I do now."

The captain stepped behind his desk and took a seat. "This is a long shot, but is there anybody still alive who was contacted by them during that earlier time?"

"Two hundred years ago?" Troi asked doubtfully.

"Two hundred and four years ago," corrected Data. "Actually there is. There were six Vulcans on the mission, and I believe one of them is still alive."

"Do you know his name off the top of your head?" asked Deanna. She was only half kidding.

"No, I do not." Data frowned as if this were a serious failing. "But I will find out."

"Make it so," ordered Picard.

The android hurried out of the ready room, and the counselor crossed her arms and looked at the captain. Despite his polite reserve, she could still feel Picard's irritation. "I was only vaguely aware of Gemworld until a few hours ago," she explained. "Now I feel as if I *grew up* there! I didn't plan on making you take a detour."

"Maybe we won't have to," said the captain resolutely. "I'm still prepared for this to be a false alarm."

His combadge beeped. "Bridge to Picard," said Riker's voice.

"Yes."

Riker continued, "Starfleet says there are no ships in the vicinity of Gemworld. It's off all the main routes. As for investigating, since we're on a non-critical mission, they say we should use our discretion."

Troi grinned, despite trying to keep a professional demeanor. "It's nice that they trust us."

"Maintain course," ordered Picard, not yet convinced.

"Yes, sir. Riker out."

As soon as he had signed off, another voice interrupted. "Data to Picard."

"Go ahead."

"I have located the Vulcan crewmember," reported the android. "Unfortunately, Captain T'Mila died seventy-nine minutes ago in a Vulcan hospice. She was suffering from Bendii Syndrome. It seems that she awoke from a nap in great agitation, insisting that she had to report to an unknown ship. She collapsed and died shortly afterwards. Her caregivers attributed her agitation to the delusional effects of Bendii Syndrome. However, it would seem to me—"

"I can draw the conclusion," answered Picard. "Set a course for Gemworld, maximum warp."

"Yes, sir."

"And notify the staff there will be a meeting in the conference room at twenty-two hundred. Picard out." The captain looked at Troi and scowled. "There will be a lot of crewmembers upset about this. Although Melora Pazlar won't be one of them, I'm sure."

"We're doing the right thing," Deanna assured him.

Now that she thought about it, she realized she had no idea what they would find there. Melora had talked about destruction and dire threats in her dream, but there had been nothing like that in Deanna's dream, except in the ancient past.

She suddenly had an uneasy feeling that her vision of Gemworld had been sugarcoated, like the rock candy it resembled.

A display case full of elegant models of starships and sailing vessels, all bearing the name *Enterprise,* stood watch over an animated gathering in the conference room. It was animated because several of the participants had no idea why they were there, or why the ship had abruptly changed course. For once, there wasn't a war to explain it. Troi felt sorriest for Beverly Crusher and Geordi La Forge, who had been taken completely by surprise.

She gazed out the panoramic window. The stars blurred past at warp speed, attesting to the fact that they were headed somewhere in a great hurry.

"This all started because of a dream?" asked Crusher in disbelief. "Who had this dream?"

"I had one of them," answered Troi. "A new crewmember, Melora Pazlar, had the other."

The doctor blinked her green eyes thoughtfully. "Yes . . . I just scheduled her for physical therapy. She should be at her appointment now. Maybe I should give her a complete physical before we put too much faith in anyone's dreams. No offense, Counselor." Troi nodded in acknowledgement.

"The captain and Data are on their way," answered Riker. "Let's hold off discussions and suggestions until they get here."

La Forge leaned forward, looking mildly irritated. "But, sir, we've assembled two special teams for the graviton polarimeter test and the pulse-compression wavelength measurements. We've been preparing for weeks—are we just going to scrap the tests?"

"They'll be delayed," answered an authoritative voice. Everyone turned to see Captain Picard enter the conference room, followed closely by Data.

Picard took his place at the head of the table. "I'd like to thank everyone for their patience and understanding. Our change in plans is as much a surprise to me as to everyone else, but we've lost contact with a Federation planet. We know this because we have on board the only representative of that planet in Starfleet. She's Lieutenant Melora Pazlar, and she'll be here as soon as she finishes her therapy. She's Elaysian, from the planet Gemworld."

La Forge gazed at the captain with his white ocular implants. "Isn't that an artificial planet?"

"Data," said the captain, "will you please brief us on Gemworld."

Before the android could begin, Troi found herself speaking up. "Excuse me, sir. May I brief everyone? I know that's usually Data's job, but I've been studying this planet, both while I've been awake and asleep."

Nonplussed, Data turned to Picard to see if he was amenable. The captain nodded. "Go ahead, Counselor."

After everyone had settled into their seats, Deanna began. "It's true, some scientists in the Federation consider Gemworld to be an artificial planet because it requires a network of forcefields to hold its class-M atmosphere. There's hardly any gravity. A spherical, metallic cage encompasses the planet, and this shell contains the forcefields, hydrogen scoops, solar collectors, dark-matter collectors, oxygen generators, and other equipment essential to maintain the planet."

Now La Forge sat forward with interest, and she could tell he was beginning to come around. She went on, barely having to think about what she was saying. "The Elaysians are only one of six sentient species who live on the planet. Their name for it translates roughly as 'Gemworld,' and it's easy to see why. Nothing is left of the original planet except for mammoth crystals in an array of colors. Can you imagine great gemstone arcs, monoliths hundreds of meters high, and gigantic clusters of crystals?"

Troi's hands swept the air as she described these wonders, and everyone was gazing at her, apparently transfixed. Somewhat embarrassed, she lowered her hands.

"Gemworld is not artificial," she concluded. "It had conventional origins, with a class-G yellow sun. In fact, it may be one of the oldest inhabited planets in the quadrant. Gemworld flourished for eons and should be long dead by now, but the inhabitants have worked hard to give it a second life.

"Two billion years ago, it was an ocean world, rich in minerals and lifeforms. In this supersaturated solution, the mammoth crystals began to grow, and they gradually took over. As the crystals became like land masses, the water evaporated, and a myriad of unique species began to take hold. After more years, the inhabitants learned how to stimulate and control the growth of the crystals."

These events were vivid to Deanna because of the dream images in her mind. She wanted to describe all the tumult and triumph of that era, but she kept her tone factual and to the point.

"In time," she went on, "the water receded, and they learned how to use other matter to feed the growth of the crystals, replacing the need for a solution. They used fractal models to stimulate the crystals because fractal geometry kept the structure sound while providing infinite variety and expansion. Natural evaporation and dehydration caused the crystals to weigh less than the oceans and converted matter, so the planet began to lose mass.

"When the seas were gone, the inhabitants used the core of the planet to feed the crystals, reducing the planet's mass even further. They had to build the shell and its forcefields to hold in the atmosphere. Millennia later, most of the gravity has disappeared, but the shell is still working. Over the years, it's been upgraded to collect fuel for the crystal and protect the atmosphere. In return, the crystal affords multi-plane housing and sustenance for billions of beings."

"That really sounds like something!" said La Forge, impressed by her descriptions. "Have you been there?"

"Only in a dream. One of the species, the Lipuls, achieved first contact with the Federation through dream telepathy." For several minutes, Troi went on in greater detail about the Lipuls' dreamships, her dream, and Melora Pazlar's dream. She also mentioned the aged Vulcan, T'Mila, who had died mysteriously about the same time she had woken up from her own dream.

When she was done, Beverly Crusher shook her head in awe. "Well, that's that, isn't it? All I can say is . . . when do we get there?"

"Thirty-one hours and sixteen minutes," answered Data. The android swiveled his head to look at Troi. "That was an excellent briefing. I enjoyed it."

"Thank you."

"What exactly do we think has happened to this planet?" asked La Forge.

"We don't know," admitted Picard. "When you only have dreams to work with, the information is a little vague. A subspace relay near the planet is definitely nonfunctional."

The captain looked apologetically at Troi. "Counselor, I'm sorry I doubted you. It's plain to see that you've been there, in spirit if not in body."

"I feel that way. But we should really hear from Lieutenant Pazlar. She knows a lot more than I do."

The captain nodded and tapped his combadge. "Picard to Barclay. Is Lieutenant Pazlar finished?"

"Yes, sir! We're on our way."

La Forge slashed a finger through the air. "Why can't we do the graviton experiments on Gemworld instead of Primus IV? It should be easier there, if they have breathable atmosphere."

"If we can get their permission, I don't see why not," answered Picard.

"That should mollify the troops," added La Forge with a smile.

A moment later, Pazlar limped into the room with Reg Barclay right behind her. She looked around at the expectant faces, turned to Deanna, and grinned broadly. "It worked, didn't it? They contacted you."

"Yes, we're on our way to Gemworld," answered Troi. "But I still don't know what's wrong there."

"Neither do I," said the Elaysian, her smile fading. "Maybe *they* don't even know."

Reg Barclay hadn't spent so much time on the bridge since his training days at the Academy. Due to his budding friendship with Melora—and her trust in him—he had been assigned to assist her. He was included in every meeting and planning session— although there wasn't much they could plan since they didn't know what to expect. He certainly learned more about Gemworld than he ever expected to know. It sounded like an amazing place—it had to be to produce someone like Melora Pazlar.

Now that she wasn't struggling to make them believe her dream and take her home, the Elaysian turned into a dynamo. She put in long hours on the bridge, manning sensors, tracking ships in the region, monitoring subspace traffic, and trying to contact her planet. Barclay worked right beside her, and he never saw her grow discouraged when the long hours failed to produce any further information. To everyone's disappointment, there were no further dreams.

He came to realize that Gemworld was in one of the most sparsely inhabited sectors of the quadrant, where only one of a thousand solar systems was inhabited. There were no space lanes near Gemworld either; it was far off the beaten track. Even the Dominion had ignored it during the recent war, deciding there was nothing to plunder in the entire sector. No wonder the Lipuls had needed to go to such great lengths to make contact with others.

Reg made sure he was on the bridge as they approached their destination at maximum warp. The bridge was a bit more crowded than usual, with himself, Pazlar, and Deanna Troi at auxiliary consoles. Captain Picard sat in the command chair with Commander Riker beside him; Data was on ops, and Ensign Yontel, a blue-skinned Bolian, staffed the conn.

"Anything on the scans?" asked Riker.

Melora shook her head. "There are still unusual levels of thoron radiation, but the sensors don't pick up anything else."

"Commander," said Data, "we are now close enough to get Gemworld on visual."

"On screen," said the first officer.

A spherical object appeared on the viewscreen, floating in the depths of space. It hardly appeared to be a planet, at least at a distance. After studying it, Barclay decided that Gemworld looked like a snowflake made of colored jewels, encased in a delicate, silver filigree ball. He was also reminded of a clump of potpourri he had seen at his grandmother's house, encased in a perforated metal ball to allow the floral scents to escape.

"Remarkable," said Captain Picard, sitting forward in his chair. "Quite unlike anything I've ever seen."

"When you're on the planet," said Melora, "you don't really have a sense of the shell. It's just a distant part of the sky."

"ETA is in five minutes," reported Data.

The bridge crew watched in awe as they drew closer to the remarkable planet. Reg could understand how an observer could claim that Gemworld was artificial, yet it was too beautiful and improbable to be artificial. Nobody would have ever designed such a conglomeration; it had to evolve over time, as Troi had told them. To Reg's mind, it was more like a bionic planet. Too fragile to exist on its own, it had to be protected and supplemented with technology.

Data frowned slighly at his instruments. "Lieutenant Pazlar, you said that the shell collects dark matter."

"Yes," she answered, not looking up from her console. "Among other fuels."

Data continued, "I am picking up unusual gravitational readings that may indicate a higher-than-usual concentration of dark matter."

"Can you be more specific?" asked Picard.

The android shook his head. "No, sir. The Federation has never pursued dark matter as a viable energy source, and our understanding of that material is limited. Our sensors cannot even detect it, although they can detect the side effects of its presence."

Melora smiled. "We can't detect it either, but we know it's out there. We've collected dark matter for centuries, although always in small amounts and combined with other fuels. When you've run out of almost every natural resource on your planet, you become very creative."

"Then it isn't a concern?" asked Picard.

She shrugged. "To be truthful, I don't know what's a concern at the moment."

"Coming out of warp in one minute," said Data.

The captain glanced at Commander Riker, who instantly ordered, "Shields up. Bring us out of warp five thousand kilometers from the shell."

"Yes, sir," answered the Bolian on the conn.

Barclay tensed, and everyone looked up from their boards. Even at close range, Gemworld appeared unreal and inconsequential, despite its huge size. If it weren't inhabited, thought Reg, it could pass as the largest Christmas tree ornament in Federation space.

"Mr. Yontel," said Riker, "this won't be a standard orbit."

"Adjustments are programmed in," answered the conn. "We're coming out of warp in ten seconds."

As soon as the *Enterprise* dropped out of warp, the ship was jolted by an invisible force. Like a paper plate caught in the wind, it flew backward toward a gaping rift in space. The anomaly was black and opaque, outlined against the stars like a gash in the firmament.

On the bridge, the viewscreen went blank. A massive electromagnetic pulse surged through the ship, and the conn and ops stations exploded in a hale of sparks. Everyone was thrown out of their seats as acrid smoke billowed through the bridge. Data, his uniform blackened and smoldering, stood calmly, looked around, and strode to an undamaged auxiliary console.

"Taking over conn," he reported, but no one responded. The command chair was empty, and Captain Picard lay sprawled on the deck. Riker was there, too, both of them unconscious. "I believe Ensign Yontel is dead," added Data.

Barclay blinked away the stinging blood in his eyes and struggled to sit up. He realized that everyone in the circle of stations around the command chair was either dead or unconscious. Those in the outer circle of auxiliary stations had fared better. In a panic, he crawled across the deck, under the smoke, looking for Melora.

"Data! What happened?" shouted Deanna Troi, staggering to her feet.

The android's fingers were a blur as he worked his console. "An unknown singularity has disrupted all of our systems and is pulling us into a rift. I am attempting to compensate. Would you mind taking command?"

"Computer, Troi assuming command!" she announced.

They were jolted again, and Barclay was pitched forward onto his face. With relief, he found himself staring eye to eye with Melora. She appeared to be pinned to the deck. "I don't know what's happening!" she said with a groan. "My anti-grav suit isn't working."

"Not much else is working either," said Reg.

"You're bleeding," she said, reaching with difficulty for his face.

"Barclay, take a count of casualties and alert sickbay!" ordered Troi. She gave the fallen Riker, Picard, and Yontel a worried glance as she staggered to Data's side. "Can we get away from that thing?"

"We are at full impulse and unable to escape its pull."

Reg rolled onto his back, did a quick count, and tapped his combadge. "Bridge to sickbay! Medical emergency! Three crewmen unconscious . . . others with minor wounds."

There was no response, and they were rocked again. The whole ship shuddered an instant before it was plunged into darkness, followed by emergency red lighting. As smoke and sparks billowed across the charred stations and fallen bodies, a Klaxon blared in alarm, and Reg held his mouth to keep from screaming.

Chapter Five

"PUT A TRACTOR BEAM on the shell!" ordered Commander Troi as the *Enterprise* slid inexorably toward a monstrous rift in space.

The android didn't hesitate to obey the order. A tractor beam shot from the bow of the crippled ship and stretched across several thousand kilometers of space. It locked onto the delicate shell which surrounded Gemworld, and the fragile metal filigree held.

Data reported to Troi, "Our descent has been halted. Routing all available power to emergency life-support and tractor beam."

The dreadful shaking stopped, although the smoke, emergency lighting, and blank viewscreen made it clear that they were in trouble. Troi whirled around,

63

looking for Barclay, and she was relieved to see him hovering over Captain Picard with a first-aid kit and tricorder. Melora Pazlar came crawling on her stomach from behind a bulkhead, ripping off her anti-grav suit.

Troi couldn't worry about them when the whole ship depended on her and Data. She turned back to the android and asked, "If we got inside the planet's shell, would we be protected?"

"Possibly," conceded the android. "Gemworld appears to be stable, despite proximity to the rift. The problem is having enough propulsion to get away from it."

"Cut the ship's gravity!" shouted Pazlar from the deck. "That's what's attracting us to the rift, and why my anti-grav suit has gone crazy—it's our artificially high gravity. Cut it, and stop the attraction."

Deanna and Data looked at one another. "I could divert the extra power to the thrusters," said Data.

The Betazoid tapped the nearest comm panel, and her voice echoed throughout the ship. "All hands: Brace yourselves. We'll be losing gravity for a short time."

She nodded to Data, who executed several overrides in order to deprive the *Enterprise* of one of her most crucial systems.

Troi got a good grip on the back of Data's chair, but she was still caught off-guard when the gravity left the deck beneath her feet. She floated upward, her mind disoriented because her body was. The Betazoid almost let go of the chair in order to grab her legs, but she managed to calm herself and keep a grip on the chair.

She turned and saw Melora Pazlar, now stripped down to thin elastic and a few braces, go soaring through the cabin. She flew toward Barclay, who was clutching Riker and Picard and watching his medkit form a floating cloud of bandages, hyprosprays, and vials. The Elaysian caught all three humans and drew them together in a tight circle. When she needed to change position or get a boost, she used her long-toed feet to push off or grab the furniture, keeping her hands free to hold the humans. Palzar was so graceful and natural that Troi felt even more helpless and klunky.

Data stayed in his seat, calmly working the controls. "We are pulling away from the anomaly. Openings in the shell are large enough for us to pass through. With such low gravity, I can plot an orbit inside, or I can maintain our position."

"Can we get farther away?"

"Negative. Until we are safe, we must keep our tractor beam locked on the shell. Also we have no warp drive, and damage and casualties are reporting in from all decks. We need a safe port."

Troi gulped at the seriousness of their predicament. "Pazlar, is it safe to just fly through the forcefield?"

"The shell will recognize us as Starfleet and allow us to pass," answered the Elaysian. "Getting out is different."

"Okay, head for safety," she told Data.

While the android piloted the crippled starship,

Troi turned her attention to the wounded. At least she hoped they were only wounded. It was too late for Ensign Yontel. He was covered in burns, and his wide-open eyes stared puzzledly at the blank viewscreen as he floated over his charred station. Barclay had recovered enough to use his tricorder, and he was checking Riker while Pazlar steadied the captain in midair.

In an effort to reach them, Deanna wheeled one hand helplessly, while she clutched the back of Data's chair with the other. "How are they?"

"They're alive," answered Barclay. "N-Not too badly off. I'd say it was concussion that knocked them out."

Troi finally let out the breath she had been holding, it seemed, since they came out of warp. "Keep them stable until the medteam arrives."

"I'm not sure I reached sickbay," admitted Barclay. "They never responded."

Deanna tapped her combadge. "Troi to Crusher. Is there a medteam headed to the bridge?"

"Yes," answered the weary doctor. "Although not quickly. The turbolifts and transporters aren't working. Since I'm talking to you, I have to assume the captain and first officer are casualties."

"They're alive, but unconscious. As far as we can tell, it's from concussion. We have one dead up here, too."

"More than that shipwide," muttered the doctor. "Before you put the gravity back on, give us all a chance to get back to the deck."

"Good idea. Troi out." She turned to Pazlar. "That was quick thinking about the artificial gravity."

The Elaysian smiled. "I'm always looking for good reasons to do without it. That's why I'm in Starfleet—to convince you rootfeet that you don't need gravity."

Data cocked his head and scanned his instruments. "We have just entered the planet's atmosphere."

"Normally that means we're about to crash," remarked Troi.

"Not this time. We are no long being pulled into the rift. Its effect seems to end at the shell. We are in stationary orbit three kilometers beneath the shell."

"We're not in danger of hitting the crystal, are we?"

"No, sir. The crystal growth does not extend this far."

"Anything else we should be concerned about?"

Data surveyed screen after screen of readouts. "Thoron radiation remains higher than normal, although it's not at dangerous levels. That would account for the subspace interference. Oddly, the rift still does not appear on our sensors."

"How is that possible?"

The android swiveled his head to look at her. "This is conjecture, but it may be a dimensional rift. We also picked up unusual gravity readings, which may indicate unusual quantities of dark matter. The two are probably related."

Deanna ducked as a figure came swooping past. It was Melora, who somersaulted over a console and grabbed the back of a chair, coming to a graceful stop a few meters away from them. Somewhat defensively she said, "There's never been any problem with the dark matter before."

It was hard to argue with someone floating over her head, but Deanna tried. "Something has gone awry here, though. You've got a singularity out there that nearly destoyed the *Enterprise,* and Lipuls are sending out dream SOSs. And nothing shows up on our sensors. Dark matter, a dimensional rift—we need to find some answers."

When no one spoke for several seconds, Data interjected, "Shall I restore gravity?"

"Just a moment." Troi twisted around, trying to find the comm panel on the nearest station. When she couldn't reach it, she ordered, "Patch in my combadge to the whole ship."

"Yes, sir." Data worked his console. "Go ahead."

"This is Commander Troi," she said. "Captain Picard is fine, but he has been hurt, as have many of you. Please remain calm. We're inside the shell that surrounds Gemworld, and we're safe from the singularity that nearly destroyed us. We're about to restore gravity, so I urge everyone to work their way to the deck. Don't try to stand up, just get your whole body as close as you can to the deck . . . or sit in a chair. Remember, when gravity comes back, you'll fall, and so will any objects that are floating near you. You have five minutes."

She nodded to Data, and he worked his board. He still looked calm and collected, seated at the auxiliary console as if nothing were wrong. "How come you're not floating?" she asked.

"I activated the magnetic implants in my posterior," he answered. "Everyone should have them."

"Excuse me, Commander," said Melora Pazlar. "Breathable air—my *home*—is just on the other side of that hull. If you could transport me out, I could fly out there, and I could try to contact my people. They must have seen us . . . and they could be heading this way."

"Lifeforms are approaching," concurred Data.

"Please beam me out," begged Pazlar, *"before* you put the gravity back on."

Troi looked at Data, and the android said, "We have the capability to perform one short-range direct-transport from here."

"Please," asked the Elaysian, fixing Deanna with her intent blue eyes.

She sighed. "Grab the communicator off your anti-grav suit."

With a swift push off the ceiling and a short flight, Pazlar retrieved the combadge off her discarded anti-grav suit. Troi could see Reg Barclay watching the Elaysian with pride and affection, delighted to see her in her native element.

"Energize," ordered Troi. She had never seen anybody so pleased to be leaving the *Enterprise* as Melora Pazlar. The young Elaysian was beaming as her body dissolved in a swirling cloud of glimmering lights.

A shout distracted Troi, and she turned to see Will Riker tip upside down in the air. He had just returned to consciousness to find himself floating above a damaged bridge.

"Relax, Commander," said Reg Barclay, trying to

calm him. "We're going to get gravity back in a minute."

Riker saw the unconscious captain and twisted unsuccessfully to look in his direction. "Is he all right?"

"He's all right, and the ship is safe," answered Deanna. "Right now we need to get everyone down to the deck before we restore gravity."

She explained briefly what had happened while they secured the captain and hovered close to the deck. Will took Deanna's hand and smiled. "Quick thinking, Commander."

"All in a day's work." She returned his smile and his grip.

"Five minutes have elapsed," reported Data.

"Restore gravity," ordered Riker.

All over the ship, thuds sounded as people and objects dropped to various decks. The bandages that had escaped from Reg's medkit fluttered down, littering the bridge. Will and Reg secured Ensign Yontel's body and covered it with a thin blanket from a survival kit.

The Jeffries tube at the rear of the bridge opened, and three medical workers crawled out, looking rather bedraggled after traversing the ship without the benefit of gravity or turbolifts. They immediately tended to the captain and brought him back to consciousness, then they patched up the cut on Reg's forehead.

The medteam cautioned Picard and Riker to go to sickbay, but of course both of them ignored the advice. Data explained matters to the captain, and there were damage reports, casualty reports, and system checks. The reports yielded little good news. Finally the turbolifts started working again, and medteams and repair teams were able to disperse quickly throughout the ship.

With the viewscreen out, Troi had almost forgotten where they were until a report came in from a repair crew.

"Captain!" said an amazed voice. "This is Lieutenant Oswell. You've got to come down to the forward observation lounge. You've got to see it!"

"See what?" demanded Picard.

"It's . . . it's impossible to describe . . . it's like a welcoming party. Sir, you've got to see it. Oswell out."

"Data and I have things under control here," said Riker. "And we'll keep trying to get a message to Starfleet."

"Counselor, Mr. Barclay," said Picard, rising from an auxiliary station. "Please accompany me."

"Yes, sir," answered Troi, anxious to see what had brought them all this way . . . into such peril.

As they rode in the turbolift to the forward observation lounge, Picard rubbed his head. "Are you all right, sir?" asked Barclay with concern.

"Yes, but I think I will drop by sickbay after this. That way, Dr. Crusher won't chase me down, as she's certain to do otherwise."

The turbolift doors opened, and they stepped into a broad foyer, which led to the observation lounge and the dining room beyond. Even from a distance and a side angle, Deanna could see something she had never seen before through the panoramic window: blue sky.

Normally the window was filled with stars, nebulae, or the curve of a planet—simple sky looked odd. Two members of a repair team stood gaping out the window, but they scurried off to work when they saw the captain coming.

As Troi trailed the captain to the window, her jaw succumbed to the newly restored gravity. Barclay gasped, and the captain let out a sharp breath. All three of them reached out to touch the window, as if they couldn't believe what they were seeing.

Just outside the hull of the *Enterprise,* the blue sky was filled with hundreds of Elaysians—flying, floating, soaring. With their billowing white outfits, they looked like winged beings from the mythology of a thousand different cultures. Some of them waved, and the three stunned observers waved back. Floating among them were small hovercraft, nets, and ropes, which Troi assumed were used for hauling passengers. It was shocking enough to see humanoids this close to the ship at all, not to mention without spacesuits, surrounded by blue sky, and flying.

"Now that's something you don't see everyday," said Barclay in a hoarse whisper.

Captain Picard smiled like a boy at the circus. "They're remarkable. What a unique culture this must be. But it's a little disappointing that we can't see the crystals from here."

"What's that thing?" asked Barclay, pointing down.

Deanna leaned over the wooden handrail to see what appeared to be a rocket shooting toward them. It left a long, dark vapor trail behind it, stretching out of view. But there was no flash of flame, and the object seemed too slow to be a rocket. As it drew closer, Troi realized the craft had several legs.

"Is it a landing probe?" asked Picard.

"Maybe it's a satellite," guessed Reg. "Or equipment the Elaysians need."

"At least they don't seem to be concerned about it," said the captain with some relief.

Troi was willing to believe the craft was unmanned, until she saw the legs rhythmically opening and closing. The object changed course slightly, and the vapor trail twisted around like some sort of cable. She wondered if it was an umbilical cord to the surface.

"It's . . . it's moving," said Barclay.

"Yes, I saw," agreed the captain. "What is that trailing behind it? Some sort of tentacle?"

That was what it looked like now, thought Deanna. In fact, the approaching object seemed to look more organic and animated the closer it came. The spindly legs, of which there had to be a dozen, opened and shut as if pushing the tentacle out behind it. It was more like a web, she realized, a stiff web which kept pushing the gangly creature ever higher.

The being finally stopped several meters beneath the horde of hovering Elaysians. Two of the humanoids dropped down to touch the creature, which looked black and spiny, almost like a sea urchin. The newcomer sat perched atop its gently swaying tentacle, like a bird's nest atop a flagpole. From her reading and her dream memories, Troi realized she knew what the creature was.

"That's an Alpusta," she said.

"Of course!" exclaimed Reg. "It's bigger than I thought it would be. What's it doing?"

"Studying us," answered Picard. "We need to make contact with the inhabitants."

"Look, it's Melora!" said Reg happily. "I mean, Lieutenant Pazlar."

They followed his gaze to see a blond Elaysian come streaking toward them. She was gripping one of the small hover-platforms like a swimmer grips a lap board, letting it pull her along. She turned it off about thirty meters away from them and glided the rest of the way, bouncing to a stop on the hull with her fingers and toes extended like miniature shock-absorbers.

Barclay waved, Troi smiled, and Picard tapped his combadge. "Picard to Pazlar."

Melora quickly found her combadge in the billowing white folds of her traditional clothing. "Pazlar here." It was disconcerting to hear her voice coming from the captain's combadge when she was floating only a couple of meters away on the other side of the convex window.

"This is quite a welcoming party," said the captain. "But we've taken serious damage, as you know. Do your people have an explanation about what's going on here?"

"Plenty of them, but none they can agree on." Melora lifted her arms to show the triangular sails underneath. "And, Captain, I'm sorry that I'm out of uniform, but I had to discard my anti-grav suit during

74

the emergency. If you want to be able to fly, you'd better be able to catch a wind current. You can do it in this apparel."

"That's understandable . . . under the circumstances," answered Picard. "But I expect you to comport yourself as if you were wearing a Starfleet uniform."

"Yes, sir." She looked around at her fellow Elaysians and the lone Alpusta. "We have representatives from the Elaysians, Alpusta, and Lipuls who want to meet you."

"What about the other three races?" asked Picard.

"Maybe in time we can meet them," said Pazlar. Troi sensed a tension in her voice at that answer, and the Elaysian quickly changed the subject. "I know I transported out, but our scientists don't advise using transporters again until we find out exactly what's causing that rift."

"The *Enterprise* is not fit to go anywhere at the moment," said Picard, "but we should be able to use our smaller shuttlecraft without problems. They will also give us islands of gravity on your world."

"Good idea, sir. Our Exalted Ones request that you send a small party, and that it include Counselor Troi. I wouldn't mind personally if Lieutenant Barclay also came with you."

"No transporters?" Reg asked with surprise and relief. He sounded quite debonair as he replied, "I'd be delighted to visit your planet."

Picard's combadge chirped. "Bridge to Picard!"

"Go ahead, Number One."

"We have to put up shields!"

They stared in horror at Melora and the other Elaysians, who would likely be vaporized if they put up shields now.

"Belay that!" ordered Picard. "We can't—"

Without warning, a barrage of rocks thudded into the underside of the hull, and the Elaysians were scattered by a shower of stones zooming toward space. Deanna stared out the window and noted with alarm that they weren't rocks but broken crystals—dark, dangerous shards pelting everything in sight. The ship took a tremendous beating—it sounded like a rockslide was pounding the hull—and Melora barely dodged a fusillade of deadly missiles. Some of the other Elaysians weren't so lucky. They were struck in the onslaught. The Alpusta shrunk into a spiny ball and descended swiftly through the dark hailstorm on its retractable web.

The *Enterprise* couldn't escape, and they couldn't put up shields—they were as helpless as the Elaysians trapped in the crystal storm.

Chapter Six

SHOOTING UPWARD THROUGH the atmosphere of Gemworld came a deadly shower of broken crystals, raking the *Enterprise* and hundreds of Elaysians caught in midair. Those who could reach hover-platforms used them to escape to the nacelles and hull of the *Enterprise*, looking for protection. The others scattered in all directions, but there was no escape for most of them from the onslaught of dark, gleaming shards.

Reg Barclay peered out the window of the observation lounge, looking desperately for Melora in the chaos. He was unable to spot her among the scores of panicked Elaysians.

"Picard to bridge," said the captain's voice beside him. "Report."

"We're taking a beating," came Riker's voice. "The

hull is holding—no breaches yet. Data says it should be over . . . about now."

As abruptly as it began, the assault stopped. A few straggling chunks drifted past the observation lounge window on their way off the planet, but the worst of the crystal storm had passed. Nevertheless, there were scores of wounded Elaysians floating in the air outside the ship, and scores more desperately rushing to their aid. It was one of the most surreal and disturbing sights Barclay had ever seen. He thought he saw Melora in the mayhem, but he couldn't tell.

"What caused that?" demanded the captain.

Riker answered, "Apparently part of the crystal structure of the planet just broke off. It acted like an avalanche, smashing more crystals and growing bigger as it rushed outward. Data is trying to figure out where the impetus came from, since there isn't much gravity on the planet."

After a pause, the first officer continued, "It looks like there was a gravity spike, perhaps caused by dark matter. We had no warning on that avalanche, and we didn't realize how many Elaysians were out there. As soon as we can, I want to clear this area and put up shields."

"There are a lot of wounded out there," said Picard grimly, "but we can open the hatches to get them. I'll contact sickbay, then I'm leading an away team to the surface. You stay on repairs, Number One."

"Yes, sir."

"Picard out."

"What can I do?" asked Counselor Troi.

"You and Barclay go to shuttlebay one and pick out a small personnel shuttlecraft. Make sure we have as many supplies and portable instruments as we can carry—we don't know what might be useful. I'll be along as soon as I can."

Reg only half heard this as he continued staring out the convex window at the desperate mayhem outside. "They . . . they need help, sir."

"We'll take care of them," promised Picard. "Load the shuttlecraft."

"Yes, sir," snapped Troi. She pulled on Barclay's sleeve. "We're here to help them, so let's get going."

"Yes . . . sir." Although he realized he had to go, the worried lieutenant could barely pull himself away from the scene of carnage outside the window. He couldn't pick Melora out in the swarm of Elaysians, but he had a feeling that she was all right. She had become accustomed to hardship during her ten years of service in Starfleet. All of that had to be for some reason. Maybe her experiences could help her help her planet, now when they needed it most.

"I'm coming," he said, hurrying after Troi.

He reached the turbolift just as the doors were closing, and she looked at him impatiently. She wasn't in her usual, kindly counselor mode—she was Commander Troi now, the woman who helped Data save the *Enterprise* only an hour ago. Now she was going to help save this ancient world of billions of sentient beings, even though their own ship was a wreck. The inhabitants of Gemworld didn't know how lucky they were to get this particular crew, thought Reg.

"Shuttlebay one," she told the turbolift computer. "You know, Reg, I understand that you care about Melora, but you're going to have to put your feelings aside if you want to help these people."

"I know . . . I'm trying."

"Does she feel the same way about you?"

"What way?" he asked with a nervous laugh.

The turbolift doors opened at their destination, and she gave him a knowing look. "I've been there, Reg, and I know. Keep your mind on business—you'll do a better job. And you won't get hurt."

She brushed past him on her way out of the turbolift, and he sighed. *Is it written all over my face?*

Barclay followed Troi into the cavernous shuttlebay where it was almost as chaotic as the scene outside the ship. When the artificial gravity was cut, most of the shuttlecraft had been secured in time, but a few hadn't been. Repair crews were working on two craft that appeared to be slightly damaged, and they were inspecting several others.

Troi picked out a bullet-shaped Type-7 shuttlecraft, which looked to be in pristine condition. It would be big enough to carry supplies and an away team of up to six, but not so big as to crash into those spindly crystals at every turn. She ordered a harried work crew to get it ready for launch, and they dropped what they were doing to comply. Meanwhile, the two of them gathered up tricorders, portable forcefield generators, jetpacks, environmental suits, jackets, survival gear, and a miniature science probe that could be launched from the shuttle.

They nearly had the small craft loaded by the time Captain Picard strode into the shuttlebay, accompanied by Data. The captain looked with dismay at the damaged shuttles, but he marched straight toward them, concentrating on the job at hand.

When he drew closer, Reg could see a new bandage on the captain's neck, and he gingerly touched the bandage on his own forehead. "Been to sickbay, sir?"

"Yes, and they're filled to capacity. We've opened the hatches and are bringing in some of the wounded Elaysians. Unfortunately, we can't make them very comfortable in our gravity. Lieutenant Pazlar is all right—she's meeting us outside and will guide us down."

Barclay let out a relieved sigh and tried not look too happy. "I'm glad to hear that, sir."

"I also got a hypo for space sickness," said the captain, "and I suggest you and Counselor Troi do the same."

"Even though we're not in space?" asked Reg warily.

"I'll get a medkit," said Deanna.

Data stepped into the shuttlecraft, looked around for a moment, then he poked his head out. "You have done a good job of packing. We can leave anytime, Captain."

"Take the controls, Data. Begin launch sequence as soon as we're aboard."

"Yes, sir."

"We're the only ones going?" asked Deanna.

"This is all I could spare from the repair effort."

Captain Picard managed a tight smile. "Even before your dream, I knew things were going too smoothly."

He climbed aboard the shuttlecraft, taking the co-pilot's seat. Troi and Barclay quickly followed suit, sitting in the stern among the supplies.

Reg felt a bit claustrophobic inside the cramped cabin, but it was better than using the transporter. Anything was better than using the transporter. Data ran through the pre-ignition checklist with his usual efficiency, while the shuttlebay crew cleared the area for departure. Troi gave Reg a hypo for space sickness, then gave herself one.

Finally they contacted the bridge and were given permission to launch. The immense shuttlebay doors opened, revealing the unusual sight of bright blue sky beyond. Data piloted the shuttlecraft very slowly through the doors and into the atmosphere, and his three passengers craned their necks to get a better look at their surroundings.

Above them, Reg could just make out the silhouette of the metallic shell, glimmering dully like a band of clouds. Elaysians no longer surrounded the ship, but Reg could see a few of them scattered in the distance, hovering warily. Below them, the view was staggering—interconnected prisms, monoliths, and archways of multi-colored crystals reached toward them like icicles, and descended deep into the planet like roots.

The intricate structures looked as if they could collapse of their own impossible size, and Barclay feared there would be more avalanches. But then he remembered that there was negligible gravity here, and these colorful monoliths had stood for millions of years. They wouldn't break unless something disturbed them . . . like the thing that disturbed the other bunch of crystals.

"The pieces that hit the ship didn't look like those," said Deanna. "They were darker, dead looking."

"Then perhaps it's not widespread," said the captain hopefully.

"Lieutenant Pazlar is straight ahead," reported Data. They were already traveling slowly, and the android put them into a crawl through the skies of Gemworld. Barclay leaned forward to try to get a look, and he spotted an Elaysian gripping one of the hover-platforms. She waved and zoomed off. To his eyes, she could have been any one of a thousand similar-looking Elaysians, and he felt a pang of jealousy. Pazlar was no longer dependent upon him to the degree she had been on the ship—now she could just fly away.

In the negligible gravity, it was easy to maintain a slow speed, and Data kept the shuttlecraft in a glide most of the way. As they descended, the levels of crystal began to look more and more like branches, growing in fractal patterns from a magical bejeweled bush. Among the growth were vinelike strands, which Data said were for nourishment. Reg couldn't help but feel small and insignificant in this immense wonderland, like a fly lost in a blossoming rosebush.

They passed swarms of Elaysians, who had encampments among the crystals, expecially in the crux of the larger clusters. Netting and ropes kept their meager belongings and their children from drifting away, and the smooth columns and prism walls afforded them shade and shelter.

Less frequently, the shuttlecraft passed enclaves of Alpusta, which made Reg shiver involuntarily because they looked like nests of spiders. The spiny, multilegged creatures bobbed and bounced on their retractable webs as if they were agitated at the mere presence of the shuttlecraft. The two humans and the Betazoid tried not to stare, but they couldn't help it.

Clutching her hover-platform, Pazlar zoomed ahead of them like a humanoid missile, and Data had difficulty keeping up with her. As she swooped among the glittering archways and prisms, Reg looked worriedly for telltale signs of the black crystals that had broken off, but he didn't see any.

At one point, they passed a vast agricultural level, where greenery grew in moss-like clumps atop the crystals. Data explained, "The Elaysians grow food hydroponically in the gelatinous form of the crystal. They use the inedible parts of the plant to make their ropes, nets, and clothing."

"I'd like to see that," said Barclay. What he really wanted to see most was firm ground to walk on, but there didn't seem to be any of that. Even if there were, walking was impossible on Gemworld. If they had no gravity on the ship, they could at least use magnetized boots, but those were no good here.

After a while, it felt as if they were entering the heart of a planet. Sun continued to filter down, dancing with the prisms in subdued rainbows instead of brilliant ones; but the weathered, pastel crystals attested to eons and eons of wear. Reg had no problem imagining thick seas washing over these monuments when they were new, a billion years ago. Among them, he felt no bigger than an amoeba.

Watching Melora zig and zag through the forest of monstrous prisms was also a surreal sight. Reg was reminded of romantic paintings of mermaids frolicking in the ruins of Atlantis. The deeper they went, the more the light took on an unreal quiver from all the refractions, like a mirage. Everyone in the shuttlecraft was perfectly silent, as if they had just entered a cathedral.

The chirp of the captain's combadge came like a shout intruding in a dream. "Pazlar to Captain Picard."

"Yes, Lieutenant."

"We're almost there, sir. The attendants will secure the shuttlecraft. Since you'll be weightless, may I suggest you just hold hands when you step out."

"Understood," answered Picard.

They glided slowly toward an encampment of Elaysians which looked little different from the dozens they had passed enroute, except that the nets covered a slit in the immense crystal. Reg was reminded of the mighty redwoods he had seen in California. This great monolith might once have been red, too. Now it was a pale pink color, like rose quartz.

As they slowed to a stop, Elaysians surrounded them, roping the shuttlecraft so tightly that it couldn't drift a centimeter in any direction. Data popped the hatch, and there was a mild rush of air as the pressure equalized. There was also a dry, chalky scent in the air which reminded Barclay of talcum powder and childhood. It was very disconcerting to peer out and see nothing below the open hatch but air.

Melora stuck her head in and smiled as she floated in the doorway. "The Exalted Ones are waiting. Normally there are a great many protocols we would observe, but these aren't normal times. If you'd care to exit, Captain." She backed away and held out her hand.

Picard stood and moved toward the open hatch, looking more confident than Reg hoped to look. He took Melora's hand and stepped through the hatch into nothingness. Other Elaysians hovered nearby in case he needed help, but the captain looked graceful as he floated in midair, holding his hand out to Troi.

The Betazoid bravely stepped out, giving a little gasp as her feet left the security of gravity. The captain steadied her, and she turned to Reg, held out her hand, and waved expectantly.

Involuntarily, he shrunk back in his seat, folding his arms tightly against his chest. Data noticed his reaction. "You cannot possibly fall."

"I know . . . I know." Barclay gave an anxious sigh, then he finally stood up and moved toward the open hatch. Just as he started to step out, he hesitated, and his toe caught on the lip of the hatch. His forward momentum propelled him out the door headfirst, his feet following, and Reg whooped in alarm as he somersaulted into the air.

Elaysians rushed to his aid, their hands grabbing

his arms and legs, scaring him even more. Reg tried to relax and let the experts set him right side up, but he didn't relax until he felt Troi take his hand.

"That was quite an entrance," said Melora with amusement. "You'll get used to the low gravity."

"I don't think so," answered Reg, his voice trembling and his limbs as stiff as the prisms towering around them. "Just drag me along—I'll be fine."

Data joined him, and it felt oddly reassuring to grip the android's cool, smooth hand.

"Ready," said Pazlar. She used the hover-platform to drag the linked visitors through the slit in the crystal into an immense rose-colored hall. To Reg, all of it appeared to have been hollowed out by natural forces.

When his eyes got used to the dim, rose-hued light inside the crystal, Reg gaped in amazement. All around the rough-hewn walls were jellyfish-like beings floating up and down in streams of bubbles. A contingent of Elaysians floated in a corner, looking like a heavenly choir, while spiny, long-legged Alpusta bobbed nervously on their webs in another part of the hall. In the center of the cavern was a dense cluster of spindly crystals, which blinked with a startling array of colors as if they were being illuminated from within.

Despite all the other wonders, Barclay had a hard time taking his eyes off the Lipuls. They seemed to be studying the visitors, although they had no eyes that he could determine. Was he imagining it, or did the Lipuls' rhythmic movments seem to correspond with the blinking crystals in the center?

Pazlar dipped into to a respectful bow and loudly addressed the assemblage. "Exalted Ones, this is Captain Picard, Commander Troi, Commander Data, and Lieutenant Barclay from the *Enterprise*. They are my shipmates, and they've come a long way through great danger to help us. Even now, their ship lies badly damaged inside the protection of the shell. In this time of crisis, we will have to work together to help each other."

Suddenly Reg realized that the crystals in the center were pulsing in unison with Melora's voice, as if they were translating. Pazlar turned to the Lipuls floating in the solitude of the crystal. "If not for the dreamships, we would never have known about this grave threat. Now you must tell us everything you know—about the rift, the dark crystals which break for no reason, and the lack of contact with the Federation."

A strange, synthesized voice issued from the sparkling cluster in the center. "You have done well, Daughter. We had no idea the rift was such a danger to the starship, or we would not have summoned you. Although our contact is infrequent, we have long valued our membership in the Federation. Like you, we have managed to create a peaceful union of many very different species. Our differences bring us strength and vitality."

Barclay glanced at the captain and saw him smiling in agreement at that statement.

The lights in the crystals grew still for a moment, then shimmered in unison. The voice went on, "Will the one named Data come forward and touch us, for we do not recognize his species."

Data swiveled his head away from the clump of crystals and exhaled loudly. The gust of air moved him just enough to hover over the sparkling translator. He bent down and touched a thin shard, which turned vibrant blue at his touch.

"I am an artificial being," explained the android.

"Nonsense," replied the strange voice. "You are made of elements and natural materials which we know. You are a natural being, not artificial."

"Thank you." Data smiled at what he obviously considered a compliment. "I have a theory that the singularity which threatens your world is a dimensional rift."

"That is correct," said a normal voice from the rear. The away team turned to see a male Elaysian wearing yellow robes instead of the more common white ones. He pushed off from the cave wall and soared over the visitors' heads. *Showoff,* Reg thought.

"Captain Picard, I am Tangre Bertoran, Peer of the Jeptah." The white-haired Elaysian said his title as if they should all be impressed, thought Reg. He kicked his bare feet in the air as he talked. "The dimensional rift is causing serious problems for Gemworld. It is directing a stream of dark matter at the planet, and this has accelerated the growth of the crystals severalfold. Gravity has doubled, and we fear it may quadruple. The new growth is not stable—it breaks off, as you have seen.

"Most of this dangerous, new growth is concentrated in the core of the planet, but all over Gemworld crystals are breaking. This has cut off travel routes and arteries, trapping and killing our people. Our communication system, which depends upon the crystal for transmission, has broken down. To relate it to your world, it's like a major earthquake in every city at once."

Bertoran folded his arms, as if expecting the visitors to do something immediately to rectify the situation. "And I needn't mention the danger to the entire sector if a dimensional rift stays open."

The captain nodded gravely. "We know the danger—it nearly destroyed our ship. But we're going to need a lot more information about this rift. What caused it?"

"How would we know?" snapped Tangre Bertoran. "One day, it just appeared."

"But you have been collecting dark matter," interjected Data. "Perhaps that is related."

Bertoran gave the android a condescending smile. "Very few scientists in the Federation know anything about dark matter, although some believe it constitutes seventy percent of the universe. The shell has collected dark matter in small amounts for thousands of years, converting it to a phosphor-rich fertilizer. We never know how much we'll get, but we're grateful for all the energy sources we have. Although you can't see dark matter with even your best sensors, it's all around you. It was never dangerous before the rift appeared."

"Perhaps there is a malfunction in the shell," suggested Data.

There were audible gasps in the rose-hued cavern, and the Lipuls and Alpusta became more agitated, moving with rapid jerks. Bertoran recoiled in horror, then he spun around, pushed off, and flew away from them. Accusatory glares came from most of the Elaysians, and Pazlar rushed to the captain's side.

Troi and Barclay leaned in to listen.

"Captain," said Pazlar with a pained expression, "the shell isn't just a machine, especially to the Jeptah. It's a holy relic from the days of the Ancients. It's the Sacred Protector." She glanced at Data and lowered her voice. "Sometimes you can't call a machine a machine, even when it is."

"I apologize," said Picard. "We'll all use more tact." He loudened his voice to address the chamber. "We ask for your pardon. Commander Data meant no disrespect to the Sacred Protector. But certainly any investigation of dark matter must include your dark-matter collectors."

"It's the rift you have to worry about!" shouted Tangre Bertoran. "We Jeptah will attend to the shell as we always have."

Barclay could see the captain's resolve harden even as his expression softened to its most diplomatic. "Our fates are linked together. The *Enterprise* can't leave Gemworld, and no other ships can come here as long as that rift is open. If you're destroyed, we're destroyed. To fight this thing, we have to be open and honest with each other. If we require access to the Sacred Protector, you will have to give it to us."

Bertoran raised a finger with a triumphant smile.

"And if we require your ship, you will give us access, right? Perhaps the best way to dispense with the rift is the most direct. Why don't you apply some firepower, and decimate it with quantum torpedoes? Our scientists feel that might work."

"That might work," agreed Picard, "but without a doubt it would be a suicide mission."

"We lose one ship and a volunteer skeleton crew," said the white-haired Elaysian with a shrug. "That's better than losing a planet of billions of souls."

Suddenly one of the Alpusta sprang forward on a rapidly elongating web. The remarkable creature stopped directly in front of Bertoran and bobbed up and down, blocking his view and clearly interrupting him. The Alpusta extended another web into the cluster of crystals in the center, and the shards pulsed with earthier, duller colors for a moment.

A scratchy, metallic voice intoned, "Captain Picard, you will have access to any system you desire. Current needs override old traditions. The Jeptah are on many of the teams which serve the Sacred Protector, but they serve at the will of the Exalted Ones. We will meet you at the Ninth Processing Gate on the shell in one shadow mark."

"Thank you," answered Picard, not pushing for details.

Tangre Bertoran and several other Elaysians didn't hesitate to show their displeasure by linking up and flying from the immense cavern. Melora looked concerned by this development, but she remained at the side of her shipmates, staring straight ahead.

Without warning, something moved high above them in the shadows of the crystal cavern. Reg looked up, as did Deanna, Pazlar, and the captain. What appeared to be a brown blanket, or maybe a carpet, fluttered slowly down, its fringed edges curling in the air. This flying creature, which seemed to have no front or back, head or tail, dropped down and undulated over the cluster in the center. The shards glowed more brightly than they had for any of the others, as if its life-force were double the others.

"Yiltern," whispered Melora.

The amazing creature suddenly elongated into a thick rope and flew swiftly toward the exit. As it passed over the visitors' heads, Reg gaped in astonishment—what appeared to have been one seamless creature was actually a flock of tiny bat-like things, flying so close together it was as if they were connected by a single mind. As they approached the narrow slit, the flock reformed into the flying carpet shape, did a ninety-degree turn, and slipped gracefully out.

The scratchy voice sounded again. "The debate is over. You are dismissed."

The Lipuls in the walls faded into the murky gel in which they lived; in a moment, they were all gone. The Alpusta disconnected its web from the cluster of crystals and recoiled on its other web until it had rejoined its fellows. Hushed whispers and suspicious glares came from the remaining Elaysians. In the center of the vast cavern, the glowing cluster grew dark, and even the refracted sunlight in the cavern seemed to grow dim.

"Link hands," said Melora softly.

The visitors wasted no time and followed her suggestion. They floated quietly from the heart of the aged crystal. Reg wasn't sure if they were silenced more by Gemworld and its inhabitants or by the scope of the problem confronting them. Either way, it was hard not to fear that they were in over their heads.

Commander Will Riker stood on the bridge of the *Enterprise,* marveling at the unusual images on the newly repaired viewscreen. Scores of technicians worked on the hull of the *Enterprise* in bright sunlight and blue skies, unencumbered by spacesuits and lifelines. They worked quickly because no one knew when the next avalanche might come, but at least they worked with relative ease. A few of them used jetpacks to cover wide areas, and the others maneuvered to the open hatches with magnetic boots and exo-hull gear. Under these ideal conditions, thought Riker, their molecular patches on the outer hull would no doubt hold until they could reach a starbase.

This place would make a perfect starbase, Riker decided. It would be the only one in Starfleet where a full-size ship could hang in weightless suspension in a class-M atmosphere. It was a natural, although he could never see the reclusive inhabitants giving their permission. On the other hand, the whole planet seemed a bit unreal and impermanent, even if it had lasted for billions of years. The dimensional rift and the strange gravity spikes—these might be the beginning of the end for a planet that had outlasted its natural time.

Riker paced the bridge, avoiding the technicians who were replacing the entire conn station. Despite the progress of the work crews both inside and out, he would be glad when they could clear the area and put up the shields.

"Commander," said the voice of the female Deltan on tactical. "Starfleet has finally acknowledged our message, version four-one-nine."

Riker sighed and gave her an unabashed grin. "Good job, Lieutenant." They had been trying since their arrival to get a brief message through the interference caused by the rift. The message wasn't so much a call for help as a warning to stay away. Normal subspace channels hadn't worked, but one of the obscure emergency frequencies finally had. He only hoped that Starfleet heeded the warning.

At that thought, the smile faded from Will's clean-shaven face. If Starfleet did heed their warning, then they were all alone here. They either had to save Gemworld or fall to pieces with it.

Chapter Seven

AT THE CORE OF GEMWORLD, a tiny shuttlecraft drifted slowly among clusters of dark, misshapen crystals. The ship was dwarfed by twisted prisms and spires, growing in chaotic profusion. Every few seconds, chunks of the crystal broke off and floated outward, like cold embers from a dead fire. Only the shuttlecraft's shields protected it from the deadly shards, which evaporated in colorful sparks along its hull. Clouds of black debris followed the shuttlecraft where the crystals had disintegrated.

Deanna Troi stared out the window and found it impossible to believe that these huge, black masses had not been here a few short weeks ago. Now they looked as if they were about to expand, crushing the old, bleached crystals which ringed the once hollow core of Gemworld.

It was crowded inside the shuttlecraft, with Data at the controls, Captain Picard on copilot, Reg Barclay, Melora Pazlar, and herself all craning forward from the rear seats. As beautiful and elegant as the structures above them were, these looked ugly, diseased, and weak. Yet they were growing at a tremendous rate, making the broken shards seem like casualties in a war of attrition.

Data studied his instrument panel intently, then he peered out the window. "I am very interested in the nutrient strands which are feeding the crystal. I wish we could get close enough to see exactly where they lead."

"My people checked that out," said Pazlar. "The strands are growing spontaneously from older irrigation systems that were supposed to be dormant. There's no control from the programs that are supposed to regulate them—they're taking the nutrients from the regular flow. It's as if a plant that was dead came back to life, only mutated in some horrible fashion."

"But where are the nutrients coming from?" asked the captain.

Melora looked down. "Ultimately, all nutrients come from the shell. All this unrestrained growth is causing the shell to overproduce nutrients to maintain these new strands."

"Which came first, the chicken or the egg?" said Barclay thoughtfully.

Pazlar looked puzzledly at him. "I don't understand that reference."

Reg smiled sheepishly. "I mean . . . has the crystal

growth caused the shell to go crazy? Or has the shell caused the crystals to go crazy?"

"The shell can't 'go crazy,' " snapped Melora brusquely. "The rift and the bombardment of dark matter . . . that's what's causing all of this."

"We cannot make a determination at this time," said Data. "The increased thoron radiation makes it dangerous to stay here for very long, and it is impossible to get any closer."

"It's hard to imagine this was once solid ore, like a conventional planet," said Troi.

"I remember it as wide, open space . . . a place to learn to fly," said Melora glumly. She still appeared to be in shock from the disfigurement of her fragile, jewel-like world. Until they had seen this obscene, unchecked growth, none of them had really appreciated how bad things were.

Picard glanced at the chronometer on his instrument panel. "If I'm not mistaken, one shadow mark is a bit less than an hour."

"That's right," answered Pazlar.

"Then it's time that we meet our hosts at the Ninth Processing Gate."

"Perhaps I could navigate for Commander Data," said Melora.

"By all means." The captain rose from the co-pilot's seat. Both he and Barclay needed to help Pazlar to her feet. Since the Elaysian had been flying freely most of the day, she no longer wore her anti-grav suit. Even the slightest movement was difficult for her with the shuttlecraft's artificial gravity.

After Melora got situated in the copilot's seat, she directed Data in a steady but cautious climb through the jungle of crystals. It was a relief to get away from the black cluster at the heart of the planet, but it was impossible to look at healthy crystal without seeing how deformed it could become. This aged planet had led many lives, thought Deanna, and she couldn't help but wonder if it were on its last.

While they ascended to the upper levels, Captain Picard contacted the ship and received some good news. Their message had finally reached Starfleet, outlining their own dire situation and warning Starfleet off from any rescue attempts. Repairs were also going better than expected, and crews would soon be finished working on the hull. The *Enterprise* still didn't have warp drive, but that hardly mattered at the moment. They weren't going anywhere as long as that dimensional rift loomed just outside the planet's protective shell.

"Data," said the captain, "I know we told them it wouldn't work, but would a brace of torpedoes have any effect on the rift?"

"Unknown," answered the android. "We know very little about the anomaly. It is interesting that dark matter is spewing *out* rather than being sucked in. This would indicate that any destructive actions could backfire. It also indicates an equalization is taking place."

"Equalization?" asked Troi.

The android nodded. "Just as air flows from one room to another if the air pressure is unequal, dark matter might be flowing into our dimension to equalize some sort of imbalance. Perhaps the imbalance was caused by the inhabitants collecting and converting dark matter for their own use."

"I doubt it," said Melora. "We've been doing that for centuries—why would it cause such problems now?"

"That is a good question," said Data. "I have not had enough time to study Gemworld, but I can make one observation: it is unique. Gemworld is a singularity unto itself, unlike any other known body in space, and its long-term effects on the cosmos are unknown."

Pazlar scoffed angrily. "Do you think *we* did this to ourselves?"

"Inhabitants have been known to do irreparable harm to their own planets, through accident or neglect."

"Not us," insisted the Elaysian. "We have a long history of *preserving* our planet. We've kept our culture simple, so there's no pollution, and we have nurtured every form of life. Everything we've done has been to extend the life of Gemworld. The Exalted Ones would never allow anyone to harm it."

"Nevertheless, harm is being done," said Data bluntly.

As if ignoring him, Melora turned to her instrument panel. "You want to bear zero-mark-zero-two-nine."

"Acknowledged," said Data, making the course correction. He continued to deftly pilot the shuttlecraft upward through the intricate layers of crystal growth, avoiding every sweeping archway and mammoth pillar. It seemed darker now on this side of the planet, but just barely. It was a sort of twilight, with overlapping shadows caused by the great monoliths.

"Is there never any night here?" asked Troi.

"Not like there is on most planets," said Melora. "Because Gemworld isn't solid anymore, light filters through constantly, no matter where the sun is. When I first went to Starfleet Academy, the nights were almost harder to get used to than the gravity. At least the gravity was constant. The nights seemed to come so quickly and with such finality. I used to lay awake, worrying that the sunlight wouldn't return."

Deanna shook her head in amazement. "I don't think I've met many people in Starfleet who have had to make as many adjustments as you. We have many non-humanoid species, but they have special ships outfitted just for them. But as the only Elaysian in Starfleet, you're not going to get any special ships outfitted just for you."

"I've noticed that," answered Pazlar with a smile. She glanced at Reg Barclay. "People always want to know why I'm in Starfleet, and why I've stayed so long. I've seen some incredible places, but I think I've stayed mostly for the people. Had I stayed on Gemworld, I never would have met any of you . . . or the hundreds of other officers I've served with. I can always be an Elaysian, flying among the crystals, but I'll only be young and footloose now."

"Have you ever considered the diplomatic corps?" asked Data. "It would appear that we require more contact with your people."

She smiled with amusement. "Unfortunately, I've never been very diplomatic. When I leave Starfleet, I always thought I would come home and teach my people about the Federation. We have a hunger for knowledge, even if we don't like to leave home. But if we survive this crisis, maybe that will change. Maybe I won't be the only Elaysian in Starfleet."

"We are almost at our destination," said Data. "Are there any security precautions I should know about?"

"No. The Ninth Processing Gate is a major entrance to the shell. Lots of supplies go in and out, as well as workers. I'm sure they'll be expecting us."

Troi sat forward to get a good look at the ancient machine she had heard so much about. As the shuttlecraft drew closer, what looked like gray clouds solidified into bands of metal traversing the planet like a wire mesh. As they drew closer yet, the metal bands became metal walls with odd portholes and kidney-shaped cutouts. Through the holes and gaps in the shell, she could see the shimmer of forcefields and the darkness of space beyond. It was disconcerting to see blue sky and black space so close together, with no blend between them. It felt like the shell was keeping them prisoner as much as it was protecting them.

There was considerable activity around one of the portholes. Flocks of Elaysians hovered about, and a nest of Alpusta bounced nervously on their webs. From this same opening, colorful tendrils snaked into a thick coil which descended to the surface. It looked like a giant vine, thought Deanna, and she couldn't help but to think of Jack and the Beanstalk, a tale her father had told her. In a way, that's what this was—a magical world floating on top of the real world.

As the shuttlecraft glided slowly toward the opening, Troi revised her opinion. Now that she clearly saw the bolts, pits, welds, and patches in the shell, she realized it was a machine—perhaps the grandest machine ever built, but a machine nevertheless. This made the playground of spires and prisms below them seem all the more unreal, like hothouse tomatoes growing in the winter. In a way, Gemworld was nothing but the galaxy's biggest fishbowl, with air instead of water.

Data stopped the ship a safe distance from the gate. Once again, Elaysians encircled them and tethered the shuttlecraft, showing a lot of enthusiasm but very little efficiency. Troi could sense that all this special treatment was beginning to grate on the captain. He wanted to stride briskly wherever he felt like going—not wait until it was safe for them to be escorted, floating and helpless.

"We seem to be secure," reported Data uncertainly.

"Open the hatch," said the captain impatiently. He was already on his feet, waiting to get out, then he stepped back and motioned to Lieutenant Pazlar. "After you."

She tried to get up and groaned. "I could use a hand."

Barclay and the captain came to her aid and helped the Elaysian to the door. She leaped for joy off the shuttlecraft and whirled around like a swimmer in midair. "In time, flying will come to you like second nature," she assured them.

Deanna didn't feel as if she were flying yet, but their exit from the shuttlcraft was more orderly than the first time. Even Barclay made it without a problem. One of the Alpusta broke off from its fellows and swooped toward them on its web, its legs pumping slowly. Troi almost ducked with alarm, but she maintained her friendly demeanor while she tried to float without pinwheeling her arms. She hoped the Alpusta knew how to control its flight.

It did, extending its leg to the shuttlecraft and stopping just in front of them. It was impossible for her to tell if this was the same Alpusta who had spoken to them at the gathering of the Exalted Ones, but it carried itself regally. She supposed it might be ten meters across if its legs were outstretched, although its spiny black torso was only a meter or so across. The Alpusta seemed to have as many eyes as legs; they were mounted on thin stalks which swiveled curiously as it regarded the visitors.

She noticed a green crystal hanging like a belt beneath the Alpusta's torso and above its numerous legs. The crystal glimmered, and they heard the same metallic, synthesized voice they'd heard earlier in the chamber of the Exalted Ones.

"I am Jrojak of the Exalted. Hold my web and follow me into the Sacred Protector."

From his thoracic region, a silky, glimmering web shot forward about three meters. Captain Picard grabbed it gamely and held out his other hand to Troi. She was glad for his strong, confident grasp. Melora pulled Reg over and took Troi's hand, while Data took

Barclay's free hand and the rear position. Like a chain of paper dolls, they were soon trailing after the Alpusta in a jerky ride into the interior of the shell.

Although the inhabitants seemed to use little technology in their homes among the crystal, the interior of the Ninth Processing Gate was a technological marvel. The corridors were cylindrical, and monitoring stations were everywhere—on the floor, ceiling, and walls. Most of these stations were unstaffed but inspected frequently by teams of fast-moving Elaysians. Snaking along the curved walls were narrow chutes and tubes, which looked like colorful veins. Materials seemed to be moving briskly through these conduits.

They stopped for a moment when the corridor became congested with workers. Deanna bent forward to inspect a bluish conduit full of liquid, and to her surprise a Lipul shot past, causing her to bolt upright in alarm.

"Steady there," warned Captain Picard with a sympathetic smile.

A moment later, they were in motion again, going up or down in branching corridors as the Alpusta desired. Troi knew they were moving laterally inside the shell, but it felt as if they were plunging deeper and deeper into a highly sophisticated complex. Some of the walls were illuminated with diagrams and flow charts; other walls were lined with filters, canisters, and apparatus she couldn't identify. Through tinted windows, she got glimpses of laboratories, testing equipment, and research facilities. At least that's what she guessed they were as the Alpusta whisked them along without comment.

Troi glanced at Data and saw that the android was bursting with questions, but he showed restraint and remained silent but curious. There would be explanations later, or they would have to deal with Captain Picard. Reg and Melora conversed in low tones, and Troi imagined that Reg was getting a more informative tour than the rest of them.

They entered what appeared to be a drinking room. There was nothing else you could call it, thought Deanna. Both Elaysians and Alpusta lined up politely to drink from long sip tubes immersed in swollen green bladders, fed by veins of liquid in the wall. They weren't offered any of the refreshment, and the procession moved on.

They passed through a long, narrow chamber that looked like pictures Troi had seen of the engine room of an old transatlantic steamship. Great pistons churned, and hydraulic pumps and bellows wheezed. Here Alpusta seemed to be in charge, and the spider-like creatures swarmed all over the aged machinery, tending it lovingly. This machinery needed no explanation, thought Troi; without gravity to aid in the flow of materials, all the hydraulics and pumps were necessary. It was the first time that she got a feel for the incredible age of the shell.

The procession continued on, led by the stoic Alpusta. Briefly they passed a window which opened on the space side of the shell. Troi glimpsed row upon row of collection dishes, standing in the shadows of much larger hydrogen scoops. Before any of them could really get a good look, they had bobbed past the window.

There were suddenly fewer workers in the circular corridor, and the walls appeared jewel-like, as if made from the crystal. The passageway ended at what appeared to be a fortified hatch—almost a vault. It was guarded by two Elaysians wearing yellow robes, and Deanna recognized the white-haired one as Tangre Bertoran, the man who had argued with them in the hall of the Exalted Ones. *The other one must also be a Jeptah,* decided Troi. Neither one of them looked happy to see the group of outsiders, even with an Alpusta and an Elaysian escort.

"I regret to say that this portion of the shell is closed to you," said Tangre Bertoran in no uncertain terms.

"What's in there?" asked Captain Picard.

"Programming systems, high-level access."

Pazlar pushed off from the wall and zoomed to within a few centimeters of the Jeptah's face. "These people have risked their lives to help us. How dare you defy the wishes of the Exalted Ones!"

He returned her glare. "For eons, the Jeptah have tended and protected this holy relic, and it has tended and protected all of us. Never in our long history have we opened the inner workings of the Sacred Protector to the eyes of outsiders. It was understood when we joined the Federation that we did not have to share our technology."

"Believe me," said Barclay bravely, "we could

d-duplicate everything we've seen here. Maybe it would take a while, but it took you a while. The Federation will still be here tomorrow, but that's hard to say about Gemworld. All it would take is for you to lose the forcefield, and you lose your atmosphere."

"Precisely!" bellowed Tangre Bertoran. "Why do you think we are so protective of the workings of the shell? A moment's sabotage could kill every living creature on Gemworld!"

He ignored the others and appealed directly to the captain. "You are a man of honor, a hero in the Federation. We know this. Can't you accept the fact that we know when the shell is working properly? Do what you do best—destroy the rift out there! We don't have any weapons, or we would do it."

The captain's lips thinned, but he replied calmly, "We don't merely destroy everything we find in space. Until we know what created that rift, we don't know how to deal with it. We need information. I'd like to remind you that the Lipuls contacted *us.* Perhaps you should discuss your concerns with them."

"You can't change anything here, anyway," insisted the Elaysian. "There are protocols even *we* must follow, and none of the senior engineers are present. It would do you little good to even—"

With a swift, violent motion, the Alpusta picked up the Elaysian with half a dozen of its legs and hurled him headfirst down the corridor. Flailing his arms and legs, Bertoran finally managed to stop his momentum and bounce off a wall. He whirled around and glared at the Alpusta. "Jrojak! You will answer for this!"

The Alpusta turned its forest of stalked eyes on the other Elaysian guarding the door. He swiftly punched a code into an entry pad, and the hatch popped open with a rush of air. The Elaysian backed away as Jrojak swept past, dragging the captain, Troi, Barclay, Pazlar, and Data along in its wake.

They entered a room that was unlike any programming center Troi had ever seen. The walls of the tubular chamber were covered with small drawers. Between the rows of drawers, clawlike switches clicked with numbing regularity. An access panel lay open, its sparkling circuitry revealed, and there was one monitoring station like the ones they had seen throughout the complex.

The far wall was covered with a tapestry made from coarse cloth. As Deanna peered more closely at this wall-hanging, she noticed that it had numerous small pockets.

Another Elaysian tried to scurry from the chamber, but Pazlar stopped her. "Don't go," she said. "Please tell us what's happening here."

The Elaysian looked uncertainly at the Alpusta, and the green crystal on its belt glimmered. "Speak, our daughter," said the metallic voice.

She gulped and nodded. "I am not Jeptah. I understand how serious this is."

"Then help us," said Picard, "so we'll know how to help you."

The Elaysian motioned around at the tiny drawers. "These are the repositories—you might call them master circuits—made from the living crystal." She pushed off and floated to the wall-hanging with all the pockets. From one of the pockets, she took a red crystal shard about thirty centimeters long. It looked like one of the spiny crystals from the cluster they had seen in the hall of the Exalted Ones.

Crystal in hand, the technician drifted toward a drawer over Troi's head and opened it. Very carefully, she shoved the shard into its slot, and the accompanying switch began to tick softly. "It is that simple," she explained, "but it is not simple. It usually takes an acolyte the equivalent of twenty years to learn to program the shell. All the functions are available, but not all the crystals are available."

"What do you mean, they're not all available?" asked the captain.

"The six master crystals are in the possession of the senior engineers, one from each of the sentient species. We can program many functions here, but access to critical systems is limited to the six senior engineers. None of them are present on the shell at this time."

Troi stared in amazement. "How could they not be present in this time of emergency?"

"There are serious problems in the rest of Gemworld," answered the Elaysian defensively. She shook her head in frustration at having to deal with these outsiders. "The senior engineers are high-ranking dignitaries. There's no one more important, not even the Exalted Ones. They are the only ones who are able to make substantive changes in the shell programming."

"Perhaps we should recall them," said Barclay.

The captain raised his hand, quelling other suggestions. "I'm sure there's much we can learn from . . . I'm sorry, I didn't catch your name?"

"Haselma," answered the programmer with a slight bow. She glanced uneasily at the Alpusta. "If it's the wish of the Exalted Ones, I will show you what I know, and how it relates to the crisis. You will have to send me your most intelligent engineers—this technology was advanced a million years ago."

Captain Picard smiled confidently. "I think Commander Data and Lieutenant Barclay will be able to keep up with you."

His combadge chirped, and a voice said, *"Enterprise* to away team."

"Picard here. Go ahead, Number One."

"We should be putting up shields now, but we have a problem. We're surrounded by about a thousand Elaysians, and they refuse to go away. We can't use thrusters or impulse engines for fear of injuring them."

"Did they say what they want?"

"Yes, access to our engine room, torpedo room, and weapons systems. And one more thing, they're all wearing yellow."

"Our friends, the Jeptah," said Picard with consternation. "Data and Barclay have to stay here on the shell, but the rest of us will return immediately. Picard out."

The captain turned and looked at Data, wishing that he didn't have to leave anyone on the shell, where they didn't seem to be entirely welcome. "Perhaps we need to send for security."

"I will be security," said a metallic voice, and they turned to see the Alpusta bobbing slowly on its web.

"Thank you," said Picard with apparent relief. "Lieutenant Pazlar, if you'll lead the way out."

The young Elaysian looked chagrined by these developments. "I'm very sorry, sir, for the problems we're facing. I knew some of my people were mired in tradition, but I didn't think they would try to hamper us. These are frightening times—it's bringing out the worst in us."

"You're not accountable for every member of your species," said Picard with sympathy. "Data, don't hesitate to contact the ship if you need help. As soon as we can spare more people, we'll send them over."

"What precisely are we looking for, sir?" asked the android.

"A connection between the shell and the dimensional rift. Check on their dark-matter collectors, too. Let's use the process of elimination to rule out the obvious. Maybe this shell has nothing to do with it."

"Yes, sir."

Troi noticed Melora giving Reg a worried glance. He nodded confidently. *Good work, Reg,* the counselor thought. *You've come a long way.* The Elaysian took the captain's hand, and he in turn took Troi's hand. Deftly bouncing from wall to wall, Melora quickly picked up momentum, and they were soon flying down the tubular corridor.

Chapter Eight

CAPTAIN PICARD COULDN'T HELP being reminded of Gulliver and the Lilliputians as he cautiously piloted the shuttlecraft toward the *Enterprise*. Suspended in the blue sky, festooned with ropes, the *Enterprise* looked more like a dirigible than a starship; and thousands of yellow-garbed Elaysians swarmed all over her. They were apparently trying to tie the ship down, or tie themselves to her. More and more of them were arriving every minute, and a long chain of towed Elaysians stretched across the sky like the ragged tail of a kite.

Beside him in the copilot seat, Melora Pazlar lowered her head in embarrassment. "I can't tell you how much I regret this, sir. I don't know what's taken hold of them."

113

"Fear," said Deanna Troi. "It's a strong motivator, not always for the best."

"Don't they realize how dangerous it is out here?" said Picard in amazement. "The new crystals are breaking off as fast as they grow, and with the gravity increasing—"

He didn't finish his statement because he knew his ship's counselor was right. They were locked in fear, striking at the wrong enemy, and rational discourse would not be easy.

Troi observed, "The Jeptahs' reaction to us is a classic case of 'killing the messenger,' because they don't want to hear what we're saying. We're raising questions they can't begin to raise themselves."

"Any ideas about how we can get them to leave?" asked Picard. He slowed the shuttlecraft down to a controlled glide. In another hundred meters, the path would be blocked unless the throng of protestors voluntarily parted for them. Instead the Jeptahs seemed to be drifting into the shuttle's path, forcing Picard to go even slower.

Melora clenched her teeth in anger. "I wish we could stun them all."

"That seems a bit drastic," said the captain, mildly amused. "And we would also have to transport them all to the planet. No, there doesn't seem to be anything to do but hear them out."

As the shuttlecraft drew perilously close to the Elaysians, Picard applied forward thrusters and brought them to a complete stop. Then he popped the hatch, letting fresh air and sunshine pour into the small craft, which refreshed his weary spirits. Gemworld was a special place, but all the things that made it special also made their job difficult.

Elaysians fluttered around them, peering into the shuttlecraft with a mixture of curiosity and anger. Picard went to the open hatchway and surveyed the crowd of yellow-garbed humanoids, who were scattered into the sky as far as he could see. Off the bow of the shuttlecraft was the *Enterprise,* seen from an angle Picard had never expected to see, unless he were floating in the darkness of space. With all the ropes hanging from it, the starship looked like a metallic Moby Dick—a monster dwarfing everything in sight.

"I am Jean-Luc Picard, captain of the Enterprise!" he called out to the Elaysians. "Do you have a spokesperson, someone I can talk to?"

"Tangre Bertoran," came the answer, which hardly surprised Picard.

"Someone get Tangre Bertoran!" His name was shouted aloud and carried across the wind by a chain of voices.

"We demand to be let onto the ship!" shouted one of the Jeptah. This cry was taken up for several moments, but Picard didn't react. He wasn't going to negotiate with an angry mob, not when he could talk to the main instigator.

Melora Pazlar appeared in the doorway, glaring at her fellow Elaysians. The captain could tell that she was about to explode. "Now would be a good time for diplomacy," he cautioned her.

She took a deep breath and nodded. "I'm just so disappointed with them. I knew that *I* was short-tempered and demanding, but I didn't think so many other Elaysians were."

"Do you have any police, or anyone we could call for assistance? To reason with them?"

Melora shook her head. "We haven't needed law enforcement for millennia. The Exalted Ones might be able to reason with them, but it would take time to convene them and send a delegation back here. The Jeptah have never been shy."

"So I gather," replied Picard.

When a few of her fellows gazed at her with curiosity, Melora granted them her most charming smile and nothing else. Deanna Troi also came to the hatch and waved, but they pointedly ignored her. While they waited, the captain contacted the bridge and told Commander Riker that the shuttlecraft was just outside the hull, trying to negotiate a withdrawal of the protestors. Riker wished him luck.

Finally the curtain of Elaysians seemed to part, and a small procession zoomed toward them. Tangre Bertoran was in the lead, with his own hover-platform, and about six associates followed in his wake.

The white-haired Jeptah looked defiant as he approached Captain Picard. "Ah, Captain, I knew we would meet again. We've shown up for our reciprocal tour of the ship. We would also like to *use* your weapon systems, as you used the Sacred Protector."

The captain sat down in the hatchway and dangled his legs in midair. "You do know how dangerous it is out here, don't you? Another avalanche of broken crystals could occur any moment. The only reason we would like you to leave is so that we can put up our shields."

Bertoran frowned, and the triangle on his forehead stood out in tight relief. "You violated the sanctity of the Sacred Protector and the rules of the Jeptah."

"And so you wish to violate our sanctity and our rules," said Picard evenly. "You've done so, in a most impressive way. We can't even leave, for fear that our thrusters and impulse engines will harm the protestors. Are your people tying themselves to the *Enterprise?*"

"The ropes are symbolic," answered Bertoran. "It means that you are bound to us by the rule of law. We have command of your ship while it is within our shell."

"So what are your demands?" asked Picard.

"That you stop invading the Sacred Protector. That you allow us to inspect your weapons systems and engine room, and that you destroy the rift with your weapons."

Picard felt Pazlar stir behind him, and he turned to see her sputtering with anger at this popinjay and his demands. He gave her a knowing smile and whispered, "How far will any of them be able to get once they come onto the ship?"

She brightened immediately. "Oh, they'll be miserable. They have no idea what it's like to move around in gravity."

Picard turned to the multitude of Elaysians, floating

all around like an assemblage of angels. He rose to his feet and waved like a politician. "We will be happy to meet the demands of Tangre Bertoran!" That proclamation was followed by a surprised clamor of voices and a startled look on Bertoran's face. Picard went on his best populist manner. "But we can't take all of you. Perhaps your esteemed leader and a small party, but the rest of you must disperse, so that we can put up shields."

Now there was grumbling, and several Elaysians flew forward, vying for Bertoran's ear. He waved them back and proclaimed, "They won't leave until after we've been aboard."

"Sorry, no deal then," said Picard flatly. "We have to put up shields as soon as possible. We're not going to fire weapons or do anything else until our shields are up. You get what you want; we get what we want. That's only fair."

Bertoran conferred with a few of his advisors, and Picard remained pleasant but stone faced. Finally the Jeptah turned to him and nodded, and his lieutenants spread the word. "Disperse! Disperse!"

There was grumbling, but gradually the Elaysians began to take their ropes and fly away. While that was going on, Picard withdrew inside the shuttlecraft and tapped his combadge. "Picard to La Forge," he said softly.

"La Forge here," came the answer.

"I want you to prepare Holodeck One to entertain some visiting Elaysians. We'll need a bridge simulation, engine room simulation, and the torpedo room."

"They're all in memory from the recent training exercises," said La Forge. "Anything in particular?"

"This is just to buy us some time and keep them occupied," answered the captain. He glanced outside to make sure no Elaysians were within earshot. "We need to launch an unsuccessful attack against the rift—they're *not* to know it's a simulation. We'll direct-beam them from spot to spot, to alleviate the problem they'll have with the gravity. Assemble a good crew, and tell them what's going on."

"Yes, sir," answered La Forge. "Too bad Reg is away—he'd be perfect for this."

"We'll come in after the Elaysians leave. They're moving quickly, so you don't have much time. If need be, we'll go to the real torpedo room first—it's cramped and claustrophobic."

"Don't worry about it, Captain, we'll be ready. I'm on my way to the holodeck."

"Thanks, Geordi. Picard out."

Pazlar stared in awe at the captain, and he gave her an innocent smile. "They're not the only ones with advanced technology."

Geordi La Forge stood on what looked like the bridge of the *Enterprise,* watching his handpicked crew go through the motions of flying the ship. On the viewscreen was the same scene of improbable blue skies that was on the real viewscreen on the real bridge. The last of the Elaysian protestors were soaring into the distance, mere specks in the clear, azure sky. All of the stations mirrored their duplicates on the genuine bridge, and La Forge checked the readings on an auxiliary engineering console. It all looked perfect, but the chief engineer still felt uneasy and distracted. His mind was still on several problems in engineering.

"They've put up shields," reported Ensign Ganadee, the bald-headed Deltan on ops.

"That means our guests are on the ship." La Forge strode to the command chair and sat down, tugging nervously at his tunic. "They're going to direct-beam from the shuttlebay. So look lively—they could be here any minute."

"Yes, sir," came several responses.

A few moments later, half a dozen figures materialized in sparkling columns in front of the turbolift. Four of them were Elaysians wearing billowy clothes, and the other two were Captain Picard and Counselor Troi.

"Captain on the bridge," said the tactical officer.

La Forge recognized the woman in the white robe as Lieutenant Pazlar. She coped with the gravity much better than her fellow Elaysians. Within seconds, all three of them slumped to the deck, and the captain rushed to assist a white-haired individual.

"Ensign Ganadee, help our visitors," ordered La Forge.

"No, no . . . remain at your stations," said the white-haired Elaysian, breathing heavily. His companions just sat on the deck, looking as though they had been stunned. "The gravity . . . is much worse than I expected."

"I'm afraid we can't adjust it," said Captain Picard. "We need to be operating at peak efficiency."

"Understood," grumbled the white-haired man.

With considerable effort, Picard, Troi, and Pazlar got the visitors situated in empty seats at auxiliary consoles. The captain finally turned toward Geordi and gave him a surreptitious wink. "Report, Mr. La Forge."

"We've just put up shields," said La Forge, "and repairs are continuing on schedule. Hull repairs are finished, and we expect to have warp drive on-line in about eight hours."

"You won't leave then, will you?" asked an Elaysian worriedly.

"No," answered Picard, "we couldn't if we wanted to, as long as that rift is out there. Allow me to make introductions: Commander La Forge, this is Tangre Bertoran, a Peer of the Jeptah and an Exalted One. The members of his party are Ebrek Optullo and Tereya Nolora. Commander La Forge is one of my most trusted bridge officers."

"Thank you, sir," answered La Forge, trying not to crack a smile.

"You have a very impressive bridge," said Tangre Bertoran, gazing around at the detailed holodeck simulation. "I wish I could get up and explore." He turned to Melora Pazlar and shook his head in amazement. "How do you ever get used to this horrible gravity?"

"I never get used to it," she replied, "but I learn to cope."

Captain Picard rubbed his palms together. "Before we get down to business, I believe you wanted to see engineering and the torpedo room."

"Yes," answered Bertoran. He tried to stand up, but the struggle against gravity was overwhelming. "I would like to, but movement is so difficult. I assume your weapon systems and engineering are in good working order?"

"Every station on the ship suffered during our encounter with the rift," answered Picard. "But we have the resources to launch one quantum torpedo. Don't we, Commander La Forge?"

"Yes, sir. Everything is in readiness."

Captain Picard looked gravely at the Elaysians. "We're in no condition to go anywhere, and flying into the rift would be suicide. So we'll have to fire the torpedo from here. How will your forcefields react to it?"

Bertoran sat forward and groaned at the effort. "It isn't normally a defensive forcefield, although it can be set for that. It's designed to let large, solid objects pass through while restricting the flow of gases and liquids. I assume your quantum charge can inflict zero-point disruption?"

"On a starship, yes," answered Picard. "But our torpedoes are designed to pierce deflector shields and ships' hulls—they've never been tested on a dimensional rift before."

"Of course not," said Bertoran, sounding less confident than he had earlier. "But it's worth a try."

The captain stepped closer to the Elaysian and fixed him with his sternest gaze. "I want it understood that if we try this, and it's unsuccessful, you'll stop telling me how to do my job. And you also won't surround the ship with Jeptah and stage more protests. We're all on the same team, and we're trying to solve problems, not create them."

Bertoran scoffed. "I hate to make promises I can't keep. I don't control all the Jeptah."

"All right," said Picard, "just give me your personal assurance that *you* won't lead any more protests against us."

"All right," muttered Bertoran. "You have been more cooperative than I thought you would be."

"I want to end this as much as you do." The captain strode to the tactical station and looked at the young officer's readouts for a moment. "Target the rift, using our original coordinates where we came out of warp. You'll have to extrapolate the position of the rift. Just make sure you don't hit the shell."

"Yes, sir," she answered, plying her console. Ensign Belkin played her part well, thought Geordi, as she initiated the torpedo training program, with a few modifications. After a few moments, she reported, "Torpedo targeted."

"On screen."

"Yes, sir," answered the ops officer.

Suddenly the scene on the viewscreen shifted to a tight view of the bow and the forward torpedo bays.

"Prepare to fire . . . on my mark." Picard held up his finger and paused dramatically. "Fire!"

On the viewscreen, a cylinder of light shot from the forward bays and streaked into the blue sky. Another angle showed the blazing torpedo shooting through a kidney-shaped opening in the shell and zooming into space. The Elaysians sat forward, staring hopefully at the viewscreen, and La Forge felt momentarily guilty about the deception. But he knew the captain well enough to realize that he wouldn't be doing this unless it was necessary.

The impressive flight of the torpedo continued into space for a second before it was swallowed up by a gaping maw in the firmament. There was no explosion—nothing happened. The light of the torpedo blinked out.

"Any change in sensor readings?" asked Picard.

"No, sir," answered Ensign Ganadee on ops. "There appears to be no effect."

Bertoran let out a deflated breath of air and sunk back in his seat. "It didn't have any effect at all?"

"None that we can determine," answered Picard. "I'm sorry, but I always thought it was a long shot."

"What about phasers?" asked another Elaysian.

"They're a broad-spectrum, short-range weapon," answered La Forge. "They probably won't even make it through your forcefield."

"All right," said Picard with finality, "we've tried to destroy the rift, and that didn't work. Now let's try to learn what caused it. I've got two people still on the shell looking for answers, and it would help greatly if you could assist them."

Bertoran shook his head in frustration. "We've done everything within reason to fight this thing, but how can you fight something you can't see . . . something that's from another dimension?" He shrugged his bony shoulders. "Perhaps this is something we can learn to live with, as we've learned to live with so many disasters in our history."

"Unless you enjoy this gravity," said Melora Pazlar, "you're not going to learn to live with it."

With a scowl, Tangre Bertoran rose uncertainly to his feet. He had the musculature to stand, thought La Forge, he just didn't have the practice.

"We are ready to go," said the Elaysian. "Don't worry, I will keep an eye on your two crewmembers."

The captain nodded congenially, but La Forge could tell from increases in electromagnetic pulses around his skin that he *was* worried. He also seemed relieved, because this visit was probably going to be short and uneventful, except for their deception.

"We're not beaming anyone off the ship," he said, "but Lieutenant Pazlar can take you home in the shuttlecraft. We'll beam you directly to the shuttlebay, if you're ready."

"I'll turn off the gravity in the shuttle," Pazlar assured them with a smile.

Bertoran and his cohorts conferred for a moment, but it was clear they wanted to get off the ship and out of its oppressive atmosphere. Since Geordi had occasionally felt disadvantaged in his life over his blindness, he could relate to them.

"We're ready," said Bertoran importantly. "Thank you for your cooperation."

"My pleasure." The captain tapped his combadge. "Picard to transporter room two. Have you still got a lock on our visitors?"

"Yes, sir."

"Take Lieutenant Pazlar first, and direct-transport them to the shuttlecraft. One-by-one sequence."

"Yes, sir."

The fake bridge crew stood at attention or dutifully worked at their stations as the Elaysians disappeared one by one into a sparkling flame of light. When they were all gone, Picard's congenial smile vanished, and his shoulders slumped. He looked at La Forge and shook his head. "I despised having to do that."

"I felt a little funny about it, too, sir, but I don't think you had any better options," offered the engineer helpfully. "We couldn't just shoot a quantum torpedo into that thing without knowing more."

"Of course not, and we couldn't let them set up camp, draped all over the hull. We had to put up shields." The captain paced the simulated bridge. There were other courses that could have been taken but none more expedient than this. He'd like to think there wouldn't be any more trouble with the Jeptah, but that seemed too much to hope.

The captain shook off his momentary gloom and nodded proudly at the young crew. "At any rate, well done, all of you. Sorry to have taken you away from your posts, but this was necessary. Mr. La Forge, there will be a briefing when Data and Barclay get back from the shell."

"I'll be ready. I've got a lot of questions."

"Don't we all." The captain started toward the turbolift door and said, "Computer, end program."

The turbolift door changed into a pair of gleaming metallic doors, and the walls turned into a black-and-green grid. The doors parted, and Captain Picard stepped from the empty room into a busy corridor.

Five hours later, Captain Picard strode into the briefing room, where he was met by Beverly Crusher, Deanna Troi, Melora Pazlar, and Geordi La Forge. They rose from their seats, and he waved them back down. "Thank you for coming on such short notice. The shuttlecraft has just returned again from the shell, and Data and Barclay will be here in a moment. I wanted you to hear their report, in case you have any ideas on how to proceed."

Melora let out a sigh of relief. "I didn't think they would have any problems, but I'm glad they're back."

"Let's hope they have some answers." The captain turned to Dr. Crusher. "How are things in sickbay?"

"It's calmed down," she answered, "but we still have too many full beds. We finally transferred the last of the Elaysians out, and that's helped. And we need to schedule a service for the seven crewmembers who died. I sent you the list."

"I saw it," said Picard, shaking his head at the inexcusable loss. "I can't say I knew many of them well, except for Yontel. I'll talk to Riker and decide on a good time to do this." As if there was ever a good time for a funeral, he thought.

The door to the conference room opened, and Data strode in, followed by Barclay, whose eyes immediately fixed on Pazlar.

"Away team reporting back," said Data. "We were able to confirm my theory that their dark-matter collection has increased dramatically, sixteen-fold, which is commensurate with the increase in crystal growth. Gravity is increasing at a lesser, variable amount, but it is enough to cause havoc with the unstable crystal."

"Then they'll have to cut back," said Picard. "Or better yet, stop collecting dark matter altogether."

"The fault does not lie in the dark-matter collection alone," answered Data. "Production of all their energy resources has increased sixteen-fold, although many of the resources have been limited by availability. With the rift, there has been plenty of dark matter available."

The captain frowned, perturbed that Gemworld's inhabitants hadn't tried the simplest solution. "Then they should cut back on all their energy collection."

"I am afraid it is not that simple," answered Data. "Energy collection is not a separate system but is governed by other systems. My new theory is that the fractal multiplying program, which controls crystal growth, has been tampered with. It seems to be in an endless loop of increasing production. But we cannot be sure until we obtain access to that code, and that is one of the second-level protocols, which require a senior engineer."

"And let me guess," said Troi, "there aren't any of them around."

"That is true." Data frowned slightly as he chose his next words. "The shell is designed to keep working at all costs, which is logical given the disastrous results if it ever failed. Despite its size and complexity, every subsystem is integrated to a remarkable degree. You cannot shut down one subsystem without shutting down many other subsystems, and that is simply not allowed. The shell is not like me or the *Enterprise*, designed to be shut down and repaired. It is more like a human being, designed to grow and compensate for system failures, but never shut down. Shutting down would result in disaster."

"So there's tremendous resistance to change," concluded Picard. "That's one reason why high-level access is limited to only six senior engineers, who are never around."

"Correct," answered Data. "Almost all the current workers are maintenance workers, because the programming for the system was optimized millennia ago. No one on the shell can access either the core fractal program or the dark-matter collection routines. We require one of the senior engineers."

Geordi La Forge scowled with incomprehension. "What do we have to do to convince these people this is serious?"

"You don't understand," said Melora Pazlar glumly. "We *know* it's serious, but we can't believe that our Sacred Protector could be at fault. We have depended upon the shell, and all the traditions that have surrounded it since the days of the Ancients. You saw the reaction you got when you said it was only a machine. We've always regarded the shell as infallible."

Reg Barclay cleared his throat. "Excuse me, but the shell's crystal computer isn't at fault. Programmers have a saying: 'Garbage in, garbage out.' Somebody messed up the programming, and only six senior engineers have access to the programming. Ergo, one of them must have started this whole mess."

Pazlar scoffed. "That's preposterous."

"It would seem a far-fetched conclusion," agreed Picard, "but you can't overlook its underlying logic. One thing is certain: we've got to get at least one of those engineers back to work so we can examine the programs."

Pazlar hobbled toward the door. "I'll get right on that, sir. I'm going to prove you wrong, Lieutenant Barclay. We will find a logical explanation for this. Or we may find that the rift *did* appear spontaneously and is causing all of the problems."

"Mr. Barclay, go with her," ordered Picard. "Take a shuttlecraft—it will be faster and safer."

The Elaysian whirled around as quickly as she could. "With all due respect, Captain, I think I can handle a protocol matter with my own people by myself."

"Lieutenant, some of your people have proven to be very intractable. I don't want anybody from this crew going anywhere on this planet alone. Do I make myself clear?"

She lowered her head. "Yes, sir."

The captain granted her a slight smile. "Besides, it always helps to view a situation from two different sides. While you hunt down these engineers, try to find out when each of them was last on the shell."

"A little detective work," said Barclay, rubbing his hands together. "I don't mind that at all."

"We'll check on it, Captain." Melora shuffled out the door, barely waiting for Reg to catch up.

"I could give you more detailed descriptions," said Data, "but until we inspect the programming, we can draw no conclusions. Their technology is both more sophisticated and more primitive than ours, owing to its advanced age. The shell is a remarkable combination of traditional circuitry and organic components made from the crystal."

The captain sighed. "At some point, I would love to hear about their technology in detail, but right now we need to finish repairs."

"What we really need is some sleep," insisted Crusher. "We've been here for sixteen hours now, and most of us were up a shift or two before that. Did Barclay sleep at all?"

"He slept on the shuttlecraft," answered Data.

"All right, Beverly," said Picard with a weary smile. "Mr. Data, you have the bridge. I'd like to send a probe into that rift, even if the chances are slim that we'll learn anything. So think about what kind of sensors would be most useful."

The android nodded thoughtfully. "I will make preliminary readings. If the other dimension contains a dark-matter nebula, which seems likely, we might be able to detect trace gases associated with a nebula."

"Make it so," said the captain.

"One more thing," said Dr. Crusher. "I just want to remind everyone that there are some severe side effects associated with weightlessness. Muscle loss, atrophy, nausea, cramping. I know it's pretty out there, but take your hypos and try not to stay off the ship for extended periods."

"If my projections hold true," said Data, "Gem-world will soon have gravity again, but it will no longer be pretty."

That was not the cheery note on which Picard would have hoped to end the staff meeting, but it was fitting. "All of you have things to do," he said, "with sleep being primary among them. Dismissed."

Chapter Nine

REG BARCLAY FLOATED in an uncomfortable silence a few centimeters above his seat on the shuttlecraft. He was uncomfortable not because of the weightlessness but because of the icy curtain of silence Melora Pazlar had strung between them. She hadn't spoken to him since they left the briefing aboard the *Enterprise*. True, she had to pilot the shuttlecraft, and there were plenty of obstacles among the glittering crystals, but she could acknowledge his existence, couldn't she?

He thought about tightening his lap belt some more, but he didn't want to appear to be frightened of the low gravity. More than anything, he wanted Melora to feel that he was sympathetic to her, but how could he be sympathetic if he was scared of low gravity? So the lanky lieutenant floated nervously above his seat, trying to cross his legs and appear noncha-lant.

Under the best of circumstances, Reg wasn't com-fortable making small talk, and this was even more torturous. He didn't even know where they were going; but it couldn't be the shell because they were headed the wrong direction. He had to trust that she was on-mission, which was to get one of the six se-nior engineers back to the shell. There was no other way to gain access to the high-level subroutines.

Reg decided that he was within his rights to ask where they were going. After all, it wasn't top secret, and he was an integral part of the away team. Never-theless, he had to screw up his courage to even clear his throat, which he did. That guttural sound didn't get a reaction from Melora as he had hoped, so Reg grew bolder. "Uh, I was just wondering . . . w-where are we going?"

She ignored him, and Reg felt a flash of anger, which spurred him to try again. "Come on, Melora! You can't ignore me the whole trip—you've got to talk to me sometime."

"But not until I have to," she snapped back.

"Well . . . you can at least tell me where we're going."

She sighed impatiently. "The Hold of the Regal Oneness."

"Oh, that clears it up," muttered Barclay. "I was worried we were going to the hold of the Twoness or Threeness."

She seethed angrily at him. "I can't believe you

suggested that one of our senior engineers sabotaged the shell. What could possibly be the motive for that?"

Barclay gulped. "I was just drawing a logical conclusion. If you hang around Data enough, you end up doing that. Please forgive me—it's nothing personal."

"I know." Melora slowed the craft down, as much to give herself a moment to think as to avoid a large cloud of dark, shattered crystals floating in the air. A few of the shards sizzled on the shuttlecraft's forcefield. "It's just that I haven't been back here in so long, and I feel like I don't belong. My loyalties are divided. I never questioned any of our traditions before, but now I do. Gemworld is the same place I left . . . but it's not."

She shook her head in amazement. "When I was growing up here, I thought it was a paradise, a place where there was never any strife or ill feelings. Now for the first time I see that some of us are petty and small-minded. Also, the Lipuls summoned us, but my own people don't seem to want us. I've never noticed the philosophical difference between our species before. I thought we were always in agreement."

"Well," said Reg, "you left here a child and you came back an adult. You lost your innocence along the way. Fighting in a war will do that to you."

Despite her silky blond hair, Melora's face looked as dark as the cloud of broken crystals. "And I've heard all of you talk about Gemworld: 'It's artificial, it's a skeleton, it should have died a million years ago.' And, you know, I look around here, and I can't help but to agree with you. Now I've seen young planets in their prime, and I know this planet is more preserved than alive. Who have we been fooling all these years?"

"Melora, you're . . . you're dead wrong," insisted Reg. "Gemworld is a beautiful place, a triumph of the will to survive. You've built, you've adapted, and you've lived in peace forever. Your people don't have to apologize for anything you've had to do to survive. So what if Gemworld doesn't look like a thousand other planets? We're all impressed with it, even if we can't figure it out exactly."

Melora gave him an appreciative smile, then turned back to her instruments. "Thank you, Reg. I'm sure glad I ran into you in the corridor and not somebody else."

He looked down sheepishly. "Uh, no, I think I ran into *you.*"

"No, I wasn't looking where I was going. That's me, full speed ahead! Good thing my full speed on a ship isn't too fast."

"Then I can stop feeling guilty?"

"Yes." Pazlar laughed. "You feel guilty too often, Reg. You act like you're always being punished for something."

"Well, I was kind of a mischievous child," admitted Barclay. "And even now, I still seem to mess up a lot and irritate my crewmates. I guess I'm never quite sure if people like me, or if they're just putting up with me."

"Your shipmates seem to like you just fine," answered Pazlar. "And whatever mistakes you've made, you still have a really good record—lengthy service on the *Enterprise* and every vessel you've been aboard."

"You checked my record?" asked Reg, not sure if he should be pleased or annoyed.

"Only because I didn't want to bring somebody aggressive down here to Gemworld. I wanted to bring somebody like you . . . nice."

"Why, thank you," said Reg, now certain he should be pleased. "I did some checking on you, too."

"You did?" Melora smiled, actually sounding pleased.

"But not your record," admitted Barclay. "It was more like scuttlebutt."

"Oh," she said knowingly, "one of my favorite parts of Starfleet—scuttlebutt. You found out that I like human men."

"Uh, yes," said Reg, certain he was blushing. "I mean, I found out you were involved with a couple of human men."

She shrugged. "Yup, humans are my weakness. But I move around far too much to have any kind of real involvement. It's odd, but I seem to be attracted to men who are rather shy and insecure—maybe they remind me more of home. Tangre Bertoran not withstanding, most Elaysians are mild mannered."

But Barclay was barely listening; he was still rerunning in his mind the part where she said she was attracted to men who were "shy and insecure." Could that mean him?

"Yes," he said, trying to agree with her. "Tangre Bertoran—a great man!"

She frowned puzzledly at him. "That's debatable. So, why aren't you attached? You've been on the same ship with the same crew for as long as I've been in Starfleet."

"I haven't met the right woman," he said, shrugging his lanky shoulders. "Remember, I'm shy and insecure."

Melora smiled. "That's what they all say."

Now that the conversation had turned to *his* love life, or lack thereof, Reg felt a desire to change the subject. "We are chasing down a senior engineer, right?"

"Yes. On the shell, they told me that the engineer who represents the Elaysians is at the Hold of the Regal Oneness. Despite the title, it's nothing but a communal storage area, but an important one. It serves a wide area, and if something were to happen to those stores, the whole region would be in turmoil."

"How much farther?"

"We're almost there," she answered. "See how many people live around here?"

Barclay peered out the window, and he finally noticed a few small details which revealed that these rainbow-hued crystals were indeed inhabited. Filmy nets were strung in the crux of one massive cluster, and hover-platforms were tethered nearby. Some greenery grew in clumps from a large prism, and thick nourishment strands snaked through the crystalline structures.

Looking as hard as he could, Reg couldn't see any actual Elaysians flying around or watching from their homes, as they usually did. Melora mentioned it first. "I don't know where everybody is. Maybe we'll find out."

Without warning, a shaft of dark shards rose from deep in the planet and plowed into the tiny shuttle-craft. It was buffeted by the impact, but the shields held as a shimmer rippled across the bow. Reg flinched while Melora calmly piloted them away from the deadly debris. When he opened his eyes, he saw the deadly cloud whoosh past them, put into motion by an unexpected gravity spike.

Melora looked intent as she piloted the shuttlecraft back onto course, and they picked up speed. Reg was going to inquire about the wisdom of that, given what had just happened, but he remembered that Melora was the kind who plowed full speed ahead. She was worried about her people and their food storage, and she wanted to reach them as soon as possible.

In short order, they saw Elaysians hovering in the distance, and Melora slowed down the shuttlecraft, to Reg's relief. They cautiously approached a large cluster of yellow crystals that seemed to be completely enshrouded in green nets, with a swarm of Elaysians frantically adding more nets. As they drew closer, Barclay could see why—there were huge rips in the net where discolored black crystals had poked through. In fact, the mutated crystal seemed to be growing from every nook and cranny of the storage area. Some of the dark growth had crossed paths with the healthy growth, and several of the yellow prisms were broken and cracked.

Melora gently applied thrusters to bring the shuttlecraft to a stop, and they both braced themselves to stop their own momentum. This time helpful Elaysians didn't crowd around to tether them—they kept working. Their frantic efforts reminded Reg of people stacking sandbags to hold a swollen river in its banks, with just as much chance of success. No one paid attention to the visitors as Melora popped the hatch and leaped from her seat, sailing into the dim blue sky. With a gulp, Reg floated uneasily from his seat, and Melora had to reach back in and help him through the hatch.

Gripping his hand, she pushed off from the shuttlecraft, and they sailed toward the nearest expanse of netting, which clung like moss to a large yellow prism. As they drew closer, Reg could see a huge clearing beyond the netting, but it wasn't clear—it was filled with smaller nets and bundles of supplies, many of them impaled on gray, misshapen crystals that grew everywhere like weeds.

She allowed them to drift into the net, which caught them gently and held them in place. Reg and Melora hung there for several minutes, staring at the frenzied activity and the awful destruction. Elaysians wearing environmental suits were working on the mutant spires, trying to cut them with whirring hand saws. Black clouds of dust floated over the work crews, attesting to their efforts. To Barclay, it was disconcerting to see these alien technologies in this unlikely place, and he couldn't imagine how Melora felt.

"The thoron radiation," she said worriedly. "That's why they need the suits. It's not dangerous in small quantities, but concentrated it can cause radiation sickness."

"I know," answered Reg, "but they can't saw down all the new growth—it's sprouting too fast. They'll have to abandon this site."

"They can't," she said worriedly. "There's nowhere else to take the stores. All of the large spaces are being eaten up by the dark crystal."

A worker in regular garb floated past them, studying a tricorder, and Pazlar yelled at him. "Excuse me! Where is the senior engineer, Zuka Juno?"

He was about to ignore her until he noticed Barclay's Starfleet uniform. Then his expression grew disdainful. "He's very busy right now. I suggest you go back to your ship, where it's safe."

Melora pointed behind them. "Do you see our shuttlecraft?"

"Yes."

"Zuka Juno will join us there in five minutes, or we'll open fire on the nets with our phasers."

"You wouldn't do that!" shouted the Elaysian, aghast.

"I would. Once I destroy the nets, Zuka Juno won't be busy anymore. Come on, Lieutenant." She grabbed Reg's hand and deftly pushed off a nearby facet. They drifted lazily back toward the shuttlecraft.

"This shuttlecraft doesn't have any weapons," whispered Barclay.

"You know that, and I know that. But *they* don't."

In short order, all of the Elaysians took notice of them, and much of the work stopped as the workers considered this new threat. Although it was as weightless in the shuttlecraft as out of it, Reg felt safer inside. He monitored thoron readings, while Melora hovered impatiently just outside the hatch.

"How much time has elapsed?" she asked Barclay.

"Almost five minutes," he answered. "I can cycle through the landing lights, which might frighten them a bit."

"Go ahead."

Reg put the tiny craft through the most impressive light show he could muster, and the Elaysians began to scatter. After a few moments, a section of netting parted, and a thin, older Elaysian emerged, gripping a hover-platform. He was followed by an entourage of two or three more Elaysians, all of whom looked angry enough to bite through the crystal. This disgruntled party cautiously approached the shuttlecraft, and Reg powered off the lights.

A violet light glowed on the chest of the older Elaysian. As he came closer, Reg could see it was a crystal shard on a metal chain. Melora crossed her arms and floated in the hatchway, waiting for him.

The older man's voice shook with rage. "Whose side are you on, my daughter? I can't believe you would threaten to destroy this precious hold!"

"I don't have to destroy it," she answered. "The crystal is doing that."

He bowed his head, conceding the fact. "What do you want?"

"I want you to come with us to the shell. Our Starfleet engineers want to know why dark-matter collection has increased sixteen-fold. They want to know why this is happening."

Zuka Juno snorted derisively. "They want to inspect our programming."

"Well it's high time somebody did, isn't it?" snapped Pazlar.

The two Elaysians—one young, one old; one wearing a Starfleet combadge and the other a violet crystal—stared stubbornly at each other. Finally Zuka Juno lifted his hands in resignation. "Do we have to go in that vehicle?"

"I've turned off the artificial gravity, and it will be fast." She moved back to allow the engineer to enter before her. Barclay floated toward the rear of the craft, almost banging his head on a fire extinguisher in the process. Melora situated the distinguished Elaysian near the front of the craft, then she hovered over the pilot's seat, checking the readouts.

"Hi!" said Reg with false cheer. "I'm Lieutenant Reginald Barclay."

The Elaysian regarded him with pale eyes. "Still planning on shooting us?"

"No," he answered sheepishly. "We don't have any weapons."

Pazlar quickly shut the hatch. "I'm sorry I had to lie back there, but this is important."

Zuka Juno sighed heavily. "Everything is important these days. There are crises everywhere, and nobody knows what to do. We are losing our homeworld to this foul growth! I don't really think inspecting a few lines of code will do much good."

"We're just looking for some answers," replied Melora. "We're not alone in this—the *Enterprise* crew can help us, if we only let them." She fired thrusters and slowly pulled away from the yellow cluster.

Barclay tried to sound nonchalant as he asked, "Um, when was the last time you were on the shell?"

"We were all there, the senior engineers, for a personnel review," answered the Elaysian. "Halfway through, the deformed crystal was reported for the first time. There were suddenly problems everywhere, and we postponed our meeting to calm the populace. Why do you ask?"

"Oh, it's nothing, really," answered Reg quickly. "I was just curious about when the programming of the shell was last changed."

The old Elaysian shook his head. "The programming has not been changed substantially since before I was born. We don't have any reason to change it."

"What about now?"

"I'm going with you, aren't I?" muttered Zuka Juno, grasping the violet crystal which hung from his neck. "I'd be very surprised if centuries-old programming caused all of this. It's the rift."

Melora shot Reg a glance, which seemed to signal that he shouldn't press for more answers now. They had done their job. Now they had to be patient and follow protocols. Barclay found a seat and tightened his lap belt until his skinny frame fit as snugly as possible. With a sigh, he leaned back in his chair, hoping he could sleep but not expecting more than a fitful doze.

Deanna Troi reclined gratefully in her bed, glad to get a moment's rest after the heady events of the day. It wasn't often she got to take over the bridge in the middle of a crisis, then spend hours flying in a wonderland. But even the incredible sights of Gemworld were almost anticlimactic after their dealings with the Exalted Ones and the Jeptah. It all added up to sensory overload. This was one night when she wouldn't have to dream, thought Troi. Her imagination couldn't possibly match the reality all around them.

Tomorrow she would have to deal with the emotional overload of losing seven crewmembers. She could comfort grieving friends and spouses, but the ongoing tension on the ship was proving to be more difficult to deal with. Although they seemed safe inside this metal cocoon surrounded by jewels, everyone knew it could crumble apart in an instant. The rift was too unpredictable and Gemworld too fragile—the shell didn't seem to be enough, with its arrogant programmers and arcane protocols. Every member of the crew knew that the *Enterprise* couldn't escape, and nobody could rescue them.

Deanna shook off her troubled thoughts and picked up a padd to do a little reading. But she found that she barely had the energy to focus her eyes, and she let the padd drop to her bed. Music, she thought, would be more soothing.

To her surprise, it wasn't a nice concerto she ordered up, but a sound effect. "Computer, put on a sound . . . the ocean at the beach."

The cry of a seagull greeted her ear, and waves lapped gently at an unseen shore. With a rhythmic lull, the waves washed up and down the sand, and Troi could feel herself floating in a cradle on the tide. Since she had actually been floating that day, her body aided the illusion, and her muscles went as limp as a Lipul floating in its crystal. Real perception and dream perception intermingled, and she felt herself floating away though a dozen different substances— water, gelatinous mass, the crystal, the air, the shell, and even space.

She thought it was the Lipuls' dreamships calling her, and she turned to look for them in the luminous starscape. But their ghostly, billowing sails were nowhere to be seen. Instead she felt the draw of a presence just outside the protective shell, something that was close but oddly far away. It terrified Deanna to think that she was alone—a fleet of one—but there was the attraction of the deep unknown, lying so close at hand.

If only I could see it as well as I can feel it. With her mind, she probed the emptiness of space and found it wasn't empty. Inside the darkness was an even greater darkness, alive and roiling with attraction and energy. It didn't reveal itself, but it knew she was there, like a suitor waiting in the shadows for his beloved to sneak out of her house.

Suddenly her mind was flooded with incredible images of worlds and wonders that dwarfed the amazing things she had already seen. Fantastic creatures, planets, vistas, and anomalies danced and faded before her, and Troi felt as if she were plunging through the history of a thousand worlds. It was too much. She almost fled in terror to the realm of consciousness.

Before she could escape, the blackness enveloped her in soothing comfort, and the images stopped. She could feel the knowledge and wisdom of the entity that enticed her. It seemed to say that she could cross the greatest barrier, and all the knowledge it possessed would be hers. She would be no mere humanoid anymore.

Troi had seen lights beckon to her before—on a runway or a starship—but she had never seen a beacon of darkness before. But there it loomed—a black gash where stars had never existed, where nothing existed except for this mysterious welcome. Transfixed, she drifted toward the gaping maw, hoping she could cross and see the identity of her suitor. It wanted her so badly, and it was willing to give so much to get her.

On the way to the ultimate barrier, some inner voice told her that she had to look. She had to *really* look. Deanna had been fooled before, and she knew too much about the nature of attraction to believe her feelings alone. When she peered into the blackness, she fully expected to see a kindly face full of wisdom. Her mind opened, and she used whatever nascent abilities she had to see beyond the veil.

The images came again—only now they were beastly and horrible. Elaysians screamed as skin peeled off their faces; writhing Lipuls were skewered on dark spires; whole planets crumbled into black dust; and stars were obliterated from the night sky. Land and water burned, and knowledge was eclipsed by cruelty and degradation. The friendly face she expected to see was nothing but a monstrous, gaping mouth—anxious to swallow everything!

An unrelenting feeling of fear washed over Deanna, like the waves washing onto the shore. Her mind filled with the deaths, disease, and destruction she had witnessed in her eventful life. It was as if an unseen power were dredging up these memories, feeding on them, forcing her to look at the horrors already in her mind. *This is you,* was the message. *We're alike!*

"No!" shouted Troi, bolting upright in her bed. The darkness of her quarters seemed to engulf her, as if she couldn't escape from the black presence. A gash began to grow on the metallic bulkhead in front her; it lengthened and widened, and she saw swirls of blackness within. The swirls pulled her in like a whirlpool, drawing her out of her bed.

It's never going to leave my mind now that I've let it in! Troi turned to run, but the darkness and fear overwhelmed her, squeezing her mind and roaring in her ears until her senses shut down. Deanna Troi screamed back, and she just kept screaming as she smashed a row of picture frames with her clenched fists. She attacked the shelves and wall hangings, ripping and slashing her dearest belongings.

It's all closing in. . . . Coming to get me!

Chapter Ten

THE DOOR TO SICKBAY WHOOSHED open, and Captain Picard strode briskly into the receiving room, where he nearly ran into Commander Riker, who was pacing with his head down. The first officer gave him a stricken look, then he composed himself and straightened to attention.

"Deanna is still with the doctor," he said, "and they won't let me see her."

"What happened?" grumbled the captain. He had been awakened from a deep sleep by the news that Commander Troi was in sickbay . . . being held in restraints.

Riker heaved his broad shoulders in bewilderment. "She was found wandering the corridor in her night-clothes, screaming."

149

"Any idea what brought this on?" asked the captain.

"I haven't been able to talk to anyone," answered Riker with frustration. "They're all busy. When I last saw Deanna, she was headed to bed, like the doctor ordered."

The captain strode over to a broad window which offered a view of a trauma center with several beds, all of them occupied. None were occupied by Deanna Troi, however. Beyond this open area, there were doorways leading to private examination rooms and operating rooms. He saw medical personnel moving among the patients, and he wanted to bang on the window to demand their attention. But the captain refrained, knowing that he wasn't the master of this place. One of the workers finally noticed him, and she pressed a comm panel on the bulkhead and spoke to someone.

From one of the examination rooms, Dr. Beverly Crusher emerged, brushing back a strand of copper-colored hair. She looked harried and haggard, as if she hadn't followed her own advice to get some sleep. Perhaps Beverly had been woken from a peaceful slumber, too, thought Picard. When there was an emergency on the *Enterprise,* sleep was the first thing to suffer.

As she approached them, she managed the wisp of a smile. "Hello, Jean-Luc, Will."

"How is she?" asked Riker with concern.

"Sedated. You can see her, but she's just sleeping." Crusher grimaced in frustration. "I tried to keep her awake—to ask her questions and find out what happened, but she wasn't responsive."

Gemworld: Book One

"Did she say anything at all?" asked Picard.

"Quite a bit, but none of it made any sense."

"Like what?"

Crusher looked pained as she replied, "Like something was trying to get her. Like there was a rip in the bulkhead in her quarters. She said something about 'it' being in her mind, but I don't know what 'it' is. I can tell you, there's no medical cause for her condition. With her symptoms, I would normally call in the ship's counselor, but she is the ship's counselor."

"What will she be like when she wakes up?" asked Riker.

The doctor shrugged wearily. "I honestly don't know. Maybe she'll be fine, or maybe she'll be like she was when they found her—screaming and incoherent."

"Do you know what she was doing?" asked Picard.

"From her dress, I'd say she was in bed. They found her in the corridor outside her quarters, and I guess her quarters were also in disarray."

"We can find out from the computer if there were any intruders in her quarters," said Picard, starting for the door. "Do you want to come, Number One?"

The first officer again looked stricken with worry. "If you don't mind, sir, I'd like to stay here . . . in case she wakes up."

"She won't wake up for hours," said Crusher with a sympathetic smile. "I'll call you first, Will."

"Thank you." The first officer nodded to the captain, and the two of them strode briskly into the corridor.

* * *

151

Captain Picard sat at his desk in his ready room, and Commander Riker looked over his shoulder, grimly watching a security video log taken in Troi's quarters after the incident. On the log there was ample evidence of her rampage: overturned furniture, ruined artwork, smashed glass—her tidy quarters had become a disaster area.

Neither one of them could imagine Deanna doing this, but the commentary on the vidlog made it clear that there had been no intruders. They watched brief interviews with the two crewmembers who subdued her in the corridor, and both of them seemed genuinely alarmed by their encounter with the distraught counselor. Picard was tight lipped as he turned off the small viewscreen.

"No intruder," muttered Riker. "Nothing happened to her. She was asleep, then she woke up and went crazy."

The captain stroked his angular chin thoughtfully. "Or something happened to her *while* she was asleep. Something that wouldn't show up on any video log."

"A bad dream?" asked Riker skeptically.

"Don't forget," said Picard, "it was a dream that brought us here."

"Do you think the Lipuls did this to her?"

"I don't know. But if she doesn't recover soon, we're going to pay them a visit." Captain Picard rose from his desk, a worried look on his face. "Now I wish I had sent a security team with Pazlar and Barclay."

"But how can Pazlar be in danger? She's one of them."

"Panic can bring out the worst in anyone, and I'm afraid our hosts are near panic." Picard thought about the fear and anger he had seen on the faces of Tangre Bertoran and the other Jeptah. The rift didn't just threaten their planet—it threatened everything they believed in, everything they held to be true, especially the myth that the shell would protect them forever.

"We could send a security team," suggested Riker.

"No, it's better to keep a low profile. For now." The captain's jaw clenched. "But I won't hesitate to disturb the Lipuls if Counselor Troi doesn't recover."

"Thank you, sir," answered Riker with relief. "By the way, I've scheduled the service for our lost crewmembers at twenty-two hundred hours. Is that all right?"

"Fine," answered the captain. "I'll give the remarks."

The first officer nodded, but he gazed toward the door, still obviously distracted by his concern over Troi's condition.

"Go on to sickbay," said Picard softly. "I'll take the bridge."

"Thank you, sir." The big man bolted from the ready room, leaving Captain Picard alone with his own worries, which extended not only to his ship's counselor, but to several hundred crewmembers and a crumbling world of two billion souls.

Somehow the Elaysian senior engineer, Zuka Juno, managed to float in the cockpit of the shuttlecraft while still looking heavy and pompous. Maybe it was the way the elder engineer crossed his arms and scowled continuously, thought Reg Barclay. On the other hand, Melora Pazlar managed to float like some ethereal being, even as she kept her hands firmly grounded on the controls.

Reg was sure that he floated as gracefully as he walked, ran, or did anything else physical, which wasn't too gracefully. The gangly lieutenant kept bumping his head, elbows, and knees, even though he had the whole stern of the shuttlecraft to himself. He thought about sitting down again, but being weightless and sitting felt like the worst of both worlds. It seemed to make his stomach queasy, too, no matter how many hypos he took.

A violet crystal bobbed behind Zuka Juno's shoulder; it was attached to a lanyard coming from his neck. The shard both marked his rank and served as a security device for top-level access. It was the whole reason they had come, and Reg was somewhat alarmed about the lackadaisical way he wore it. *What if it got lost?*

The lieutenant said very little, hoping that the two Elaysians would talk to each other and he could eavesdrop. But an icy silence had fallen over the shuttlecraft and her occupants; it was evident that Zuka Juno considered this interruption to be a waste of time. Mutant, malformed crystals were threatening their food supply, their housing, and every other form of infrastructure on Gemworld—and humoring two minor Starfleet officers must have seemed like a low priority. Barclay wondered how helpful the senior engineer would be once they got back to the shell and its mysterious programming room.

"The shell is in sight," reported Pazlar.

Reg looked up from his troubled thoughts, and he instantly banged his shin on a protruding shelf. Stifling a cry of pain, he gazed out the window at the rapidly approaching bands of gray silhouetted against the pale blue sky. Even Zuka Juno looked up from his pouting long enough to observe the immense shell. What a triumph of engineering and determination it was, thought Reg, a paean to the will to survive.

Then again, he had spent several hours on the shell, and he had spotted the patches, seals, welds, solders, and kludges—the spit and shellac that was holding the thing together. The repairs were impressive, too, but also troubling. There was no "plan B," no backup system. Nothing but the Sacred Protector kept the fragile planet intact, and it had started failing in its job.

They closed quickly on the Ninth Processing Gate, but there were no crowds of Elaysians and Alpusta to greet them and secure the shuttlecraft. The nourishment strands still pulsed with life, and the forcefields sparkled like dew on a transparent leaf. An occasional worker soared from the kidney-shaped opening and flew off, but overall the place felt deserted. Reg imagined that travel had gotten difficult for the average denizen on Gemworld, and maybe people had returned home to be with their families. By now, some of them had to be thinking that these were the last days for their ancient civilization.

They braced themselves in order to stop their own momentum when the shuttlecraft stopped. With Melora's help, Barclay exited from the shuttlecraft without incident, and he watched as Melora tethered their craft. Holding her hand, he floated confidently into the shell. Once the staff realized that a senior engineer was in their midst, workers emerged from circular corridors all around them, and they soon had a sizable escort. They were whisked through the corridors in an officious manner. Reg got a little queasy from all the bouncing off the walls and sharp turns. He worried that the hyposprays for space sickness weren't working.

Reg tried to look for markings and details in the corridors, so that maybe he could find his way out on his own. But it was hopeless. Without any up or down, he was unable to get his bearings and was soon lost in the cylindrical passageways.

No true believers from the Jeptah stopped them this time. They were taken immediately to the ancient programming room, where crystal shards were inserted into the living crystal to unleash programs that had been written and optimized centuries ago.

The Elaysian technician in the room shrunk back from Zuka Juno's withering gaze; she tagged up on the wall and shot out of the room, leaving the three of them alone.

The senior engineer ignored Reg and Melora as he made his preparations. First he laboriously studied page after page of readouts on the monitoring station. Zuka Juno seemed to know his way around the instruments, which gave Barclay some hope that they would be successful in finding a cause for all the problems.

The V-shaped ridges on the Elaysian's forehead deepened as he read. Reg figured he was learning about the dark-matter collection shooting sky-high, along with the fractal overproduction. When Juno glanced up and saw the Starfleet officers staring at him, he scowled and turned his back to them.

Melora wasn't as shy as Reg, so she asked point-blank, "Are they right about the fractal program running in an endless loop?"

"I can't say for sure," blustered the Elaysian. "Something has stimulated production of crystal—inferior crystal, at that. But the program is designed to compensate for changes in operating conditions, and that rift is a large change. Perhaps these cycles will end on their own, once the rift is dealt with."

"But what if it's causing it?" asked Reg.

The senior engineer shot him a disdainful look. "What you suggest is quite impossible. I think I know this machinery better than you, Lieutenant."

"We are going to look at the code, aren't we?" asked Melora, deflecting his anger away from Reg.

"I suppose." With a scowl, Zuka Juno twisted gracefully in midair, caught a handle, and pulled himself along the curved wall to the top row of tiny drawers. Without looking, his hands crept across the small drawers and clicking relays to a panel made from blood-red crystal. The surface of this nondescript little nook looked chipped and aged, and he ran his hands over it with loving tenderness.

After a moment of silent communion, Zuka Juno gripped the violet shard floating around his neck and brought it to his lips for a kiss. Then he opened the drawer and shoved it into the glowing red crystal. A miraculous light burst forth, filling the room with twinkling rainbows and dancing sparks of gold. Had there been any gravity, Reg's jaw would have dropped open.

The monitoring station blinked through a sequence of readouts, and all three of them maneuvered into position to see the screen. Melora and Reg hung back in order to let the senior engineer reach the actual controls.

The readouts were going by too fast for Barclay to gather much from them, but he could see that Zuka Juno was keeping up with the scrolling code. The senior engineer kept a placid expression on his face, but Reg could see his eyes dashing back and forth, up and down across the screens. Those pale, wise eyes couldn't hide his immense disbelief and fear.

"Stop it for a second," ordered Pazlar.

The old engineer's hands hovered over the instruments, but they halted and began to tremble. With alarm, Melora reached over his shoulder and began pounding on the board, but her actions had no effect whatsoever. Screens full of obtuse computer code kept scrolling past, with no way to stop it, no way to end it.

"It's frozen, isn't it?" demanded Melora.

The elder Elaysian was certainly frozen, floating in front of the screen, staring at it as if it were his tombstone. Angrily, Melora grabbed him by his billowing white robes, spun him around, and shook his body. In her grasp, the once arrogant engineer now seemed as frail and helpless as the oldest spires on Gemworld.

"You can't stop it, can you?" shouted Melora, tears welling in her intense blue eyes.

He gulped and finally seemed to hear her. "Uh, no," he answered in a cracked voice. "It's encrypted . . . in an endless loop."

"Can you break the encryption?"

"No." He shook his head, then buried his face in the billowy sails under his arm.

Seeing this reaction, Reg twisted his hands nervously. He wanted to pace, but his feet dangled in midair; so he kept clapping his hands as he spoke. "It's just as we suspected . . . only worse. Somebody sabotaged the shell, then they encrypted it so nobody can fix it. This may look bad, but I'm sure Data or Geordi can break the—"

"No one can break it," answered Zuka Juno, snapping out of his stupor. "Only those who put it on— maybe not even them."

"And who put it on?" asked Melora.

He turned away evasively. "That's hard to say."

"No, it's not," she insisted. "Only six beings had access to this level of programming—the six senior engineers. Isn't that right?"

"You've got to give me time to think about all of

this. The repercussions—" Juno couldn't finish the sentence, and his face reverted to a stunned mask of fear.

"The repercussions are that everybody on this planet is going to die! Everybody on the *Enterprise* is going to die!" Melora laughed derisively and tossed her silky blond hair. "I apologize, Reg. I told you it couldn't be possible that someone from Gemworld could destroy their own planet, but that's apparently what happened."

Barclay cleared his throat, trying to find something to say in response to this devastating news. "Well, my people almost destroyed their own planet. We survived because we're like you. We just kept trying to hold things together. Of course, Earth is younger, not quite as fragile as Gemworld is."

"Yes," grumbled Pazlar. "One tiny bit of corrupted code, and billions of years of history and survival are about to vanish. What are we going to do about this, Engineer Juno?"

The old Elaysian shook his head slowly, eyes wide, as if he had just seen his own mortality. "It's not just the fractal program," he murmured hoarsely. "There's also the rift out there."

"But if you stop collecting dark matter," said Reg, "you have a chance to stop it before it destroys everything."

No sooner had he said those words than he remembered Data's report to Captain Picard. The shell was designed like a human being, not a machine. It was not a collection of subsystems that could be turned on and off as needed; it was a single entity, designed to compensate for changing conditions but never to stop working. At the moment, it was compensating for a fractal growth program run amuck by sucking all the dark matter from another dimension. One of the keepers of the secrets had betrayed them.

Zuka Juno looked at Reg with a mixture of shock and horror. "I have to convene the Exalted Ones and ask for their opinion."

"There's no time for that!" snapped Pazlar. "We've got to get the other senior engineers back here!"

"Uh . . . one of them is a mass murderer," Reg reminded her. "Did all six of them have access to this room?"

"Yes," answered Zuka Juno, "except for the Gendlii, of course, who must send a proxy. The Lipul engineer has access via the crystal stream behind these panels."

"Okay, the Gendlii is out," said Reg, making a mental note. He wasn't sure what a Gendlii was, but he was glad to hear that at least one of the six engineers could be eliminated from suspicion. "Who is his proxy?"

"Tangre Bertoran. Perhaps you know him."

"Oh, we know him," Reg assured the engineer. "I think it's time to contact the *Enterprise* and tell them the bad news." He lifted his hand to strike his combadge, but Juno reached out and grabbed his wrist. The old engineer's grip was surprisingly strong.

"Please, think about what you're doing," begged the elder Elaysian. "There will be panic . . . a complete loss of faith. We must keep this a secret for now, until I can inform the Exalted Ones. We must prepare our people first."

"I think they're mature enough to know the truth," said Melora. "Go ahead and contact the *Enterprise,* Reg."

"I want to *find* the one who did this," insisted the aged Elaysian, his hand and his voice shaking with anger. "If we act too quickly and bring in your crew, he might be driven away. Give us a moment to handle this internally—a small delay won't affect anything. Please."

He seemed so sincere that Reg was forced to glance at Pazlar. She seemed torn by indecision, and Barclay could understand how they might want a short period to digest this news before outsiders got involved. "All right," he said, "but we'll go with you."

Juno gave them a weak smile and pointed to the blinking monitor station. "Perhaps I should stay here and do what I can—maybe there's something I've overlooked. You go, my son, to the Exalted Ones and speak to them in my place."

"Do you think they'll believe me?" asked Reg. "Nobody has so far."

"They will if you carry this." The senior engineer pushed off from the monitoring station and floated to the small red panel above them. He extracted the violet shard and handed it to Reg, brown lanyard and all.

The crystal twinkled for a moment when Reg held it, and he flinched. But it didn't burn or hurt him; in fact, it felt strangely cool and energizing. It was like holding an icicle with his bare hands. The shard was about the same size as an icicle, and Barclay was reminded of winters back in the midwest, when he used to throw snowballs at the icicles hanging from the rain gutters.

Melora proudly put the fiber lanyard around his neck and tightened it like a noose. "You're a proxy for a senior engineer," she said. "That's a great responsibility."

"Are you . . . are you sure you want to do this?" asked Reg doubtfully. "I don't have much experience being a dignitary."

"You are the one, my son," insisted the elder engineer. "You diligently tried to warn us about this when no one was listening; now you must continue this thankless task. With that gem, they will know you have my blessing. Hurry."

"Come on, Reg," said Melora, taking his hand.

The lanky engineer grasped the violet shard with his other hand, certain that someone had made a mistake. It felt as if they had given him the key to the city, but for all the wrong reasons. Although Reg was honored, he didn't want to be the voice of doom for all of Gemworld.

Lying on metal girders were seven corpses in black body bags bearing Starfleet insignia. The funeral took place in a cavernous space in the *Enterprise* that was occasionally used for sporting events, such as soccer. Three of the deceased were members of a field hockey team which had reigned as champions of the *En-*

terprise for two years. It made sense to hold the service here, thought Picard, since it was going to be a bit different, anyway.

Because they couldn't use the transporter or torpedoes to dispose of the bodies in space, as was traditional, they had fallen back on a little-used but acceptable alternative method. Captain Picard was a traditionalist when it came to funeral services—and he had performed a great many during the war—so he was uneasy about these changes.

The crowd was large, consisting of almost everyone who wasn't on active duty. They stood in a semicircle around the six small pyres. There was an air of quiet, except for a few sniffles. Will Riker was speaking, reading the name of each fallen crewmember and listing his or her accomplishments. Picard recalled faces, especially Yontel's, and snippets of conversation in passing. Now those youthful personalities were gone, and the entity that was the *Enterprise* was diminished.

Commander Riker finished reading the biographic part of the program, and he nodded to the captain. Picard cleared his throat and lifted his chin, all the better to project his stentorian voice.

"Around the turn of the last millennium," he began, "a fleet of one hundred thirty-one sailing ships had a race on one of Earth's oceans—from Sidney, Australia, to Hobart, Tasmania. As the race progressed, a storm blew in, but there are often storms in those waters. Most of the yachts plowed ahead, hoping to win the race. But the storm quickly turned into a rare hurricane, such as was never seen in those waters before. Scores of ships were disabled or capsized.

"For two days, primitive aircraft performed hundreds of daring rescues. When it was over, six sailors from three different vessels had perished. Two of their bodies were never recovered."

The captain scanned the array of faces, skin colors, and species, marveling at the incredible variety of his crew. Despite their many differences, they were closer now to each other than they were to their own families, and each death affected every one of them. Picard noted the absence of Counselor Troi, who would normally be moving among them, giving comfort and consolation where needed. By now, all of them knew of her distress, and it had to be one more worry they shared.

The captain continued, "When we entered this solar system, we lost seven brave shipmates in an unforeseen tragedy. Like those sailors of centuries past, we fly into danger, never knowing exactly what we will face. For all of us who travel in space, or upon the untamed sea, or in any hostile environment—we know that we are tempting the fates. There are places where nature and physics don't want us to be, but we persist in going there, anyway. Because challenge and exploration are in our nature."

He hardly needed to add that Gemworld also fit that description—a hostile environment that harbored life despite its true nature. "In space, we know we will meet threats that we would never meet if we remained safely in our armchairs, but that has never deterred us.

Exploration of the unknown can be both thrilling and tragic, but none of us would live our lives any differently.

"At that long-ago memorial service for those six sailors, Hugo van Kretschmar, the commodore of the local yacht club, had these words to say. I think these sentiments hold just as true for our fallen comrades now as they did then, for those lost sailors:

" 'We will miss you always,' " intoned the captain, quoting a man who died three centuries ago. " 'We will remember you always; we will learn from the tragic cirumstances of your passing. May the everlasting voyage you have now embarked on be blessed with calm seas and gentle breezes. May you never have to reef or change a headsail in the night. May your bunk always be warm and dry.' "

He nodded to Commander Riker, who barked, "Present arms!"

Six crewmembers with phaser rifles stepped forward, holding their rifles in a shouldered position. "Take aim!" ordered Riker, and the squad lifted their weapons and drew a bead on the six body bags resting on pedestals. "Fire!"

With their rifles, they blasted the bags with gleaming beams until they vaporized, leaving nothing but a slight trail of steam. There was silence at this somber, unexpected sight, and the captain wished he had something uplifting to say to his crew. But he didn't. Vaporizing the bodies might have been efficient, but it only served to remind everyone what dire straits they were in.

Silently the crowd began to file out the doors at either end of the cavernous room. Riker thanked the six members of the firing squad, who themselves looked shaken from dispatching their comrades in such a fashion. The captain lowered his head, knowing the service had ended on a disturbing note.

The other thing that had ended was his patience. He lifted his chin and tapped his combadge. "Picard to bridge."

"Data here."

"I want to find out what we're up against," declared the captain. "Prepare the probe."

Chapter Eleven

DEANNA TROI LAY UNCONSCIOUS in a private room in sickbay while Dr. Beverly Crusher stood at the foot of her bed checking her vital signs on the overhead screen. Except for her brain waves, which were slightly more active than usual, Troi's vital signs were all within normal ranges. She appeared to be sleeping peacefully, almost angelically, with her raven hair streaming outward across the pillow from her radiant face.

That would last only about another fifteen minutes, thought Crusher, until the sedatives began to wear off. At that time, there was no telling which Deanna Troi would return to them—the trusted counselor or the delusional patient.

As a friend, Crusher hated what she had to do next;

as a doctor, she had no choice. She bent down and made sure that the heavy-duty restraints on her comrade's arms and legs were tight, but not tight enough to cut off circulation. Deanna hadn't appeared to be a danger to others, but she could easily injure herself if she became destructive again. It was better to be overly cautious than sorry. The restraints were the main reason the doctor hadn't wanted Will and Jean-Luc to see her patient. They might get the wrong idea.

Or perhaps they might realize how serious it was.

With a troubled frown, Crusher gazed at her colleague, shipmate, and friend, thinking how painful life would be on the *Enterprise* if she didn't recover. She could mend the burns, broken bones, and diseases she saw every day, but a damaged psyche was beyond her bag of tricks. Deanna should be at a starbase, under the supervision of a team of counselors, but knowing that didn't do either one of them any good. They were trapped here, far removed from help for her condition. It wasn't in Beverly's nature to be pessimistic about a patient's chances, but she didn't think the terror she had seen in Troi's eyes would leave easily.

Her combadge beeped, snapping Beverly out of her oppressive thoughts. "Crusher here," she answered.

"Doctor, this is Nurse Ogawa. Commander Riker is in the receiving room."

Crusher nodded to herself, knowing that she couldn't hold him off forever. "Tell him I'll be right there. And, Ogawa, let's have somebody standing by with Counselor Troi—she could wake up any time."

"Don't worry, we won't leave her alone," promised the senior nurse.

When Crusher entered main sickbay, she found Will Riker pacing. The big man whirled around and stared expectantly at her, his clean-shaven face making him look more boyish than he had in years. "Any change?"

"No," she answered softly, "but the sedative will be wearing off in fifteen or twenty minutes. The next time she wakes up should tell us a lot about her condition."

"Can I see her?"

"Why don't we wait until she's awake," said Beverly pleasantly. "I'll let you buy me a cup of coffee until then."

Riker looked uncertain about leaving Deanna again—after all, it wasn't that long ago that he had rediscovered his feelings for her. But Crusher smiled and took his arm, guiding him out the door and into the corridor before he could mount a protest. With any luck, thought the doctor, the next time he saw her, she wouldn't be strapped down and unconscious.

"*Enterprise* to away team," said Captain Picard from the command chair in the center of the bridge. When there was no answer, he tapped the combadge on his chair again. "Picard to Barclay. Come in, away team."

"They may be out of range," suggested Data, plying the ops console. "Interference from the new crystal growth has drastically reduced our effective range.

When we last got a fix on the shuttlecraft, they were at the shell, but our scanners indicate they have left the shell. They will probably go deeper into the planet."

Picard nodded, trying to temper his worry and impatience. Experience had taught him that the Elaysians, Lipuls, Alpusta, and other denizens of Gemworld were not the easiest to get along with, and he had best let the away team do their job. He had faith in both Barclay and Pazlar. Their movements clearly showed they were traveling far and wide, trying to gain access to the computer codes. Once they did, another piece of the puzzle would be uncovered.

The captain knew it was up to him to turn over a large chunk of that puzzle himself. Tangre Bertoran and the Jeptah had been right about one thing—the rift was connected, and they couldn't ignore it. They had to find out more about this invisible singularity which spewed dark matter, thoron radiation, and destruction in equal measure. If it truly was a dimensional rift, they couldn't even guess what was on the other side.

The captain had stared down a black hole before, but at least he knew what awaited him on the other side of a black hole—nothingness, nonexistence. Another dimension, one full of dark matter, could be more alien than anything ever seen in their galaxy. Despite the captain's wealth of experience, that was a sobering thought.

Picard kept recalling what Data had said about imbalance and equalization. If the rift were left open, dark matter might keep flowing between the two dimensions until they were equalized. First Gemworld would be destroyed, then the solar system, the sector, the quadrant—and both dimensions. The rift would widen until it consumed the cosmos.

"Mr. Data," said the captain, "prepare to launch the probe."

"Yes, sir." The android deftly worked his board for a few seconds. "Without accurate sensor readings, targeting is problematic. I will be forced to make an approximation of the rift's location."

Picard smiled slightly. "I trust your guess, Data."

"Course laid in," reported the android. "Probe is ready for launch."

"Fire when ready."

Data tapped his console. "Probe launched."

The captain looked up at the viewscreen to witness a scene very similar to the simulation he had viewed on the holodeck with the Jeptah protestors. The probe zoomed through an opening in the shell and streaked into space. Scanners picked up the blip outside the shell as it soared toward a jagged gash in the starscape. At least that's how Picard imagined it.

"Sensors reporting in," said Data, scanning screen after screen of readouts. "Trace gases are consistent with a dark-matter nebula. Thoron radiation increasing exponentially, as are graviton readings, baryon particles, and gamma rays. Probe is now encountering unknown gas clouds; recognizable substances are ammonia, carbon dioxide, and water vapor."

Picard frowned, thinking those were the basic ingredients of amino acids, the building blocks of life.

Could that thing be alive? He was about to order the probe aborted when it disappeared from the viewscreen.

"Transmission ended," said Data simply.

Deanna Troi was asleep. Oblivious, until a sharp pain punctured her stomach, and a horrible whining sounded in her mind. She howled as her abdominal muscles tightened involuntarily, and she tried to sit up to ease the pain. But her arms were strapped down! All she could do was thrash about on the bed, not knowing where she was or what was happening to her. It felt as if a knife was tearing her insides out, and her head was about to split open.

In a small cafeteria a few meters down the corridor, Beverly Crusher's combadge chirped. "Ogawa to Crusher," came a familiar voice.

"Crusher here," answered Beverly, hoping it was good news. Across the table from her, Will Riker leaned forward expectantly.

"Come quickly!" urged Ogawa. "She's delirious."

Crusher jumped to her feet and reached the doorway a split second before Riker. The two of them charged down the corridor and into sickbay, barely giving the automatic doors a chance to whoosh open. An anguished scream pierced the air, urging them past rows of occupied beds and into the private examination room where they saw Nurse Ogawa and two orderlies trying to subdue Troi, who thrashed and shrieked like a woman possessed.

"Don't you know you're *killing* me! Stop it! Stop it!" she cried between screams and lunges.

"Twenty cc's of lectrazine," ordered Crusher, holding out her hand for the hypospray.

"Wait a minute . . . can't we talk to her first?" Riker rushed to her bedside, pushing the others out of his way. He gently touched her trembling, sweaty forearm. "Deanna, do you hear me? It's Will."

"Ah! No! Stop!" She cried like a frightened animal caught in a trap, while she struggled pathetically against her binds.

Riker gazed with anguish at the troubled woman. "Does she have to be tied up like this?"

"Look at her, Will," shouted Crusher over the din. "I'm afraid she'll hurt herself!"

Just then, Troi erupted with a scream that was primal, like a childbirth scream, and even Riker recoiled. Crusher glanced at Ogawa, caught her eye, and waited as the nurse placed a hypo in her palm.

Will inserted himself between them, shielding Deanna from the hypo. "Let me talk to her for just a second."

"She's in pain," said Crusher. "I don't know why she's like this, but the mind can do real damage to the body."

Riker desperately tried to grip Troi's hand, then he yelped in agony as she dug her fingernails into his flesh. Spittle flew from her mouth as she shouted, "Don't do that again! You *stabbed* me! Why? I gave to you, and you took—" Deanna grimaced and would have doubled over in pain if she weren't bound so tightly.

With considerable effort, Riker wrenched his bloodied hand away from hers and rose to his feet, a distraught look on his face. With the path clear, the doctor waded in with her hypospray.

"You wanted it!" shouted Troi, struggling against her bonds. "You wanted to know . . . now you have it all! It's in you . . . and me. Everyone—"

"I'm sorry," said Crusher as she administered the hypo.

"Unnh," moaned the disheveled woman, sinking back on her pillow. Within a few moments, Deanna Troi was again sleeping peacefully, her hair radiating outward from her serene face.

Riker scowled with a mixture of anger and helplessness. "What brought this on? Was it those damn *dreams?* She was fine before this!"

"I don't know what happened to her." Beverly shook her head in frustration. "We may never know what started this agitation . . . unless it has a physical cause I haven't found yet."

At Riker's crestfallen expression, Crusher patted the big man on the shoulder. "We'll keep looking, but the sooner we get out of here, the better . . . for her. She needs the specialists at a starbase."

"There's nothing you can do for her?"

"We'll keep her comfortable, and we'll try to talk to her again," answered Crusher. "Next time, I'll bring her around more gradually. We don't have any Vulcans on board, do we?"

"No, none at the moment," muttered Riker. "During the war, most of them went to serve on Vulcan ships, and we never got them back. You can forget about a mind-meld."

"Will, I don't know what to tell you." She patted him again on the shoulder, and they both looked down at the bound figure. Beverly didn't want to give him any false hope, and she was fresh out of words of encouragement.

"I'm going to get her out of here," vowed Riker. He strode from the examination room, through main sickbay, and out the door.

Crusher sighed wearily and rubbed her eyes. She thought about going back to bed, but instead she turned to Nurse Ogawa and said, "Let's do a complete workup again, starting with a brain scan."

Reg Barclay gaped at the magnificent hall of the Exalted Ones, with its rose-hued prisms sparkling with bubbles, glints of light, and the faint silhouette of a Lipul. As if revisiting a dream, Reg glided deeper into the hollow crystal, clinging to Melora's hand. By the time his eyes adjusted to the dim, refracted light, his expression had changed from wonder to distress.

The floor of the cavernous chamber and all of its nooks and crevices were encrusted with the mutant black crystal, growing like spiny weeds. Here and there, black clouds of crushed and broken crystal floated ominously in the air, and an oppressive silence hung over the sparse assemblage. Barclay looked around the gloomy hall but could see no Alpusta or Yiltern, and only a handful of desolate Elaysians.

From the rear of the hall, a figure zoomed toward

them gripping a hover-platform, his yellow robes billowing behind him. "Tangre Bertoran," muttered Reg, pulling back from Melora's grip.

"You let me handle him," she insisted.

When the Peer of the Jeptah reached them, he swung around to a stop and hovered dangerously close to Reg's head. The lanky engineer flinched a little, but not much, and he returned the unfriendly gaze.

"He has no right to be here," declared Bertoran, pointing at the human.

"He has every right to be here." Melora pointed to the violet shard floating around Reg's neck. "He's the proxy for Zuka Juno."

The gray-haired Elaysian looked abashed for a moment at this news, but he quickly recovered both his attitude and his sneer. "*If* that's true, then it shows that my brother Zuka has made a mockery of his esteemed office and should be replaced."

"I really d-don't want to intrude," said Barclay, gripping the shard for comfort, "but you people need to know what you're up against. Zuka Juno said you would believe me . . . if I carried this jewel."

Reg held up the shard, and it glinted briefly, which caused more commotion than his entire speech. The Elaysians waved their arms and conversed in urgent whispers, and the Lipuls bobbed with agitation inside their rose-hued crystals. Melora tried to call them to order, but it was hopeless.

She gave him an encouraging smile, but all Barclay could do was gulp. In front of him, Tangre Bertoran seethed with such anger that it looked as if he would break his hover-platform in half. Before he could denounce Reg, his constituents swooped forward, clamoring for his attention.

"You won't keep that trinket," Bertoran vowed under his breath. He gripped his disc and sped away from them.

"Now what?" asked the human worriedly.

"You're the one with the crystal," said Melora. "Use it."

Reg knew he needed help, but then he remembered that the Elaysians didn't run this show by themselves. Although few in number, the Lipuls seemed to possess considerable authority and influence. As Deanna had said, they were certainly the oldest of all the sentient races, and nobody wanted to upstage them.

He looked around and spotted a glimmer on the floor. By bending over and peering into the clumps of misshapen, smoky crystal, he was able to make out a small cluster of rainbow prisms. Reg remembered that this gemlike instrument had helped Captain Picard communicate with the Lipuls, so he gripped Melora's hand and pointed down.

She nodded and whirled around to push off the roof of the entryway. Grabbing Reg as she soared past, she dragged him into the thicket of black spires, which shattered at their touch, sending up noxious clouds of dust. Reg would have coughed himself to death, but Pazlar kept them moving briskly through the new growth. Finally they reached the rainbow cluster, which glittered like a treasure at the bottom of a sooty mine.

With Melora's help, Reg pulled off the lanyard and pressed the violet crystal into the center of the larger crystal, as he had seen the others do on his earlier visit. Melora pushed off the floor to elevate the two of them above the clouds of soot, and they watched while the aged cluster cycled through a vibrant display of colors.

After a moment, a strange, disembodied voice spoke loudly enough for all to hear: "Barclay is recognized as a proxy. Afford him all regard and esteem you would afford a senior engineer."

"Bah!" scoffed Tangre Bertoran from the back of the hall. Several other Elaysians murmured their disapproval, but no one jumped up to openly challenge him.

Melora urged Reg, "Go ahead and tell them."

Reg's mouth suddenly felt as dry as the brittle, black crystal beneath him, and he wished he had drunk more from his sip tube. He blurted out, "The fractal program on the shell is corrupted. It's in an endless loop, sucking dark matter from the rift. It's spewing it as fast as your collectors can grab it. We can't stop it—not even Zuka Juno—because the code has been encrypted. To be blunt, one of your senior engineers has sabotaged the shell."

Now the murmurs grew to shrill squawks and cries. Accusations rent the air, and the Elaysians fluttered around like a flock of starlings scattered by a loud noise. "You have to be wrong!" shouted Tangre Bertoran, shaking his fist. "Or *mad!*"

Melora dashed in front of Reg and shouted, "I didn't believe it either! Neither did brother Juno. But when we entered the programming room, opened the files, and saw with our own eyes, we had to admit the truth. Now you will have to open your eyes and see that *one* of us is a traitor. Not all of us, just one. Unless we find that being, he or she may succeed in destroying Gemworld."

From the corner of his eye, Barclay saw Tangre Bertoran descending quickly toward the glowing cluster on the floor. He tugged on Melora's shoulder and pointed. "He's after the crystal."

Using Reg as a springboard and pushing him ten meters higher, Melora went soaring back toward the cluster. Although Bertoran was moving faster than her on his hover-platform, Melora had the shorter distance to travel, and she reached the cluster a second before him. Deftly the blond Elaysian snatched the violet shard from its socket and held it up for all to see.

Then she waved the shard in Bertoran's face and crowed, "You're too late to get this one! Is that how *you* got to be proxy for the Gendlii?"

"Enough of these games!" shouted Tangre Bertoran. He gripped his own gleaming green crystal, which floated from a golden cord about his neck. "I will return to the shell, using my own proxy, and inspect the programming. If what these outsiders say is a lie—and I'm sure it is—we will charge them with blasphemy and heresy!"

That pronouncement was met with considerable agreement, and the clamor grew deafening for a few seconds. Melora floated to Reg's side and hung the violet gem around his neck. He wasn't going to say anything else, but resentment walled up within him. *We risked our own lives to save these fools!*

On top of that, he was getting very queasy. All of this put Reg in a mood to speak his mind.

He shouted, "This time, you won't survive! The Ancients would be ashamed of you. No . . . you can't be descended from the beings who built the shell!"

That insult got their attention, and several of the Elaysians stopped to glare at him.

"This is not how your ancestors survived," he told them, "by ignoring a problem. No, they . . . they survived because they *faced* every problem that confronted them—from the receding of the oceans to the loss of their atmosphere. The inhabitants of Gemworld have gotten soft. You prefer to bicker and fix blame instead of finding a solution. I'm sorry . . . that's not how the Ancients would have faced this."

When Reg caught Melora beaming at him, he knew he was on a roll. He puffed his chest out and continued, "Actually our first guess about this crisis was wrong. We thought the shell might have malfunctioned, but it turned out to be the oldest problem in the book. On earth we used to call it 'human error,' and you can use that term, although this act was not done in error. It was done on purpose. You'll claim that it can't happen, that I'm insane, or whatever . . . I've heard that all before. The question is—will you act like your ancestors? Will you do what it takes to survive? Or would you prefer to hide in this room and bicker . . . until you die?"

No one talked against him now, and no one mocked

him, not even Tangre Bertoran. Melora moved to Reg's side and squeezed his arm. "That was good," she whispered. "When you invoked the Ancients, you hit them where it hurts. Now what do we do?"

Barclay's stomach churned. Without gravity to hold the bile down, he felt it coming up. "I've got a big finish," he said with a groan.

A look of realization dawned on Melora's face, and she jerked away from him just as he vomited. Retching in a weightless environment was far worse than retching in gravity, Reg decided. For one thing, there was no obvious direction.

Doubled over in pain and embarrassment, he let Melora drag him backward out of the hall of the Exalted Ones.

Chapter Twelve

"A PRIVATE WORD with you, Captain."

From the command chair, Picard looked up at Will Riker, who had just returned to the bridge. The way the big man worked his jaw, he was obviously agitated, and the captain was curious as to why he wanted privacy. *It must have something to do with Counselor Troi.*

The captain looked around at the bridge and decided there wasn't anything that required his immediate attention. Mostly there was nothing but ongoing repairs, diagnostics, and monitoring. Soon most of the crew wouldn't have enough to do to keep their minds off their predicament. Picard wished the probe had told them more about the dimensional rift, but all it had done was confirm some of their worst suspicions.

Until they heard from Barclay and Pazlar, their next step on Gemworld's behalf was uncertain.

"You have the bridge, Data," said Picard, rising to his feet. He motioned to his first officer and led the way into his ready room. Once inside, he paused for a moment to inspect his new lion fish in its cylindrical aquarium.

"Go on, Number One."

Riker shifted on his feet, looking uncomfortable. "I've just come back from seeing Deanna—"

"I know." The captain shook his head at the tragedy which had befallen one of his most trusted officers. "The doctor told me that when she woke up, she was . . . unchanged."

"That's putting it mildly," grumbled Riker. "She's delirious, completely out of it. Beverly says that we have to get her to a starbase where there are specialists."

"I understand the problem." Picard fixed his first officer with a concerned look. "But I'm not sure what you're getting at."

"I've thought about it, sir, and I believe that a shuttlecraft could escape from the rift by leaving on the far side of the planet. We'd be using the shell as a sort of shield, then we'd go immediately into warp. I'm sure we could—"

Picard held up his hand and smiled sympathetically. "Permission denied. We know too little about the rift, even after sending a probe into it. And the morale problem if people started deserting the ship—"

"But, Captain, we can't leave her like this," insisted the commander.

Picard's tone grew a bit steely. "We all feel strongly about Counselor Troi and want to see her full recovery, but this is a foolhardy plan. I'm not going to gamble your life on it, or hers. In our fastest shuttlecraft, you couldn't get to a starbase in less than thirty hours. How would you take care of her? Number One, accept the fact that we're here until we resolve this crisis."

"And if we can't?"

"Then she'll be the luckiest one among us," replied Picard. "She won't have to see the end."

His combadge chirped and a familiar voice said, "Bridge to Picard."

"Go ahead, Data."

"Lieutenant Pazlar has reported in. She will dock the shuttlecraft in approximately five minutes, and she has requested a medical team. Lieutenant Barclay is ill."

"How ill?" asked the captain, fearing a sickness similar to Danna Troi's.

"Space sickness."

He let out a relieved sigh. Although he was sure that Barclay would disagree with him, space sickness wasn't deadly. "See to it. Riker and I will meet them in sickbay. Picard out."

He turned to Riker and managed a pained smile. "This gives you another excuse to visit sickbay."

"I'm with you, sir," said the first officer, lifting his chin. "Are you sure we can't destroy that rift?"

"Perhaps we can. But we don't know how, and we don't know *what* we'd be destroying. If we can stop the flow of dark matter, maybe it will close on its own."

"That's the plan?" asked Riker.

"Until I hear a better one."

From his bed in sickbay, Reg Barclay looked apologetically at Captain Picard. "I'm really sorry I messed up, sir. I tried to convince them."

"Don't listen to him," said Melora Pazlar, gazing proudly at the lieutenant. "He did great. I really think the Exalted Ones listened to him and will cooperate with us. He can't help it if he was in a weightless environment for too long . . . and got a little sick."

"No, of course not," said Picard with an encouraging smile. "I'm sure they won't hold it against you."

Commander Riker bent over and fingered the violet crystal hanging from Reg's neck. "You seem to have picked up a souvenir."

"Yes, it's . . . it's kind of a key, like a promotion." Barclay shook his head in wonderment. "Apparently I'm now the proxy for one of the senior engineers, Zuka Juno. That means we can get access to the shell programming whenever we want, for all the good it will do us."

"Why don't you tell us exactly what happened," said the captain.

"Yes, sir." Reg glanced uncertainly at Melora. "We actually promised to keep it a secret until they had time to deal with it, but I don't suppose it matters."

"We can't wait any longer," agreed Pazlar.

In a somewhat halting manner, with frequent side jaunts, Barclay told the captain and first officer about finding Zuka Juno and bringing him to the shell. When the senior engineer accessed the primary computer code, their worst fears were realized. The code had, indeed, been sabotaged and put into an encrypted loop.

It was only logical to leave the senior engineer at work on the problem, so Barclay had gone in his place to appeal to the Exalted Ones. To give his words more weight, he had became Zuka Juno's proxy.

Melora interrupted, "He really shamed them into taking some action."

"I hope so," said Reg, shaking his head. "By now, Tangre Bertoran has had plenty of time to go the shell and verify it for himself. If we go back there now, maybe we can get some cooperation."

The captain frowned. "But we can't really stop the synergy between the rift and the shell until we break the encryption. We've got to find the one who did this."

"It could even be Tangre Bertoran," said Pazlar.

"Or one of six senior engineers who are scattered all over the planet," muttered Riker. "We need a plan B in case we never find this criminal. Is there any way to turn off the shell and reboot the system?"

"Not that we've seen," answered Reg. "As Data pointed out, the system isn't designed to be shut down."

"It would only take an instant to lose the planet's

atmosphere," said Pazlar, sounding horrified at the very idea. "We can't shut down the shell."

"The only thing in the shell that's crucial to the atmosphere are the forcefields," said Picard thoughtfully. "Maybe there's a way to keep them going. We've got to get back to the shell and talk to the senior engineers."

"I'm ready," said Barclay, struggling to sit up.

"Not you, Lieutenant," said the captain with a smile. "You've done enough for today."

"But I *am* one of the senior engineers . . . sort of." Barclay tugged on the violet crystal hanging from his neck. "Besides, I feel much better, really I do."

"The doctor said he could leave whenever he felt better," added Melora. She gazed fondly at Reg. "This time, we'll leave on the artificial gravity in the shuttlecraft."

"Very well." The captain tapped his combadge. "Picard to Data."

"Data here," came the response.

"Meet us in shuttlebay one. Commander Riker will take over the bridge."

"Yes, sir."

"On my way," replied Riker, moving toward the exit. The big man glanced at the door of Troi's room, and anguish etched his handsome features. Reg had discovered that no one in sickbay was giving out any information about Counselor Troi, and she wasn't seeing visitors. Commander Riker must have known that, too, because he lowered his head and walked out the door.

Reg looked worriedly at Melora. "We'd better have the doctor give us a few extra hypos. I think we're going to be gone for a while."

En route in the shuttlecraft, Picard, Barclay, and Pazlar went over every bit of information they possessed with Data, who was the repository of all their knowledge concerning the rift, the shell, and Gemworld. The android had studied the data from the probe as well as Barclay's new information about the shell, and he theorized a classic Catch-22: the rift would stay open as long as the shell collected dark matter, and the shell would collect dark matter as long as the rift stayed open. As long as these conditions remained in force, the dark, mutant crystal would continue to grow and choke the life out of Gemworld.

Picard had no solution to suggest. They would just have to keep gathering information until a solution presented itself. With any luck, thought the captain, maybe they could find the person who did this.

No Elaysians were seen drifting outside the Ninth Processing Gate so they tethered the shuttlecraft themselves and entered the shell. Captain Picard noted and was amused by the deference shown to Lieutenant Barclay. As Melora Pazlar led them through the tubular corridors, Elaysians and Alpusta pressed forward to see the human who wore the violet shard. When Reg nodded shyly at them, they shrunk back, as if unworthy or embarrassed. Picard soon realized that Barclay, as unlikely as it seemed, had made himself something of a celebrity on Gemworld. Now he would have to be included on every away team to the planet.

In due course, they found themselves in the dead-end passageway that led to the central programming room. Picard's hackles rose when he saw two yellow-garbed Jeptah waiting outside the vault. He reminded himself that he had his own dignitary—Reg Barclay—and so no one could refuse the team access. However, he knew this encounter wouldn't be easy when the Jeptah turned around and one of them was revealed to be Tangre Bertoran.

The Peer of the Jeptah scowled at them. "Come to gloat have you, Captain Picard? As you predicted, we're incapable of helping ourselves, and we have to depend upon our saviors from Starfleet." Picard ignored the taunt.

Bertoran reserved his biggest sneer for Barclay. "And here's the new proxy for the senior engineer of the Elaysians. What tricks have you and Zuka Juno concocted for us? Why won't he let us enter?"

"What do you mean?" asked Reg puzzledly.

"I mean, he's got the door barred from the inside. We've been standing out here for a long time, begging him to let us in."

"What does he say?" asked Reg.

"He says nothing. He refuses to answer." Bertoran looked at his fellow Jeptah. "Are you sure he's in there?"

"Oh, yes, Exalted One." He pointed to Reg and Melora. "He entered with these two and has not left since then."

"That was several hours ago," said Melora.

"I can tell from the way the hatch is locked, that he's in there," insisted the Jeptah.

Barclay pounded on the solid metal hatch and shouted, "Zuka Juno! It's me . . . your proxy! Let us in!"

There was no response, and Reg turned worriedly to the captain. "I don't get it. He said he'd be trying to break the encryption and would wait for us to return."

The captain turned to Tangre Bertoran. "Is it all right if we break this hatch open?"

"How do you intend to do that? This door is made from our strongest alloy." The Elaysian frowned worriedly. "You're not going to shoot your phasers off in here, are you?"

"There's no need for that," the captain assured him. "Mr. Data, please open this hatch."

"Yes, sir." The android floated forward and anchored his feet in the circular entryway to give himself some leverage. Then he gripped the hatch wheel with both hands and gave it a twist. The sound of snapping metal could be heard even through the thick vault, and the wheel spun freely in Data's hands.

"By the Ancients—" muttered Bertoran, staring at the android. "You *are* a remarkable being."

"Thank you." Data pushed the broken hatch, and it swung open, revealing nothing but a few sparkles of refracted light inside. "Zuka Juno?" he asked politely.

No answer came, and Captain Picard pulled himself up to the entryway to take a look. The hair rose on the back of his neck as his sense of danger was alerted. The feeling must have been widespread because no one else in the corridor spoke or moved. Data took the point and shot through the hatchway. When Picard heard no shouts of warning, he followed.

He found the android shining a light around the hundreds of small drawers that lined the cylindrical chamber. It didn't take the android long to locate the body of a thin, older Elaysian floating in the back of the room. The man's eyes stared blankly in the unmistakable stupor of death. Data efficiently drew his tricorder and took a reading, but there was no urgency or surprise in his voice. "He is dead."

"What? What is it?" shouted Tangre Bertoran, muscling his way past the others in the hatchway. He swooped into the room and followed the light to the ghastly scene in the corner, and his arms fluttered with alarm. "Help him! Is he alive?"

"No, we're too late," said Picard. "I'm sorry. Do you see any marks on him, Data?"

The android hovered closer to the corpse and inspected him with his light.

"Don't touch him!" wailed Tangre Bertoran. "Leave him alone—you must not defile the body! He can only be handled by the Jeptah."

"Is he Jeptah?" asked Data with curiosity.

"No, but that is our traditional function, even before we began caring for the Sacred Protector. We have strict protocols in these matters."

"I'll bet," said Barclay, peering into the hatchway. "Can we find out how he died?"

Bertoran whirled on the lieutenant and glared at

him before he realized that Picard was watching him closely. "Perhaps," said Bertoran with a curt bow. "That is also a function of the Jeptah. But after all, he was an old man."

"The timing of his death is rather suspicious," observed Data, continuing a careful examination without actually touching the corpse. "I see no obvious marks of foul play."

"Foul play!" echoed Bertoran with a derisive snort. "We may have accidental deaths on Gemworld, but we haven't had a murder in thousands of years."

"And this room was sealed, wasn't it?" asked Picard. "If it was locked as we found it."

"Of course," snapped the Elaysian. "There is no other way in or out. Now if you'll excuse me, I have arrangements to make." He bounced off a panel and swooped toward the hatchway.

Reg barely had time to get out of the way. "What about the program you came to see?"

"Let's have some respect for the dead," said Bertoran. "I'm sure you people don't mind working with a corpse looking over your shoulder, but I do."

As he swept past, Barclay called after him. "What about *me?* Seeing as I'm his proxy and all?"

"You're no longer a proxy," muttered the Elaysian. Reg sighed with relief, and Bertoran sneered as he added, "Now you're Acting Senior Engineer of the Elaysians. You can only be removed by the Exalted Ones, and we could never convene enough members at this time. So, Mr. Barclay, you represent me and all of our people in the gravest matter we have faced in a million years. Congratulations!"

He hurried off, and Barclay turned to the captain and gulped, as if to say he was sorry for getting so hopelessly mired in this situation. Picard felt the same way as he turned to look at the corpse floating in the air.

Data was carefully studying the dead Elaysian's mouth. "There is some liquid on his lips, probably saliva," reported the android. "I cannot get a sample without touching him."

"Don't touch him," said Melora Pazlar, staring at the android with intense blue eyes. "Please don't. It's true, only the Jeptah are allowed to touch our dead."

"What will h-happen to him?" asked Reg.

"He'll be taken to the Blood Prism and be dedicated to the Progeny."

"She means, he will be eaten," said Data, "by a sentient race known as the Frills. Their holy hunters are called the Progeny."

Picard looked up at the body hovering overhead, and he frowned sourly. "I hope that step can be delayed until we find out what killed him."

Deanna Troi fidgeted in her sleep, and she felt cloying arms embrace her and hold her against her will. For a moment, she felt as if she might have to wake up and deal with this unwelcome suitor; but in the end, the great dread that had troubled her began to lift. She felt herself melting comfortably back into the serene sleep which had embraced her for so long, before they awoke her the first time.

The threat was over. It had been dealt with. Their wickedness would not hurt her anymore, at least not for a while. She could rest and build up her strength to resist the next attack—to emerge triumphant in the end. She hadn't known it before, but she knew now that she was in the fight of her life. The new enemy was strange and clever, but it didn't know her true capabilities. She didn't really know them herself.

But she could dream, and anything she could dream, she could accomplish. That was the greatest gift they had left her, for all they had stolen.

Chapter Thirteen

MELORA PAZLAR WATCHED SOLEMNLY as two yellow-garbed Jeptah enclosed the body of Zuka Juno in a yellow fabric bag and floated him out of the programming vault. Beside her hovered Captain Picard, Data, Tangre Bertoran, and Reg Barclay. As unlikely as it seemed, Reg was the new Acting Senior Engineer for the shell, representing the Elaysians; he had the violet crystal to prove it.

Hovering near the hatchway, Tangre Bertoran watched the visitors carefully, looking for any signs of disrespect as the body was removed. To their credit, thought Melora, the *Enterprise* crew were quiet and respectful, hiding their impatience well. None of them gave the volatile Peer of the Jeptah any cause for overreaction.

Melora was beginning to regret ever involving the crew of the *Enterprise* in this disaster because the longer they stayed, the more hopeless it looked. She felt doubly bad about Deanna Troi, who was apparently in some sort of hallucinatory state. With all that was happening, she hadn't even had a chance to visit the counselor in sickbay. Barclay, Captain Picard, and everyone else were struggling valiantly to save Gemworld, but they had been thwarted at every turn by distrust and hidebound convention.

All this time, her people thought they were so resilient, able to face any peril. In reality, all it took was one deranged engineer to bring Gemworld to the brink of destruction.

On top of that, Melora was grumpy because her joints ached. She could feel the extra gravity resulting from the rampant crystal growth. In a bizarre way, her homeworld was being reborn into something that would look more like a conventional planet, even if it could no longer support the lifeforms it had supported for billions of years.

After Zuka Juno's body had been borne away, Captain Picard looked expectantly at Tangre Bertoran and pointed to the terminal. "Now will you take a look at the programming? I think you can see that it's locked up."

The Peer of the Jeptah sighed and waved at the blinking screen. "Oh, I've already assumed that it is. Zuka would have solved the problem, if anyone could. It's a shame he won't be here to help us break the encryption."

Data bobbed forward. "I do not believe the encryption is breakable. The form of biological, crystalline memory components which this system employs are a thousand times more complex than our best gel packs, and a level-eight encryption could not be broken on our equivalent subsystems."

Bertoran smiled condescendingly. "I didn't say *you* could break the encryption, but you haven't really given *us* a chance, have you?"

"We should have an alternative plan," said Picard. "Can't we find the one who sabotaged your computer? There are only six suspects."

"And one of them just died," said Bertoran. "If Zuka Juno was the one, you would never find out. If *I* were the one—and I have access as proxy for the Gendlii—you would never find out either. In fact, whichever one of the senior engineers did this, they must be quite insane. I sincerely doubt if they will ever come forward and admit what they've done, and I don't see how you can force them. In fact, I'm not even sure you'll be able to *find* them all in these troubled times."

The captain's lips thinned in anger, and Melora felt as if she should to do something to break the stalemate. "Captain, why don't we let the Jeptah work on the encryption. In the meantime, I think we can locate the senior engineers of the Lipuls and the Alpusta. The Frills and the Yiltern are going to be much harder to find."

Picard nodded grimly, not looking pleased with his limited options. "Very well. We'll investigate from that end while the Jeptah work on the encryption. If you don't mind, I'd like to leave Commander Data to help you."

Bertoran shrugged. "We don't have any more doors that need to be broken open, but you never know—he may be useful."

"I can process four hundred thousand calculations a second," said Data matter-of-factly.

"That's good to know." Melora detected sarcasm in his voice. The white-haired Elaysian motioned to the door where more of his yellow-garbed retinue were standing by. "Bring in the programmers."

As the Jeptah lined up to come in, Melora decided to lead her party out. She was no happier than the captain about Zuka Juno's death and their general lack of progress, but she knew her people well enough to realize that they would do as they promised, even if they protested all the way.

Melora grabbed Reg's arm, turned him around, and propelled him out the door and past the waiting Jeptah. "Let's get the parade started."

"I feel so helpless, like we're not doing anything," he muttered.

"So do I, but we're doing all we can . . . for now."

A moment later, Captain Picard joined them in the corridor. They watched silently as Jeptah technicians swarmed into the programming room. Data was lost in the shuffle, and Melora hoped the android would be able to assert himself. Captain Picard obviously felt he was the right one to leave behind.

"How can we find the senior engineers?" asked the captain, his mind on the task at hand.

"It won't be easy, unless they're still here." Melora turned to Reg and smiled. "As proxy for the Elaysians, you have resources we haven't used yet. For one thing, you've got an office here somewhere."

"I do?" asked Reg.

"Just a minute." Melora pushed off the wall and skirted within a meter of the nearest Jeptah. "Where is the office of the Acting Senior Engineer of the Elaysians?" She pointed to Reg, who smiled and waved.

The technician shook her head incredulously and ducked inside the hatchway to consult Tangre Bertoran. Melora couldn't hear what he told her, but the woman returned a few moments later and motioned to them with a beleaguered scowl. "Follow me."

The female Jeptah led the way down the circular corridor so quickly that even Pazlar had to hurry to keep pace while dragging Barclay and Captain Picard with her. Of the *Enterprise* crew, only Data moved efficiently in low gravity. Melora knew she had to be doubly careful with Barclay, who had shown a predisposition to space sickness. She didn't know what was in those hypos he took periodically, but it wasn't working very well, judging by the paleness of his skin. Then again, maybe he was just scared of dying, a sentiment she could understand.

To her mind, Reg had been incredibly brave, taking on a very serious responsibility in order to help them. Although he hadn't asked to be proxy to the senior engineer—and now the senior engineer himself—he had accepted the burden without complaint. If he hadn't, there would be no voice of reason in the hall of the Exalted Ones, no one speaking unpleasant truths they didn't want to hear. Plus there would have been a very nasty fight over who would succeed Zuka Juno, which would have further splintered their leaders' attention.

Melora couldn't believe that she had doubted Reg, too. The captain had been right—his impartial viewpoint had been crucial. It was her own people and the other leaders of Gemworld who had disappointed her. They couldn't envision their precious shell failing, even when the signs were all around them.

Then again, to be charitable, thought Melora, they might have recognized failure, but they couldn't foresee treachery from within. Even now, outright destruction would be easier to deal with than the painful sight of malformed crystals eating away at the structure and beauty of Gemworld. No one could have foreseen this bizarre turn of events.

The Elaysian shook off her troubled thoughts and tried to follow the route of their imperious guide. Melora discovered a subtle pattern of waves and bubbles engraved on the convex walls, and she remembered similar patterns from the communes where she grew up. They were directional marks. Although few on the planet had ever seen free-flowing water, the motif of waves, rivers, and water was strong in their culture. Melora had no problem understanding the system once she got used to it, and she realized her guide was taking them in circles.

"The most direct route," she demanded. "In case you don't know it, the Acting Senior Engineer can have you removed from your post. Not even Tangre Bertoran could help you."

She glanced at Reg and saw him about to stammer that he would never do such a thing, and she winked at him to keep quiet. The Jeptah wasn't sure what to do, until Barclay began to stroke the violet shard importantly.

"I do know a quicker way," she muttered with a slight bow. "I thought you would want to see something of the Sacred Protector, but if not . . . come with me."

The Jeptah reversed herself and led them upward through the metallic maze. With a minimum of twists and turns, they arrived at a hatch with a circular plate in front of it, like a shield. Their guide stepped aside and looked expectantly at Reg.

When he didn't act quickly enough for her, she pointed to his chest and said impatiently, "The jewel."

"Right," said Reg, sounding more confident than he looked. Melora carefully anchored herself and pushed him toward the bronze shield; with a trembling hand, he held out the gem. When he was almost touching the door, the gem flashed a faint glow, and the door opened like a camera lens retracting in slow motion.

"That's more like it," said Captain Picard with relief. He nodded to their reluctant guide. "Thank you."

She bowed curtly and hurried off, a worried look

creasing her V-shaped brow. Clearly the disciple had failed Tangre Bertoran by successfully bringing them here.

"It's dark inside there," said Barclay, peering into what was indeed a very dark chamber.

"I think you can fix that," said Melora, pushing down Reg's head and guiding him through the circular hatch.

As soon as he entered the room, lights came up. They were a soothing violet color, and they revealed what looked like an underwater scene. Bulging nets floated everywhere, all of them crammed with unusual items. One net was filled with computer padds, isolinear chips, books, manuals, sextants, and various unidentifiable gadgets. Another was jammed with the preserved remains of animals and jars containing biological specimens, some recognizable, some not. A third was full of what seemed to be personal items, such as holographic photos, plaques, and crystal samples.

Every spare centimeter of the convex walls was crammed with drawings, charts, and illuminated transparencies, depicting everything from crystal clusters to star clusters. Almost buried amidst the splendid jumble was a monitoring station and computer screen like the one in the central programming room.

"Zuka Juno was a Renaissance man," said Captain Picard, gazing around the cluttered room with admiration.

"I've never understood that reference," said Melora, "although I've heard it before."

"In terran history, the Renaissance was a period of enlightenment which followed a period of ignorance and superstition," answered Picard. "Generally 'Renaissance man' has come to mean a person who knows a great deal about many different subjects. I think that would describe Zuka Juno."

"On Gemworld, we seem to be following a reverse trend," grumbled Melora. "Our ignorant, superstitious age is now, and the enlightened age was in the past."

"Don't be t-too hard on your people," said Barclay sympathetically. "They've been safe for so long, they must have thought nothing could harm them."

"Nothing but themselves," said Picard, leaning over the terminal. "How do we find the whereabouts of the other senior engineers?"

"I think I can bring up their schedules," answered Reg, slipping between the captain and the console. "Data and I saw the technician do it when we were here the first time."

While Barclay plied the board, plowing through screen after screen of tables, Captain Picard studied the gadgets in one of Zuka Juno's nets. At the sight of one object—a slim, white, segmented board—his eyes widened with delight, and he carefully pulled it from the bundle.

"I can't believe it—a slide rule!" exclaimed Picard. He inspected the object, which had miniature rules and guides on both of its intricate faces. "This is from Earth—a primitive computing device that compares logarithms for quick calculations. This one has to be from the early to mid-twentieth century. I wonder how it found its way here."

Pazlar smiled. "As I told you, Captain, my people don't travel much beyond Gemworld, but they're very interested in collecting knowledge. It's a shame that Zuka Juno never got to see any of the places where these objects came from."

The captain nodded thoughtfully while he carefully worked the inner segment of the slide rule. "There must be a way to bring more inhabitants of Gemworld into Starfleet. I don't see why we couldn't outfit a ship to operate under weightless conditions. It's more natural in space, anyway. If Lipuls and Alpusta can function here on the shell, they could do just as well on a starship."

Melora nodded with appreciation. "Thank you for the thought, sir. If we survive this, I'm sure my people will be ready for some more cultural exchange."

Her eyes never strayed far from Reg Barclay, and she looked back at him worriedly. "Do you need any help?"

"Maybe a little bit with translation," he answered. "I think I've pulled up the minutes of a meeting of all six senior engineers. It was approximately one month ago."

She leaned over his shoulder and intently studied the document. "I remember that date. It was just after that, while all six of them were still on the shell, that a group of students found the first cluster of mutant crystal. Right after that, when problems began cropping up everywhere, the engineers scattered to their home bases."

"Except for the proxy of the Gendlii, Tangre Bertoran," said Picard pointedly. "We know he's been commuting back and forth between here and the Exalted Ones, without going home."

"Keeping an eye on things," said Pazlar. She didn't want to mention that Bertoran was the only one actually in position to harm Zuka Juno because she didn't want to admit that the senior engineer had been harmed at all. Nevertheless, Bertoran knew the shell inside and out, and he could have arranged for them to find the programming room as they had. After all, he had been the first one on the scene.

The captain and Reg knew that, too.

"The Lipul engineer hasn't left the shell," said Reg, pointing to a graph with a solid red line. "He's here somewhere."

"The Lipuls can't come and go as easily as the others," explained Melora. "But they can use the nourishment strands to get to the surface when circumstances permit."

"Let's pay a visit to the Lipul engineer before he goes anywhere," said Captain Picard decisively. Behind a bulging net, the captain found a proximity panel, and he opened the door with a wave of his hand.

Barclay moved uncertainly away from the computer terminal, tilting like a windmill. Melora gripped his arm and steadied him. "How is your medicine working?" she whispered.

He gave her a wan smile. "I do much better when I

don't have to move around so much. I was hoping I could stay still for a while."

"I'm afraid we have to keep moving," said Pazlar grimly. She glanced at the captain, who was already gliding down the corridor, learning how to push and pull himself along. Could he get them out of this disaster? Could anybody? Melora wanted to slip away to visit her parents, but there was no time for that now.

Nobody knew how much time they had left.

Chapter Fourteen

"HE'S HERE," SAID NURSE ALYSSA OGAWA, motioning to the door of the examination room.

A shadow blocked the entryway, and Beverly Crusher turned from her preparations to see Will Riker looking apprehensive as his gaze traveled from her to the sleeping figure of Deanna Troi. She was still restrained, but now intravenous tubes were attached to her arms. Not a pretty sight, but Crusher was determined to change that.

"Hello, Commander," she said. "Shall we wait for the captain?"

"No, he's going to be delayed for a while," answered Riker, moving past her to look worriedly at Troi. "How is she?"

"She's weak, and we had to feed her intravenously.

But physically, she's fine." Crusher leaned over her patient and lifted an eyelid. The pupil underneath retracted in reaction to the light, and Troi flinched slightly. "She'll be waking up soon, anyway, but we're going to help her along. Last time we let her awaken on her own, but this time it will be more gradual."

The commander didn't take his eyes off Deanna, and Beverly went on, "You don't have to stay, Will, but I thought I'd give you the option. There's a good chance it will turn into a repeat of what we've seen before."

"Then we'll deal with it," he answered, rising to his feet and stepping back. "I know you'll do the best you can."

"All right." Crusher made sure that her emergency hypos were within reach, then she nodded to Ogawa. The veteran nurse reached up and adjusted the flow of the intravenous tubes.

"We're giving her a mild stimulant through the IV," explained Crusher. After two or three minutes, Troi looked unchanged, but Beverly could see that several of her vital signs had increased in activity.

"Now we'll employ an ancient method of waking people up." The doctor nodded to Ogawa, who broke open a small capsule and swiped its contents under the patient's nose.

"A bit of ammonia, just enough to wake up her olfactory nodes," Crusher whispered to Riker. "If we can get another part of her brain working first, maybe we'll avoid a disturbance."

When Troi began to wrinkle her nose and frown puzzledly, the doctor motioned to Ogawa to stop. With a few deft movements, the nurse removed the IVs from her arm, leaving on the restraints.

More tense moments passed, while Troi twisted and stretched in her sleep, slowly discovering that she was bound to the bed. Crusher quickly prepared a hypospray. Just as the patient was about to open her eyes, the doctor applied the hypospray to her neck. Deanna instantly relaxed and slumped onto the bed, but she didn't go back to sleep. Instead she lifted her head and stared dreamily around the examination room.

"Hmmm . . . what's going on?" she asked slowly, licking her dry lips. She tried to focus her eyes on Riker, and Crusher stepped back to give her a clear field of vision. "Will? Is that you?"

"It's all right," he answered with joy and relief, rushing toward her bed. "You're going to be all right."

"I am?" she asked doubtfully.

"You had an accident," said Beverly. She pressed a button, and the restraints snapped back, drawing attention to themselves.

"Why . . . was I tied down?" asked Troi with a flash of anger.

"Because of the intravenous tubes," answered the doctor evenly. "So you wouldn't pull them loose. Let's not talk much now, all right? You've been through a lot, but I think it's permissable to give Will a hug."

Riker didn't hesitate to follow the doctor's orders,

engulfing Deanna's slim body in his biggest bear hug. Immersed in his all-encompassing embrace, she gripped him fiercely for a moment, then she went limp with relief and exhaustion.

Everything seems okay for now, thought Crusher. But they had to confront the fact that Troi was suffering from some amount of memory loss. If she wanted answers about what happened to her, there wouldn't be any.

Riker gently lowered her onto the bed and smiled fondly at her. "You're going to be just fine."

"I'm thirsty," she said hoarsely.

"We'll get you something to eat and drink," answered Crusher. "Then you'll have to sleep some more. After a little more observation, we'll see about releasing you from sickbay."

"What about the mission?" she asked worriedly. "Gemworld? And the ship?"

"They're both still here," Riker assured her. "Do what the doctor says, and I'll give you a briefing as soon as you get out. Over dinner." He gave her his most charming smile, and she gently touched his smooth-shaven cheek.

"I've got to get back to the bridge. See you later." Riker rose to his feet and strode from the room, giving Beverly a grateful nod.

The doctor tried to figure out exactly what she was going to tell her best friend. When Deanna was fully recovered, they could show her the video logs, but it was hard to tell how much she should know at the moment. The last thing they wanted was a relapse, although Crusher was fully prepared for that to happen. She would keep Deanna sedated for a while.

"What happened to me?" asked the counselor, shaking her head and staring at the marks on her arm where the restraints had held her.

"The truth is, we don't know," answered Crusher. "Since you seem to have a memory loss about it, we may never know what happened to you. But that isn't important now—all that's important is your well-being."

"Okay," muttered Troi wearily, "so I'm not going to get anything out of you, and I don't remember anything. I guess I just have to lie here and wonder why."

"I guess so," answered Crusher with her best air of harried superiority. She moved toward the door. "Besides, the only person who can figure out what happened is *you*. Nobody else was there. But relax—don't rack your brain. It's more important that you get better. If you need anything, just call. Okay?"

"Okay. Thanks."

"What would you like to eat?" asked Nurse Ogawa pleasantly.

Troi slumped back in her bed, weary and confused, while Beverly kept walking away. Crusher tried not to glance over her shoulder at her troubled patient. If she reported this incident in any detail, it would likely get Deanna relieved of duty for an extended psychological evaluation. Of course, that was in the event that they *survived* this mission.

The doctor didn't like things she didn't understand, and she didn't understand what had happened to

Deanna. Stuck down in sickbay, Beverly hadn't seen much of the vaunted beauty of Gemworld, but she didn't care about its beauty. It was dangerous here. She had a bad feeling about Gemworld. She was ready to leave.

Following the directional markings on the curved walls of the shell, Melora Pazlar led Captain Picard and Reg Barclay to another circular door. The few Alpusta and Elaysians they passed gave them a wide berth, and there was no one around to tell them what to do next. Melora knocked on the door, and Barclay lifted his violet shard and waved it about. But nothing happened.

"What's this?" asked Picard, pushing himself lower. Beneath the door, recessed into the wall itself, was a drawer similar to the ones in the programming room. Picard opened the drawer and searched for a receptacle.

"The crystal," he said, holding up his hand.

"Yes, sir." Barclay removed the lanyard from his neck and handed the crystal to Picard, who shoved it into the waiting slot.

A moment later, the doorway opened, revealing not a crowded office but a smooth facet of yellow crystal. Deep within the crystal, bubbles and glints of light danced in the slowly moving marrow. Melora and the two men peered into the topazlike depths, and she wondered whether the Lipul was even present.

The bubbles slowly increased in volume, shifting downward. Nobody moved or said a word. Finally a vague mushroom shape floated upward and drifted in front of them, opening and closing like a miniature bellows. Melora had never been so close to a Lipul, not even in her first encounter as a child, and she stared in wonder at the filmy creature. It looked fragile and helpless, although it might have lived for centuries, even millennia.

This Lipul was a dignitary, thought Melora. For all she knew, it could be the oldest living creature on Gemworld. Perhaps it had sailed on the dreamships that contacted the humans over two hundred years ago.

Still, the Lipul looked tired as it bobbed up and down in the yellow marrow, as if the effort to maintain this position was very taxing. Certainly, these were difficult days for everyone on Gemworld, perhaps more so for the oldest beings among them. They had seen so much, lived through so much, yet they faced a threat they had never seen before.

"Greetings!" said Reg cheerfully.

"Greetings," answered an artificial voice. "You are the newest."

"I guess so," answered Reg with a nervous chuckle. "Do you know . . . how it happened?"

The Lipul fluttered with agitation for a moment, then it settled down in the slow stream of bubbles. "Zuka Juno is dead. An able colleague, I will miss him. But we have you."

"Well, I don't know if I make up for losing him," said Reg sheepishly.

Melora was surprised at this vote of confidence on behalf of the Lipul, but perhaps it knew how instrumental Reg had been during the crisis. *What else did the Lipul know?*

Captain Picard pressed forward, looking impatient, and Barclay said, "May my captain speak with you?"

"Yes, if his questions are pertinent."

"They're pertinent," replied Picard. "Our ship is also endangered by the rift. Are you aware that one of the senior engineers corrupted the fractal computer program? It's in an endless loop, drawing dark matter from the rift to feed the mutant crystal. This disaster is the result of sabotage."

"So you have said," answered the Lipul, sounding doubtful. "Death and change are natural. To all events, there is a purpose."

"The purpose of the sabotage is to destroy Gemworld!" blurted Pazlar.

"Or to make Gemworld stronger," said the disembodied voice. "We do not recognize evil intentions."

"Do you know that the program is encrypted?" said Melora. "There's no way to stop it . . . no way to end the growth of the black crystal!"

"Untrue," answered the Lipul. "The end is death."

"The death of everyone!" snapped Melora, who was stunned at the Lipul's cavalier attitude. She had heard that they sometimes acted as if they were above the fray, but this was ridiculous.

"Death is the end. Also the beginning," replied the scratchy artificial voice. "The Sacred Protector is the key."

"We know that," said Melora, getting angry and frustrated. She felt someone grab her arm, and she thought it was Reg, until she saw Captain Picard shaking his head at her.

"He's right."

"What do you mean?"

"If the shell died, the crisis would be over," said the captain with cool understatement.

"But we'd lose our air!" protested Pazlar. "We wouldn't survive!"

"Uh . . . actually I think the Lipuls would survive," said Reg. "They would probably adjust to increased gravity better than the rest of you, too."

"Of course, everyone on the *Enterprise* would survive, too," grumbled Pazlar. "Just you and the Lipuls."

Picard narrowed his eyes at her, but his tone stayed friendly. "I think the senior engineer is saying that shutting down the shell would more than likely shut down the rift as well. This is a hypothetical, worst-case scenario, but it would end the crisis."

In shock over this devastating idea, Melora turned to see the Lipul bobbing serenely in its yellow gel. The Lipuls thought in vast increments of time, where generations of Elaysians were but seconds on a lengthy timeline. They cared about their neighbors, but they were also inclined to take a long-range view of things.

More than anyone, they could probably envision a great die-off of life on Gemworld because they had spent so much time trying to delay that inevitable scenario. *But not now,* thought Melora, *not during my lifetime.*

It would be worse for her, because she would have

to witness the extinction of her people from aboard the *Enterprise*. Then she and her crewmates would fly off, unscathed. Maybe they could save a few hundred Elaysians, but which ones? Who would choose?

Trying to control her emotions, Melora turned to consider Captain Picard. He wasn't here to save them, she realized, but to protect the interests of the entire Federation. Those interests lay in shutting down the rift in the most expedient manner possible. The needs of the many outweighing the needs of the few, and all that.

She could agree with him on one matter, however. The real target of this attack might not be Gemworld; it could be the Sacred Protector and the oxygen breathers. The planet, the *Enterprise,* the Federation, and the Lipuls would go on after the shell had been shut down.

If anyone is going to save the day, it will have to be me. Melora's heart raced unpleasantly at the thought of doing something that would get her thrown out of Starfleet, maybe even arrested and charged. But she couldn't let them destroy billions of Elaysians, Alpusta, Frills, Yiltern, and Gendlii.

She took a deep breath and blurted out, "Father, do you know who corrupted the program?"

"As you have said, one of the senior engineers," answered the Lipul. "This knowledge would not serve any purpose, even if you possessed it. Do what you must to kill the Sacred Protecter, and be swift."

The Lipul drifted upward, as if too weak to fight the slow, sparkling current. The artificial voice continued softly, "To the new one, have marrow in your bones. The crystal responds to you."

"Uh, sir? Mr. Engineer!" Barclay peered upward at the departed Lipul and motioned him back, but the amorphous creature was gone. Captain Picard removed the shard from the receptacle and hung it back around Reg's neck.

"I'm sorry, Captain," said Pazlar, gnawing her lip, "I don't know what came over me. I was out of line correcting you and the senior engineer. But I couldn't stand to hear that we had to shut down the shell! That might save Gemworld in some fashion—as a museum piece—but it would kill most of the life here."

"Which is why I view it as the very last resort, Lieutenant. Let's see if we have any other options." The captain scowled and gazed down the tubular corridor, as if dreading having to navigate another weightless corridor. He tapped his combadge. "Picard to Data."

"Data here," answered an efficient voice.

"What's your status?"

"As expected, we have failed to break the encryption. However, the Jeptah engineers have suggested a promising method of fooling the dark-matter collectors into collecting hydrogen, or some other harmless material. By invading the subsystems that control the collectors, we can pass a variable to the program that will effect this change. The invasion will have to take place on the space-side exterior of the shell, but the Jeptah assure me that there are Alpusta trained for this work."

"Won't the rift affect them?"

"No, they feel they can extend the forcefield enough to afford the workers protection for a short time," answered Data. "I have no firsthand experience with these systems, but the plan appears feasible."

"What a relief," said Melora with a huge grin. She gripped Reg's arm and shook him. "Isn't that great?"

"Yes," he answered with a shaky voice.

Picard gave Data a brief account of their activities, but no specifics about what the Lipul had said. *With any luck,* thought Melora, *the idea of turning off the shell will never be mentioned again.*

"It will take several hours to finalize these plans," said Data. "I will stay on duty."

"So there haven't been any conflicts with the Jeptah?" asked Picard.

"None so far. They have utilized my talents well."

"Well done, Data. Picard out."

Pazlar floated closer to Picard and gave him a conciliatory bow. "Captain, please . . . why don't I show you the one thing nobody has shown you since you've been here. Hospitality."

"Hospitality," said Picard with a wan smile. "It's true, we haven't seen much of that. But all of us have been so distracted."

"The commune of my parents is reachable in about an hour by shuttlecraft," said Melora. "I've sent them messages through the people here because our communications are down. But I wasn't sure I would have a chance to actually visit them. It's really important to me, and I would like you to meet our people outside of this place where tensions are running so high."

"I would love to go!" exclaimed Barclay. He glanced sheepishly at Picard. "If that's okay with you, sir."

The captain nodded warmly. "It sounds like an excellent idea. Thank you for the invitation."

Anything it takes, thought Melora, *to keep you from shutting down the shell.*

Chapter Fifteen

ONCE MELORA WAS SETTLED into the pilot's seat of the shuttlecraft, she put on the artificial gravity, much to Reg's relief. Captain Picard sat beside her, relegating Barclay to the stern, but he didn't care. With artificial gravity and lots of room, he stretched out on the seats and tried to doze while they soared through the azure skies of Gemworld.

Reg was jolted awake by loud thuds and a sudden swerve. He rolled off his chair onto the deck and looked up in time to see Melora feverishly working her console. The window was filled with smoky shards and clouds of mutant crystal, exploding against the shields. They seemed to be flying through an ocean of broken chunks. Pazlar put the tiny craft through evasive maneuvers, trying to avoid the worst of it.

"Hang on!" she cautioned. "We're almost through."

"Shields are holding," said Picard, studying his console.

Just as suddenly as it began, it was over, and they blasted through the noxious cloud into clear blue skies. Only these skies seemed to shimmer and bend. Reg rubbed his eyes and peered out the window at the shifting heavens.

"What's wrong with the sky?"

"It's not just the sky," answered Melora with a smile. "You were asleep when we entered, but this is a stand of sky crystals. Named that because of their color. It's hard to differentiate the crystals from the sky, but you can if you look closely."

Reg did look closely, following the bow spit as Melora steered them between the mighty monoliths. From the way one gleaming facet blended into another, he was reminded of the house of mirrors at the amusement park he used to love as a kid. As they descended, the vivid blue facets folded over onto themselves, making the walls look like an undulating prism. It was so beautiful down here, Reg tried not to think how deadly these crystals would be if Pazlar took a wrong turn into them.

The captain never took his eyes off his instruments as he performed the copilot duties. "We're only about five minutes from the coordinates," he said.

"Good," answered Pazlar. "I can taste that home cooking now."

Barclay had no sense of perspective as they zoomed deeper into the cluster of crystals. It was like descending into a canyon made of glass. Finally he caught a glimpse of dark spots ahead of them, and he feared they might be more mutant crystal.

"What's that?" he asked worriedly.

"Home," Melora answered wistfully.

As they plunged deeper, the distance between the prisms narrowed, and the facets converged into a central crux. Reg could see that the dark areas were really nets strung across the crux, and he remembered the nets he had seen before. Melora slowed down, and they passed a handful of Elaysians hovering around crevices and crannies in the old-growth crystal. Seen at close range, the aged monolith was more weathered and beaten than Reg would have imagined. He could also see the telltale signs of black crystal: ominous clouds and broken shards floating in the air like a stain.

"Normally those people would be farming," grumbled Melora. "Now it looks like they're removing the mutant growth. I wonder if the crops have been destroyed."

Reg gulped, feeling bad for Melora. Normally a person wanted to bring guests home when they could see the place at its best, not when it was threatened by disaster. The Elaysians they passed looked up from their labors with curiosity, but they looked desultory and despondent. Some of them were just going through the motions.

As the shuttlecraft glided closer to the center of the great cluster, Reg got a good look at the commune. Nets were stretched across the triangular openings in

the crux, arranged in layers, broken into small com-
partments, like bundles within bundles. Barclay
found it strange that even though there was no gravity or planetary surface on Gemworld, there was always a feeling of descending deeper, going beneath
the layers.

Melora gently applied thrusters and brought the
shuttle to a complete stop. A few Elaysians gathered
around and tethered the craft, while others peered curiously into the window.

"Oh, there's Bozwani!" said Pazlar with delight.
"And my teacher for agriculture . . . I forget his
name."

"Why don't you go ahead," said Picard, motioning
to the hatch. "I'll make sure the shuttlecraft forwards
all hails to us."

"Could I? Thank you, sir." Eagerly Melora pressed
her console and opened the hatch. "I'm shutting off
gravity now."

Reg braced himself, although that was hardly necessary after he began to float harmlessly off his seat . . .
until he bumped his head on the bulkhead. With Pazlar
dashing ahead of him, followed by the captain, Barclay had to haul himself out.

He finally made it through the hatch only to find a
mob of people fluttering around Melora. In their
haste, two of the Elaysians brushed past Picard, spin-
ning him around, and for once Reg was there to
steady someone instead of the other way around. The
two humans moved back toward the shuttlecraft and
hovered silently over the reunion.

Melora was treated like a returning hero, which seemed to surprise her, but it made perfect sense to Reg. She called many of the Elaysians by name, and they bombarded her with questions about Starfleet and her life. If anyone had a question about the rift or the smoky crystal, they kept it to themselves. This was the time to welcome home a prodigal daughter, who also happened to be famous for her unusual path in life. In fact, many of them called her "daughter," and one child called her "mother."

These were gentle people, as Melora had insisted they were, not driven types like Tangre Bertoran. The reunion was all very heartwarming, and Reg couldn't help but feel a little teary eyed.

Finally Pazlar managed to shift the attention to the visitors. "And this is Captain Picard, master of the *Enterprise*, and Lieutenant Barclay, who's an engineer aboard the *Enterprise*. He's also *our* engineer— Acting Senior Engineer for the shell . . . since the death of Zuka Juno."

This was a double dose of bad news, thought Reg, judging by the stunned reaction from the crowd of Elaysians. They looked at each other with alarm, then turned toward him with amazement, jealousy, and just plain surprise. Reg felt like a carpetbagger, an outsider who had come in to usurp the power of the locals.

He reminded himself that normal forms of communication were down on Gemworld. These people would be shocked to hear about Zuka Juno's death even without his involvement. However, they probably never thought that a midlevel Starfleet engineer would become one of their most revered dignitaries.

"All the more reason to welcome them to our homes!" declared one woman, crawling upside down across an expanse of netting. "Hello, Daughter!" she called.

"Hello, Dupanza!" called Melora excitedly. She looked as if she wanted to rush to this trusted older woman, but she stayed beside her shipmates. The Elaysians hovering in front of them backed away as Dupanza came closer. She bounced off the runners of the shuttlecraft, soared upward, and grabbed Melora in a warm hug. "My daughter, how you've grown! It's so good to see you!"

Although others had called her "daughter," Reg began to think Dupanza really was Melora's mother. At least there was a clear bond of affection between them.

Melora looked at the humans' puzzled expressions and burst out laughing. She motioned expansively at the Elaysians gathered around them. "They are *all* my parents! We are all each others' parents and children. No one knows who their real biological parents are because we time the Great Birthing for the same day, using herbs. The babies are shared, and everyone takes care of them. After you grow up, you can guess sometimes who your biological parents are by coloring and such, but no one knows for sure. As for romantic relationships, we're mostly monogamous."

She looked slyly at Reg. "Just like humans."

Dupanza broke in. "All of the races on Gemworld

observe some sort of communal child rearing. It's a tradition that unites us. So we call each other 'mother' and 'daughter' even across species. If you're still around here in two months, you can come to the next Great Birthing."

"It's quite a party," added Melora, flashing Reg those vibrant blue eyes, which were the same color as the crystal which surrounded them.

"Yes," he said quickly. "I'd love to!"

The others laughed at his eagerness, and he could tell that it had been a long time since they had much reason for joy. These Elaysians were being brave in the face of crushing disaster, but somehow the appearance of their prodigal daughter and her comical shipmates had lifted their spirits.

"A feast!" shouted one of the Elaysians. Others took up the cry. "A feast! A feast!"

"Oh, do we have enough food for a feast?" asked Dupanza worriedly.

"We're entertaining the Senior Engineer of the Sacred Protector!" cried a woman. "We must have a feast!"

"It's traditional!" shouted someone else.

As the clamor mounted, Picard held up his hands. "We may not be here very long, and we don't want you to plan anything special on our account. We're trying very hard to solve the problem with the rift, so we may be called away at any minute."

The Elaysians stared at him somberly for a moment. Then one of them held up his fist and shouted, "A feast!"

As the cry thundered around the commune, Dupanza looked at the visitors and shrugged. "I suppose there will be a feast, although we may not be serving quite as much food as usual for these occasions. I hope you don't mind, Captain Picard."

"We don't want to waste your food stores," insisted the captain.

"Thank you, but sometimes good morale is more important than a full belly," answered the Elaysian with a smile. "Come on, let me show you around."

While the energized Elaysians rushed to and fro, preparing for their feast, Dupanza linked hands with the captain, and Melora took Reg's hand. Pushing off from the shuttlecraft, Dupanza led the visitors toward the nearest net, in which there was a small slit for a door. The netting functioned not only as walls, creating rooms and homes, but as gravity, preventing the inhabitants' belongings from drifting away. Once Barclay caught hold of the net, he found that he could pull himself along rather easily, and he didn't feel so disoriented.

They moved from room to room, slipping through almost invisible slits in the walls as they worked their way deeper into the layers of the compound. From what Reg could see, the Elaysians didn't own much except for bundles of clothing and a few personal items. Their homes were simple, and they slept wherever they floated. The group passed a room full of children, who stared curiously at them, while the yellow-garbed teacher glared at them for interrupting her class.

The netting also partially blocked the light, making it darker the deeper they went into the cluster. Reg didn't care much for that, but his uneasiness was tempered by the fact that Melora held his hand and often gave it a warm squeeze. Several inhabitants greeted the only Elaysian in Starfleet, and the younger ones called her "mother."

She shook her head in amazement and whispered to Reg, "I can't get used to the children calling me 'mother.' I was young when I grew up here and when I left, but I've come back an adult."

"A famous one," added Reg with a proud smile.

"Thanks," she whispered, squeezing his hand. "We'd better catch up."

They had fallen behind Picard and Dupanza, but the way the passage between the prisms was narrowing, they had no problem catching their guide. The four of them finally emerged in a pyramid-shaped room at the very crux of the massive cluster. Here there were pantries built into the living crystal and tubes to access water from the nutrient strands. Scattered crops sprouted from troughs in the crystal, and a phosphorescent coating on the nets gave the room a dim, lavender glow. Barclay was dismayed to see a work party removing a cluster of misshapen black crystal.

"Even down here," said Dupanza sadly, "there's no escape from the unsound crystal. This is our communal room, which we use for everything from dining to the Great Birthing. We'll have our feast here, although I'm sure it will spill into the other rooms as well."

She motioned to the water tubes. "May I offer you some water? Our supply is quite pure."

"Thank you, that would be welcome," answered Picard. Barclay nodded in agreement.

While they waited, a few more well-wishers came up to Melora and welcomed her home. It seemed as if everyone knew her, or knew of her, and Reg began to think that it must have given her a great sense of security to grow up in a place where everyone considered her immediate family. The open netting made it clear that this was an open society with people who held no secrets from each other. It was a true commune, with everyone sharing the work, sharing Melora, and sharing the unfolding tragedy as their unique ecosystem fell apart.

"Quite a place," said Picard thoughtfully. "I hope we can keep it intact."

"Yes, sir," answered Reg, lowering his head. "What if we can't? How can we save them all?"

The captain's lips thinned. "We'll do the best we can. Whatever happens to them will happen to us, too."

"But the ship would survive shutting down the shell." He pointed at the happy clutch of Elaysians hovering around Melora. "They *know* that we're not at risk the same way they are."

"I don't intend to watch them all die," said Picard gravely. He looked up and smiled as their hostess returned with two small canteens with sip tubes.

"We don't need much water," said Dupanza, "but I know that other humanoids are not so fortunate. Please drink."

"Thank you," said the two humans at once. Barclay took a few gulps, surprised at how thirsty he was. The water had a slight sulfuric smell, although maybe that was his imagination. He hoped it wasn't contaminated by the dark crystal.

"So where are you staying?" asked Dupanza.

"On our ship," answered the captain.

"Such a great distance to travel," said the Elaysian, shaking her head. "Especially now, when travel is so difficult. Why don't you stay here a while and make this your base of operations. We're much closer to all the enclaves than your ship is, way up there along the shell. You have gravity on your shuttlecraft, so you'll be comfortable."

"We might consider it," agreed Picard.

Reg saw more Elaysians surrounding Melora, bombarding her with questions and greetings, and she was beaming in the glow of their attention. "You just want to keep Melora around longer," said the lieutenant.

Dupanza nodded wistfully as she watched her prodigal daughter. "That's true. She really has blossomed while she's been in Starfleet. I knew she would mature to be beautiful and confident, but this is beyond even what I envisioned. She was home once before, but I was working on the shell and didn't see her then."

"What did you do there?" asked Reg.

Dupanza gazed into the distance, and her eyes grew misty. "I was an assistant to your predecessor, Zuka Juno. It's painful to hear about his death. He wasn't ill, was he? Can you tell me anything?"

"We were the ones who found him," answered Picard. He told her briefly what had happened, adding that they wouldn't really know anything until the Jeptah had finished their investigation.

"Then I don't think you'll know anything," whispered Dupanza. "The Jeptah are very secretive, and they like to control things. They're honest and hardworking, but they don't really trust anyone but each other." She smiled at Reg. "They must be apoplectic over your having that gem."

Barclay gulped and touched the violet crystal. "That's true, they weren't very happy. I really don't know what to do with this thing."

"You wield tremendous power with that crystal," answered the elder Elaysian. "Be honest and true to your ideals. I think we could use a jolt of fresh thinking here on Gemworld. We've never faced a crisis like this before, but I imagine you have faced many crises during your exploration of the stars."

"We have," answered Reg, lifting his chin proudly. "We'll do the best we can for you."

"That's all we could ask." Dupanza gazed fondly at Melora, who was engaged in animated conversation with a large group of Elaysians. The younger ones regarded her with rapt attention. "You've brought our daughter back to us, for which I am very grateful."

Picard's combadge chirped, interrupting their idyllic respite. "Excuse me." He tapped his badge. "Picard here."

"Captain," said the unmistakable voice of Commander Data, "we are almost ready to perform the procedure. I advise you to return as soon as possible."

"We're on our way," said the captain. "Picard out." He gave his hostess an apologetic smile. "I'm sorry, but it appears that we have to be going."

"So soon? Before the feast?" she asked with disappointment. "Do you promise to return to us?"

"If circumstances permit," answered the captain. "Would you please inform Lieutenant Pazlar that we have to be going?"

"I will. Thank you for all you're doing to help us." Dupanza used the netting to work her way to the crowd gathered around Melora, and the two women conferred for a moment. After a quick hug, Melora joined her shipmates.

"Are we ready to shut down the dimensional rift?" she asked confidently.

"I hope so," answered Picard, concern etched into his furrowed brow. "I sincerely hope so."

Picard, Barclay, and Pazlar were met by Data at the Ninth Processing Gate, and Barclay was amused to see that the android had procured himself a hover-platform.

"You must rank," said Reg, pointing to the self-propelled disk.

Data cocked his head puzzledly. "I do not 'rank.' In fact, with your temporary title, you outrank me. The hover-platform makes transportation much more efficient, and we have a considerable distance to travel within the shell."

"Are they still on schedule?" asked Picard.

"Yes. The Alpusta are in final preparations for their space walk. Although I am unfamiliar with the actual procedure they will use to tap into the collectors, the theory is sound. If they can pass one variable to the program, the dark-matter collectors will switch to collecting hydrogen."

"Is there a backup plan?" asked Reg.

"No," answered the android. "We have studied every feasible option, and nothing else will correct the problem without disrupting the operation of the shell. Short of finding the engineer who actually corrupted the program, this is our only option."

"It will work," insisted Melora.

Captain Picard nodded grimly. "I hope you're right. Lead on, Data."

"Link hands," said the android.

By this time, they were accustomed to linking up, and Barclay smiled as he held out his hand to Melora. This part of being weightless he was beginning to like. Data gripped the hover-platform with one hand and Captain Picard's hand with the other, and they were soon moving steadily through the tubular corridors of the shell. As they plunged deeper, Reg noticed fewer workers than before, and he saw no Alpusta at all. He had the feeling that everyone and everything was in a holding pattern as they waited for the plan to take effect.

Eventually they entered a large, oval-shaped corridor that was packed with yellow-garbed Jeptah hovering in front of a panoramic window. The Elaysians parted to allow the visitors to enter, and Tangre Bertoran pushed off the wall and glided toward them.

The Peer of the Jeptah was grinning confidently. "Ah, Captain Picard, Lieutenant Pazlar, and our esteemed Acting Senior Engineer—welcome. We've missed you, Captain, where have you been?"

"I took them to see my enclave," said Melora, "and meet my parents."

Bertoran clapped his hands together, looking delighted at that news. "Wonderful! I'm so happy that you're taking time to see our beautiful planet. After we're done here, you'll be able to travel anywhere on Gemworld and see all of our attractions. Perhaps you'd like to visit *my* enclave."

"I certainly hope so," said Picard with a polite smile. "May I ask, have you discovered the cause of Zuka Juno's death?"

Bertoran scowled. "I've been rather busy, Captain. When we're done here, I'll get an update."

"Even after we solve this problem," said Picard, "we still have to find out who corrupted the program in the first place."

The Jeptah shook his head. "We'll have plenty of time to solve that little mystery after life gets back to normal. Trust me, this will never happen again—the dark-matter collectors will stay off-line indefinitely."

"That is wise," concluded Data.

Tangre Bertoran motioned to the window and its expansive view of the star-sprinkled void beyond. "We'll give you the best vantage point in the house. In brief, here's what you'll see: the Alpusta engineers are going to use portable devices to tap directly into the collectors. At the exact same moment, we'll pass a variable to every collector and end all of this madness. Then we'll have time to play detective, for as long as you wish, Captain."

"I only wish to see the crisis over," said Picard.

"It will be. Don't go anywhere—we'll be starting soon. Excuse me." Tangre Bertoran flew off to confer with his fellow engineers, leaving the four crewmembers gathered at the window, surrounded by milling Jeptah.

Data lowered his voice to say, "Although I am satisfied with their plan, I am not as confident as they are."

"They have to be confident," said Barclay. "They haven't got much choice." Nobody argued with him.

The four visitors gazed out the window at a vast array of scoops and dishes aimed toward space. The rows of collectors stretched into infinity, and Reg realized why there were no Alpusta at their regular posts—they were all needed for this procedure. It was hard to imagine that the peaceful starscape outside the shell harbored a deadly singularity, but the proof was all around him in hushed conversations and concerned looks. Only Tangre Bertoran, in his role as head cheerleader, seemed totally confident.

They floated in front of the window for several minutes, as the crowd of Elaysians increased in number. Melora gripped Reg's hand and gave him a brave smile, which he returned as best he could. There wasn't really anything any of them could say—the fate of billions of beings depended on what happened in the next few minutes.

Finally a chime sounded, and the conversation dropped to an expectant murmur as Tangre Bertoran rose above the crowd.

"It is time!" he announced. "May we please have quiet. Extend the forcefields!" He nodded to an assistant stationed at the only console in the room.

Although nothing looked different outside the shell, Barclay could well imagine the forcefield extending several meters into space. Both he and Melora pressed closer to the window to get a better look, and her grip on his hand tightened.

"Signal the Alpusta!" ordered Bertoran.

Hatches opened on the space side of the shell, and an army of spidery Alpusta swarmed out, bouncing across the pitted surface of the shell. Reg had seen environmental suits on humanoids, but he had never seen suits on such oddly shaped creatures. Their long, spindly legs were covered in white material with metallic boots, and their spiny, headless bodies were encased in breathing tubes. The way they labored across the shell, Reg assumed their boots must be magnetic. Under normal circumstances, they would use their weblike extensions, but they couldn't risk that with such a shallow forcefield. The rift would do to them what it had almost done to the *Enterprise*.

As he looked closer, Barclay realized that each Alpusta had an electronic device strapped to one leg. Each was apparently assigned to a single scoop, and they fanned out across the vast field of collectors.

Tangre Bertoran issued orders as he hovered over his chief technician, but everyone else who was gathered around the window fell silent. It was unlikely, thought Reg, that any of them had ever seen a sight like this before—thousands of Alpusta scrambling across the space side of the ancient shell.

Picard whispered to Data, "How long can they stay out there before being adversely affected?"

"The forcefields block ninety-four percent of the thoron radiation," answered the android. "Even so, our best estimate is that they can remain in space no longer than fourteen minutes before suffering irreversible cell damage."

Barclay gazed out the window, now realizing why the Alpusta were hurrying to reach their assigned positions. Unfortunately, they had to tap into the system in unison, so they had to wait until every technician was in place. Although it only took a few minutes, the time seemed interminable before the technician at the console announced they were all in position.

Tangre Bertoran hovered close to the terminal, and his amplified voice rang out across the room. "All stations reporting ready. Stand by for countdown!"

While Bertoran methodically counted down, Reg watched in amazement as the agile Alpusta manipulated the wires on their portable devices. Such maneuvers were easy for them, he decided, because they were used to low gravity.

"Connect!" ordered Bertoran. Like machines, the Alpusta moved in unison to jack into the collectors. "Transmit!"

There was no explosion, no sparks, no fireworks—but Reg knew something dreadful had happened. The Alpusta closest to the window suddenly went limp and slumped over—only their magnetic boots kept them from floating away. All across the forest of dishes and scoops, the Alpusta collapsed. A few managed to unplug and scurry away in time, but hundreds of them weren't so lucky.

"Feed-coil overload!" shouted Bertoran in alarm. "Disconnect! Disconnect!"

The Elaysians began to shout and mill around in panic. Barclay was jostled and knocked away from the window, but he saw Data soaring toward the console. The android pushed the stunned technican out of the way and took over the board, his fingers flying across the controls.

In the chaos, Reg crawled his way through Elaysians to get back to the window, hoping the scene outside had somehow changed for the better. But not a single Alpusta was moving, except for a handful of limp beings whose magnetic boots had failed them. They bobbed slowly in space, tethered by the wires on their portable devices.

Reg heard weeping, and he turned to see Melora staring out the window. Tears seeped from her reddened eyes and floated in the air like slow-motion raindrops.

"This is the end," she murmured. "It's the end of everything."

Chapter Sixteen

"GET THEM INSIDE!" shouted Tangre Bertoran, pointing frantically out the window at the horrendous sight of thousands of unconscious Alpusta marooned on the space side of the shell. Their limp bodies floated in the low gravity like seaweed at the bottom of a calm ocean; only their magnetic boots kept them from floating away. The blackness of space surrounded them like a funeral shroud.

There's no way to get to get them back, thought Reg Barclay. He put his arm around Melora Pazlar and tried to comfort her, but her face was frozen in grief and shock. Over the din of terrified Elaysians, he heard Captain Picard's voice. "Picard to *Enterprise!*"

"Riker here."

"We've got an emergency," said the captain. "If you

lock onto my signal, you'll find several thousand Alpusta in my vicinity, just outside the shell. Can you beam any of them to safety?"

"Just one moment, sir," replied the commander. It seemed hours before he replied, "Sorry, Captain, but we can't transport through their forcefield. Besides, we don't pick up any lifesigns outside the ship."

"No lifesigns?" echoed Picard. He glanced at Barclay, and the engineer gulped. They both knew what "no lifesigns" meant, and so did everyone within earshot.

"They're all dead!" wailed an Elaysian near them. Heartfelt cries of anguish rent the air, and Reg had never felt so helpless in his entire life.

Captain Picard clawed his way through the milling, weeping throng to reach Data, who was still working the lone console in the room. Reg didn't want to leave Melora, who appeared to be in shock, but he had to see if he could do anything to help. Following in the captain's wake, he reached the console a few moments after Picard.

"Data, is it true they're all dead?" asked the captain.

"These instruments do not furnish that information," answered the android. "Considering the intensity of the feed-coil overload, the increase in thoron radiation, and the weakening of the forcefield, it is unlikely they could survive. A few of them disconnected in time and were able to reach safety, but that is a relatively small number."

"What happened?" asked Barclay.

"I can suggest a theory. The overload was programmed to occur if any attempt was made to disable the collectors. Our unknown adversary anticipated that we would use this solution to correct the corrupted programs, and they took action to prevent it. We are dealing with a mastermind."

Picard scowled. "They're one step ahead of us at every turn . . . and they don't mind killing everybody on Gemworld to get what they want."

"What *do* they want?" asked Reg with frustration.

"To kill everyone on the planet," said a feminine voice. Reg looked up to see Melora hovering above them. Her eyes were still red from crying, but a fierce anger burned in those pale orbs.

"W-Why don't we use the *Enterprise* to destroy all the collection dishes?" asked Reg.

Data cocked his head. "Due to the rift, we are unable to position the *Enterprise* outside the shell. Due to the forcefields, we are unable to fire at the collectors from inside the shell. As before, we are left with only one viable solution: disabling the shell."

"Which isn't possible," snapped Melora, "without killing almost everyone on the planet. It's a choice between a fast death without any air, or a slow death as the planet disintegrates around us."

"The likelihood is that," replied Data, "increased thoron radiation will kill everyone before the planet disintegrates."

"Thank goodness for that!" said Pazlar sarcastically. "Excuse me, I think I need to be with my people." Pulling herself hand-over-hand, she moved across the ceiling of the oval room and joined a large group of Jeptah gathered around Tangre Bertoran.

Picard's lips thinned as he surveyed the solemn crowd. "We need to get back to the ship. Maybe our sensors can tell us something—maybe there's something we've overlooked." With a sigh, he glanced back at Pazlar, who was hugging another Elaysian. "I think we can let Lieutenant Pazlar stay here for a while."

"Sir, can I—"

"No, Mr. Barclay, you're with us." The captain nodded to Data. "Shall we go?"

"Yes, sir." The android pushed himself away from the console and retrieved his hover-platform. A moment later, the three visitors wended their way slowly out of the observation room. Barclay glanced back at the grieving Elaysians, who were weeping, hugging each other, and gazing forlornly out the window at their fallen comrades. They couldn't even retrieve the bodies, thought Reg glumly.

He was haunted by what Melora had told him at the instant of the disaster: *This is the end. It's the end of everything.*

On board the *Enterprise,* the command staff gathered in the observation lounge, and a solemn group it was, thought Barclay. He had only been in this room with this important group of officers a few times, and he wished he wasn't here now. He would rather be running third-level diagnostics down in engineering instead of trying to save a couple billion lives. Reg wasn't comfortable playing hero, especially when he had no idea how to get out of this awful mess.

At Captain Picard's insistence, he had kept the violet crystal around his neck, and he felt self-conscious about it. Why should he have this added responsibility when others were more deserving? Were La Forge and Riker staring at him? At least there wasn't much small talk as they waited for the last members of the command staff to trickle in.

The door whooshed open, and Deanna Troi and Beverly Crusher entered. This brought a welcome break from the tension, as everyone rose to their feet and looked at Troi with concern.

"How do you feel?" asked La Forge.

"Fine," she answered with a polite smile. Finally, thought Reg, there was someone else to take the unwanted attention off him. Troi took her seat and folded her hands in front of her, acting as if she hadn't been smashing furniture a day before.

"We're all present," said Captain Picard, surveying the faces of his most trusted officers. "Mr. Data, would you please brief everyone about what just happened on the shell."

"Yes, sir." In detached, unemotional tones, the android recounted the details of the failed procedure and horrific deaths of over a thousand Alpusta. La Forge frowned and looked down at the table with his opaque eyes, while Commander Riker and Dr. Crusher made notes on their padds. Commander Troi seemed lost in quiet contemplation. Reg just stared straight ahead, unable to come to terms with the immensity of the tragedy. It wasn't just the deaths that troubled him, but the death knell for the entire planet.

"There you have it," said Picard. "The grim reality is that neither us nor anyone on Gemworld has any idea what to do next. Shutting down the shell would end the collection of dark matter and, possibly, close the rift. But it would also shut off the forcefields and allow all the atmosphere to escape. Only the Lipuls would survive the loss of the atmosphere—all the other species on Gemworld would die. We couldn't evacuate more than a few hundred on the *Enterprise.* So any ideas are welcome."

Geordi grimaced puzzledly. "Are you sure we can't find the one who did this . . . who corrupted the program?"

"We'll keep trying to do that, of course," answered Picard. "But our adversary has anticipated every move we've made so far, and it's unlikely they would just surrender themselves and offer to fix their handiwork. Also, traveling on Gemworld is very difficult now, and the saboteur might belong to one of the distant, non-humanoid species we haven't even seen. No demands have been made, so we have to assume we're dealing with a mass murderer rather than a political terrorist. A very clever mass murderer."

Riker stroked his clean-shaven chin. "The problem is in the forcefields, right? Could there be some other way to power the forcefields that doesn't use the shell?"

"Hey," said La Forge, snapping his fingers, "what about the *Enterprise?* Could *we* take over powering the forcefields ourselves? I mean, we couldn't do it for very long, perhaps no more than a few seconds, but all we need to do is disrupt this endless loop for a few seconds. Isn't that right?"

The captain nodded thoughtfully. "I believe so. At any rate, it's worth looking into. Could you do a feasability study on that, Mr. La Forge?"

"Yes, sir," answered the chief engineer. "How much time do we have?"

When no one answered immediately, Data cocked his head. "That is an excellent question, Geordi. I have started running a modeling program based on the growth of the mutant crystal and the increase in thoron radiation, but I have not had time to input recent data. I will take more sensor readings and update my model as soon as this briefing is over."

"Make it so," replied the captain. "Next time we talk to them, I want to have all the facts."

"We're not beat yet," said Riker confidently.

"They'll never let you shut down the shell," proclaimed Deanna Troi, her voice cutting through the note of cautious optimism. "They're too afraid."

"I don't see that they have much choice," insisted Riker.

"Nevertheless, they'll fight you."

Reg opened his mouth to refute the counselor, but he really couldn't. Although he didn't want to admit it, Troi was probably right.

"It's too bad there's no way to evacutate everyone," said Doctor Crusher. "Or no way to give them individual breathing devices. Are we sure they don't have the technology to survive without air, even for a few seconds?"

"We'll look into that, too," answered the captain. "We're going to explore every avenue."

La Forge shook his head. "The problem is, how do we replace the atmosphere once it's gone? The shell might be able to regenerate the air over time, but how much time? It could take years."

"Once we get rid of the rift, we've got all the time in the world," answered Riker. "We could send for a whole fleet of ships to evacuate the planet."

A beep sounded. "Bridge to Picard."

"Go ahead."

"Sir, there's a ship coming out of warp!"

"What?!" exclaimed the captain with concern. "Hail them! Tell them not to."

"I have. The interference—"

The captain charged out of the observation lounge with Data, Riker, Barclay, and the others right behind him. Since the room adjoined the bridge, they reached their usual stations in a matter of seconds. Not having a station on the bridge, Barclay hovered near an auxiliary console, in case he was needed.

"On screen," ordered Picard.

"Yes, sir," answered the officer on ops a moment before Data replaced her.

At first, there was nothing on the viewscreen but the sparkling starscape. If Reg looked hard enough, he could almost see a dark rip in the glittering firmament, although maybe that was just his imagination. A brilliant glow appeared in the void, and a sleek starship emerged. Judging by her twin nacelles, she was a Federation ship. Normally a ship coming out of warp was a beautiful sight, but not now . . . not here.

"Fools!" Riker exclaimed. "What are they doing?"

"I would say they are trying to rescue us," answered Data.

No sooner had the ship emerged than it tilted at an obscene angle and began to slide backward toward the unseen anomaly. Thrusters rippled along her stern, and impulse engines were obviously on full; the ship jerked and heaved as it tried unsuccessfully to escape from the deadly singularity.

"Akira-class," said Data, working his console. "The *Summit*. They are unable to compensate for the gravitational pull of the rift."

"Tell them to use their tractor beam!" ordered Picard.

Data worked his console, then shook his head. "They are not responding. They are so close to the rift, they cannot receive our hails. Their reactor is close to overloading."

Everyone on the bridge watched in horror—helpless, unable to do anything to save the struggling ship. The captain's jaw clenched in anger, and Riker pounded a fist into his palm. Dr. Crusher slumped into a chair and lowered her head while La Forge leaned over Data's shoulder and peered at his readouts. Only Counselor Troi stared unblinkingly at the disaster unfolding on the viewscreen.

The nacelles on the *Summit* suddenly erupted, and plasma clouds blossomed outward . . . a moment before the starship exploded into a mass of silvery confetti. Even the debris couldn't escape the hungry maw of the rift, and the clouds were swept into blackness. A second later, there was no trace of the Akira-class starship.

"Lost, with all hands," reported Data.

"Why didn't they listen to us?" muttered Riker.

The captain scowled. "Because we're Starfleet, and we're always trying to do the impossible. If another ship was marooned here, we would probably try to save her."

"I'm sure they had a plan," said La Forge. He didn't need to add that plans hadn't worked very well since their arrival on Gemworld. The only plan they could depend upon was the immutable law of the universe—that all biological beings would die, some sooner rather than later.

Barclay felt a gnawing in his stomach. He wanted to say something compassionate and profound to his shipmates, but he wasn't articulate under the best of circumstances. And these were the worst of circumstances. He wished Melora was there with him, because for once, he was the one who needed comforting.

He noticed that Data continued to work his console at a rapid pace, even though nothing else was happening on the bridge. Reg stepped closer to the android and looked over his shoulder.

"W-What are you doing?" he asked.

"Taking sensor readings and completing my forecast," answered the android. His fingers were a blur, and the sensor data scrolled by so fast that Reg had no chance of reading any of it. The lieutenant stepped back and saw that Captain Picard and everyone else on the bridge was waiting for Data to complete his analysis.

After another moment, the android stopped working and turned to the captain. "Sir, I regret to say that the situation is worse than I had anticipated."

Picard stiffened his back. "Report."

"At the current rate of increase, thoron radiation will kill almost all life on Gemworld, including most of the crew, in approximately eight days."

Barclay's mouth flopped open, and Riker let out a low whistle. Captain Picard tried to keep his spine erect, but his shoulders slumped perceptibly. Both Crusher and La Forge headed for the turbolift, looking determined to pursue a solution within their own departments. Only Counselor Troi took the news with an unearthly calm, almost resignation. She stared curiously at the glittering stars on the viewscreen, as if looking for an answer in the vastness of space.

After everything they had seen that day, the idea of dying was not far from anyone's mind, but no one had realized that their time was so short.

"Eight days," said Reg softly. "That's one more day than it supposedly took to create Heaven and Earth."

"It's much easier to destroy than to create," answered Captain Picard grimly. "One thing is certain— we haven't got any more time for diplomacy. Mr. Barclay, are you ready to return to the planet?"

Barclay snapped to attention. "Yes, sir."

"Counselor Troi, do you feel up to joining the away team?"

"Yes, sir," answered Deanna, still gazing at the twinkling stars on the viewscreen. "Gemworld has lived on borrowed time for millions of years, but every loan must be settled someday."

OUR FIRST SERIAL NOVEL!

Presenting, one chapter per month . . .

The very beginning of the Starfleet Adventure . . .

**STAR TREK®
STARFLEET: YEAR ONE**

A Novel in Twelve Parts

**by
Michael Jan Friedman**

Chapter Seven

Chapter Seven

Weapons Officer Morgan Kelly took a deep breath and considered herself in the full-length mirror.

Like everyone else on the Christopher-class vessel *Peregrine,* she wore an open-collared blue uniform with a black mock-turtle pullover underneath it. A gold Starfleet chevron graced the uniform's left breast, and Kelly's rank of lieutenant was denoted by two gold bands encircling her right sleeve.

She tilted her red-haired head to one side and frowned. She had worn the gold and black of Earth Command for so long she had come to think of it as part of her natural coloring. A blue uniform looked as inappropriate as a hot-pink atomic missile.

But there it was, Kelly mused, her frown deepening. And she would get used to it. She would *have* to.

The sound of chimes brought her out of her reverie. Kelly turned to the double set of sliding doors that separated her quarters from the corridor beyond and wondered who might be calling on her.

Maybe it was the engineer she had met earlier, who had gotten lost looking for the mess hall. Or yet another lieutenant j.g., wondering if she had received her full complement of toiletries. . . .

It couldn't be a friend. After all, the lieutenant only had one of those on the ship . . . and he was waiting for her on the bridge.

"I'm coming," she sighed.

Crossing the room, Kelly pressed the padd in the bulkhead beside the sliding doors and watched them hiss open. They revealed a silver-skinned, ruby-eyed figure in a uniform as blue as her own.

"Captain Cobaryn—?" she said, unable to conceal her surprise.

He inclined his head slightly. "May I come in?"

Kelly hesitated for a moment. Then she realized she really had no choice in the matter. "Of course. But I should tell you, I'm—"

"Due on the bridge in ten minutes," the Rigelian said, finishing her declaration for her. He fashioned a smile, stretching the series of ridges that ran from his temple to his jaw. "I know. I spoke with Captain Shumar before I transported over."

"Did you?" the lieutenant responded, getting the feeling that she had been the victim of some kind of conspiracy. *I'll be the first officer in Starfleet to kill my captain,* she told herself.

"Yes," Cobaryn rejoined. "I wish to speak with you."

Of course you do, she replied inwardly.

After all, Cobaryn had taken every opportunity to speak with her back on Earth Base 14 in the aftermath of the Romulan assault. It hardly came as a shock that he wanted to speak with her *now.*

And he had gone to some pretty great lengths to do so. All six of the fleet's Christophers were supposed to leave Earth orbit in less than an hour, and the Rigelian had a command of his own to attend to. There might even be a regulation prohibiting a captain from leaving his vessel at such a momentous juncture.

If there was, Cobaryn seemed unaware of it . . . or else, for the sake of his infatuation with Kelly, he had decided to ignore it.

"Look," she said, "I—"

He held up a three-fingered hand. "Please," he insisted gently, "I will not be long, I promise."

The lieutenant regarded her visitor. He seemed to mean it. "All right," she told him, folding her arms across her chest.

Cobaryn offered her another smile—his best one yet. "First," he said, "I would like to apologize for my behavior back at Earth Base Fourteen. In retrospect, I see that my attentions must have been a burden to you. In my defense, I can only state my ignorance of human courtship rituals."

An apology was the last thing she had expected. "Don't worry about it," she found herself saying. "In a way, it was kind of flattering."

The captain inclined his hairless head. "Thank you for understanding. There is only one other thing. . . ."

But he didn't say what it was. At least, not right away. Whatever it was, he seemed nervous about it.

As much as he had annoyed her at the base, Kelly couldn't help sympathizing with the man. "One other thing?" she echoed, trying to be helpful.

"Yes," said Cobaryn. He seemed to steel himself. "If it is not too much trouble, I would like a favor from you."

She looked at him askance, uncertain of what he was asking but already not liking the sound of it. "What kind of favor?"

His eyes seemed to soften. "The kind a knight of old received from his lady fair, so he could carry it with him on his journeys and accomplish great things in her name."

Kelly felt her heart melt in her chest. It was far and away the most romantic thing anyone had ever suggested to her, and it caught her completely off guard. For a second or two, she couldn't speak.

Cobaryn winced. "You do not think it is a good idea?"

The lieutenant shook her head, trying to regain her composure. "I . . . I'm not sure what I think."

He shrugged. "Again, I must apologize. It seemed like a good solution to both our problems. After all, if I had a favor, I could perhaps feel content worshipping you from afar."

Kelly sighed. She hadn't intended to. It just came out.

This is crazy, she told herself. Cobaryn was an alien—a being from another world. What did he know of knightly virtues? Or of chivalry? And yet she had to admit, he embodied them better than any human she had ever met.

"I . . . see you've been doing some reading," she observed.

"A little," Cobaryn admitted. He looked sad in a peculiarly Rigelian way. "Well, then, good luck, Lieutenant Kelly. I trust you and I will meet again someday."

He extended his hand to shake hers. For a moment, she considered it. Then, certain that she had gone insane, she held up her forefinger.

"Give me a second," she said.

There was a set of drawers built into the bulkhead beside her bed. The lieutenant pulled open the third one from the top and rifled through it, searching for something. It took a while, but she found it.

Then she turned around and tossed it to Cobaryn. He snatched it out of the air, opened his hand, and studied it. Then he looked up at Kelly, a grin spreading awkwardly across his face.

"Thank you," he told her, with feeling.

She smiled back, unable to help herself. "Don't mention it."

Still grinning, the captain tucked her favor into an inside pocket of his uniform, where it created only a slightly noticeable bulge. Then, with obvious reluctance, he turned, opened the doors to her quarters, and left her standing there.

As the doors whispered closed again, Kelly had to remind herself to breathe. *Come on,* she thought. *Get a grip on yourself.*

Cobaryn's gesture was a romantic notion, no question. But it hadn't come from Prince Charming. It had come from a guy she didn't have the slightest feelings for.

A guy from another planet, for heaven's sakes.

Now, the lieutenant told herself, if it had been the Cochrane jockey who had asked for her favor . . . *that* would have been a different story. That would have been unbelievable.

Chuckling to herself, she pulled down on the front of her uniform and put on her game face. Then she tapped the door controls, left her quarters, and reported to the bridge.

Where she would, in her own unobtrusive way, give Captain Shumar the dirtiest look she could muster.

Hiro Matsura got up from his center seat on the *Yellowjacket* and faced his viewscreen, where the image of Director Abute had just appeared.

The captain wasn't required to get up. Certainly, none of his bridge officers had risen from their consoles. But Matsura wanted to show his appreciation of the moment, his respect for its place in history.

For weeks they had talked about a Starfleet. They had selected captains and crews for a Starfleet. And now, for the first time, there would actually *be* a Starfleet.

"I bid you a good morning," said Abute, his dark eyes twinkling over his aquiline nose. "Of course, for the United Federation of Planets it is *already* a good morning. More than two hundred of our bravest men and women, individuals representing fourteen species in all, are embarking from Earth orbit to pursue their destinies among the stars.

"Before long," the director told them, "there will be many more of you, plying the void in the kind of ships we've only been able to dream about. But for now, there is only you—a handful of determined trailblazers who will set the standard for all who follow. The Federation is watching each and every one of you, wishing you the best of good fortune. Make us proud. Show us what serving in Starfleet is all about."

And what *was* it about? the captain wondered. Unfortunately, it was still too soon to say.

Of course, Matsura knew what he wanted it to be. The same thing Admiral Walker wanted it to be—a defense force like no other. But as long as Clarisse Dumont's camp had a say in things, that future was uncertain.

Abute smiled with undisguised pride. "You have my permission to leave orbit," he told them. "Bon voyage." A moment later his image vanished, and their orbital view of Earth was restored.

Matsura didn't take his eyes off the viewscreen. He wanted to remember how the sunlight had hit the cloud-swaddled Earth when he left on his first Starfleet mission. He wanted to tell his grandchildren about it.

"Mr. Barker," he said finally, "bring us about."

There was no response.

The captain turned to his left to look at his helmsman. The blond man ensconced behind the console there was staring back at him, looking a little discomfited. And for good reason.

His name wasn't Barker. It was McCallum. Barker had piloted Matsura's ship when it flew under the aegis of Earth Command.

The captain had wanted to take the helmsman with him when his ship became Starfleet property. However, he had been forced to adhere to Abute's quotas, and that meant making some hard decisions.

"Mr. *McCallum*," he amended, "bring us about."

"Aye, sir," said the helmsman.

The view on the screen gradually slid sideways, taking the clouds and the sunlight and a blue sweep of ocean with it. In a matter of moments, Earth had slipped away completely and Matsura found himself gazing at a galaxy full of distant suns.

They had never seemed so inviting. "Full impulse," he told McCallum.

"Full impulse," the man confirmed.

The stars seemed to leap forward, though it was really their Christopher 2000 that had forged ahead. As it plunged through the void, reaching for the limits of Earth's solar system and beyond, Matsura lowered himself into his captain's chair.

McCallum, he told himself, resolving not to forget a second time. *Not Barker. McCallum.*

Aaron Stiles eyed the collection of haphazardly shaped rocks pictured on his viewscreen, some of them as small as a kilometer in diameter and some many times that size. A muscle twitched in his jaw.

"Mr. Weeks," he said, glancing at his weapons officer, "target the nearest of the asteroids and stand by lasers."

"Aye, sir," came the reply.

Out of the corner of his eye, the captain could see Darigghi crossing the bridge to join him. "Sir?" said the Osadjani.

Stiles turned to look up at him. "Yes, Commander?"

Darigghi tilted his long, hairless head, his deepset black eyes fixed intently on the captain's. "Sir, did I hear you give an order to target one of the asteroids?"

Stiles nodded. "You did indeed, Commander." Then he turned back to Weeks. "Fire lasers, Lieutenant."

The weapons officer tapped a control stud. On the viewscreen, a red-tinged chunk of rock was speared mercilessly by a pair of blue energy beams. Before long it had been transformed into space dust.

Stiles heard the Osadjani suck in a breath. "Sir," he said, "are you certain you wish to do this?"

The captain shrugged. "Why wouldn't I?"

Darigghi licked his fleshy lips. "This asteroid belt is a most intriguing phenomenon," he replied. "I believe that is why we were asked to analyze it in the first place."

"And analyze it we did," Stiles pointed out. Then he glanced at Weeks again. "Target another one, Lieutenant."

The weapons officer bent to his task. "Aye, sir."

The first officer licked his lips a second time. "But, sir, it is irresponsible of us to destroy what natural forces created."

The captain eyed Darigghi. "Irresponsible, you say?"

The Osadjani nodded. "Yes, sir."

Stiles grunted. "I suppose that would be one way to look at it. But let me offer you another one, Commander. You see, during the war, the Romulans used this asteroid belt to hide their warships. When we finally found them and dug them out, it cost us the lives of three good captains and their crews."

Darigghi's eyes narrowed. "But what—?"

"What does that have to do with the activity at hand?" Stiles said, finishing his exec's question for him. "Simple, Commander. No hostile force is ever going to hide in this belt again."

The alien didn't know what to say to that. Of course, that was exactly the result the captain had desired.

Turning to the viewscreen, Stiles settled back in his seat. Then he said, "Fire, Mr. Weeks."

The weapons officer fired. As before, their lasers ate away at a sizable hunk of rock, reducing it to debris in no time.

Darigghi looked on helplessly, licking his lips like crazy. Ignoring him, Stiles ordered Weeks to target another asteroid.

Alonis Cobaryn sat at a long rough-hewn table in the gargantuan Hall of the Axe, which was located on a world called Middira.

By the light of the modest braziers that lined the soaring black walls, Cobaryn could make out the immense crossed set of axes wielded in battle by the founder of Middiron civilization—or so the legend went. He could also make out the pale, hulking forms of his hosts and the mess of monstrous insect parts they considered a delicacy.

First Axe Zhrakkas, the largest and most prominent member of the Middiron Circle of Axes, offered the captain a brittle, amber-colored haunch. "Eat," he said insistently.

Truthfully, Cobaryn had no desire to consume the haunch. However, his orders called for him to embrace local customs, so he took it from the First Axe and sank his teeth into it.

He found that it was completely tasteless—at least to his Rigelian senses. Considering this a blessing, he ripped off a piece of the haunch with his teeth and began chewing it as best he could.

"Have you reviewed our proposal?" the captain asked Zhrakkas, speaking with his mouth full in the manner of his dining companions.

The First Axe's slitted blue eyes slid in his guest's direction. "I have," he growled, spitting insect splinters as he spoke.

"And what is your reaction?" Cobaryn demanded. After all, he had been told to be firm with the Middirona—firm and blunt.

"I did not see anything that made my blood run hot," said the First Axe. "There is that, at least."

The Rigelian took another bite of the insect haunch. "Then you understand we mean you no harm? That the creation of our Federation does not portend badly for you?"

Zhrakkas grunted. "I understand that you say it."

"I do more than say it," Cobaryn assured him, forcing a note of titanium into his voice. "I mean it."

The First Axe made a face. "We will see."

It was the best response the Rigelian could have hoped for. Pressing the matter might only have made his host wary, so he let it drop. Besides, there was another subject he wished to pursue.

"I want to ask you something," said Cobaryn.

Zhrakkas shrugged his massive, blue-veined shoulders. "Ask."

The captain leaned forward. "As I understand it," he said, "you trade regularly with the Anjyyla."

The First Axe lifted his protruding chin. "Among others."

"However," Cobaryn noted, "the area between here and Anjyyl is reputed to be rife with interstellar strings, which, as you know, would be most dangerous to a vessel passing near them. I was wondering—"

Zhrakkas's eyes grew dangerous under his brow ridge. "The space between here and Anjyyl is *ours*—no one else's. If your Federation has any intention of trespassing in Middiron territory—"

The captain hadn't expected such a violent reaction—though perhaps he should have. "You misunderstand, First Axe. We have no intention of trespassing. We merely seek to increase our store of knowledge."

The Middirona's mouth twisted with mistrust. "Why would you need to increase your knowledge of what takes place in *our* space?"

By then, Zhrakkas's fellow councilors had taken an interest in the conversation as well. They glared at their guest with fierce blue eyes, awaiting his response.

The Rigelian sighed. Obviously, he had placed his mission here in some jeopardy. He would have to salvage it somehow—and quickly—or be the cause of a potentially bloody conflict.

Unfortunately he could think of only one way to do that. Gritting his teeth, he pulled his fist back and drove it into Zhrakkas' shoulder with all the power he could muster.

Though he was clearly unprepared for the blow, the Middirona barely budged. Then he looked to Cobaryn for an explanation.

"The First Axe needs to hone his sense of humor," said the captain, effecting his best human grin.

Befuddled, Zhrakkas looked at him. "My sense of humor?"

"Absolutely," Cobaryn pressed. "I thought when I poked my haft where it did not belong, you would find my impertinence amusing. But, no—you took my question seriously. Admit it."

The First Axe looked around the table at his peers. "I did no such thing. I knew it was a joke all along." He smiled, exposing his long, hollow fangs. "But I decided to turn the tables and play a joke on *you.*"

And then Zhrakkas expressed his feeling of good fellowship the way any Middirona would have—by hauling his meaty fist back and returning the captain's blow with twice the force.

Cobaryn saw it coming, but dared not try to get out of the way. Not if he wanted to hang onto the respect of the Middirona.

The First Axe turned out to be even stronger than he looked. His punch knocked the Rigelian backwards head over heels. The next thing he knew, Cobaryn was sprawled on the floor—and his shoulder hurt too much for him to even contemplate moving it.

Seeing him lying there, Zhrakkas got up and walked over to him. Then he pulled the captain to his feet.

"I like you," the Middirona said. "Your people and mine will be two blades of the same axe."

Trying not to wince at the pain in his shoulder, Cobaryn nodded. "I certainly hope so."

Connor Dane leaned back in his chair and studied the stars on the screen in front of him. They didn't look much different from any other stars he had seen, even if they constituted the part of space now known as the Romulan Neutral Zone.

Dane's eyes narrowed. "Let me get this straight."

"All right," said his science officer, a white-haired man named Hudlin. He was standing next to the captain with his arms folded across his chest, an expression of impatience on his wrinkled face.

"Our long-range scanners," Dane began, "have detected a wormhole out there in the Neutral Zone. And like any other wormhole, it's probably not going to be there for long."

"That's correct," Hudlin confirmed.

"But while it *is* there," said the captain, "you'd like the chance to study it at close range—even if it means entering the Neutral Zone, violating the treaty we just signed and risking another war."

The science officer frowned. "With all due respect, sir, we don't have to go very far into the Neutral Zone, and it's highly unlikely that the Romulans would notice us. As you're no doubt aware, the war served to thin out their fleet considerably."

True, Dane conceded. Of course, the same could be said of the Federation. "So you really don't think we'd get caught?"

"I really don't," said Hudlin.

The captain grunted. "I'll tell you what, pal—I think you're in luck. You see, between you and me and the bulkhead, I don't give a rat's fat patootie about this Romulan Neutral Zone everybody's so impressed with. On the other hand, I don't give a rat's fat patootie about your wormhole."

The science officer stared at him, clearly more than a little confused. "But you said I was in luck."

"You are. You want to get a little closer to that wormhole? Be my guest. Just don't get me involved, all right? I hate the idea of having to explain something like this to a court-martial."

And with that, Dane got up from his chair and headed for the turbolift. Naturally, he didn't get far before he heard from Hudlin again.

"Sir?" said the science officer, hurrying to catch up with his captain. He looked around at the other bridge personnel, who were looking on with undisguised curiosity. "Where are you going?" he asked.

Dane shrugged. "To my quarters. I figure I'll get a little shuteye. But don't worry—you've got all the leeway you need. Just try to bring the ship back in one piece, okay?"

Again he headed for the turbolift.

"No!" Hudlin exclaimed.

The captain looked back at him. "No?"

The science officer swallowed. "What I mean is . . . I can't command the ship. I'm only a science officer."

Dane feigned surprise. "Hang on a second, Mr. Hudlin. There's a wormhole out there just begging to be examined with short-range sensors—and you're going to let that kind of opportunity slip through your fingers? What kind of scientist are you?"

The man couldn't have looked more frustrated. "But I've had no tactical training. What if—"

The captain regarded him. "What if you run into some Romulans?" He allowed a note of irony to creep into his voice. "It's highly unlikely that they'd notice us, don't you think? Especially after the war thinned out their fleet so much."

The other man frowned. "There's no need to be abusive," he responded. And without another word, he retreated to his science station.

Dane returned to his center seat, where he was greeted again by the stars that filled the Neutral Zone. "There's no need to be abusive, *sir,*" he said under his breath.

* * *

Bryce Shumar was three weeks out of Earth orbit when he finally found what he was looking for.

The Tellarite vessel on his viewscreen was a collection of dark, forbidding spheres, some bigger than others. The deep creases between them served as housings for the spacecraft's shield projectors, weapons ports, scanner arrays, and audio-visual transmitters, while a quartet of small cylinders, which spilled golden plasma from unlikely locations among the spheres, provided the ship with its propulsion capabilities.

More to the point, the vessel was far from any of the established trade routes. And from the time it had picked up Shumar's ship on its long-range scanners, it had done its best to elude pursuit.

Unfortunately for the Tellarite, there wasn't a starfaring vessel in the galaxy that could outrun a Christopher 2000. It hadn't ever been a question of whether Shumar's craft would catch up with its prey; the only question had been *when*.

Mullen, Shumar's first officer, came to stand beside the captain's chair. "Interesting ship," he noted.

"Ugly ship," Shumar told him. "Probably the ugliest I've ever seen. And when you run an Earth base, you see all kinds."

The younger man looked at him, no doubt uncertain as to how to react to the remark. "I have to admit, sir, I'm no expert on esthetics."

"You don't have to be," said Shumar. "Some things are ugly by definition. That Tellarite is one of them."

"Weapons range," announced Wallace, the helm officer.

The captain leaned forward. "Raise deflector shields and route power to laser batteries."

Forward of his center seat, Morgan Kelly manipulated her tactical controls. "Aye, sir," came her reply.

Just like old times, thought Shumar. He turned to Klebanov, his navigator. "Hail the Tellarite, Lieutenant."

The woman went to work. A moment later, she looked up. "They're responding," she told the captain.

"On screen," he said.

Abruptly, the image of a porcine being with a bristling beard and a pronounced snout assaulted his viewscreen. "What is the meaning of this?" the Tellarite growled.

Shumar could tell the alien was covering something up. Tellarites weren't very good at duplicity.

"I'm Captain Shumar," he said, "of the starship *Peregrine*. I have reason to believe you're carrying stolen property."

"I'm Captain Broj of the trading ship *Prosperous*," the Tellarite answered, "and what I carry is my own business."

"Not so," the human pointed out. "It's also the business of the United Federation of Planets."

Broj's already tiny eyes screwed up even tinier. "The United *What?*" he grunted, his tone less than respectful.

"The United Federation of Planets," Shumar repeated patiently. "An organization of which your homeworld is a charter member."

"Never heard of it," said the Tellarite.

Another lie, the human reflected. "Nonetheless," he insisted, "I need to search your vessel. If you haven't got anything to hide, you'll be on your way in no time. If—"

"Sir," said Kelly, a distinct note of urgency in her voice, "they're building up laser power."

Shumar wasn't the least bit surprised. "Target their weapons ports and fire, Lieutenant."

Out in space, the *Peregrine* buried her electric-blue fangs in the other ship's laser banks. But Shumar didn't see that. What he saw was the wide-eyed apprehension on Broj's face as he anticipated the impact of Shumar's assault and realized that the human had beaten him to the punch.

Suddenly, the Tellarite flung his arms out and lurched out of sight, revealing two other Tellarites on a dark, cramped bridge. A console behind them erupted in a shower of sparks, eliciting curses from Broj's crewmen and a series of urgent off-screen commands.

When Broj returned, his eyes were red-rimmed and his nostrils were flaring with anger. "How dare you fire on a Tellarite ship!" he snorted.

"As I indicated," said Shumar, "I'm acting under Federation authority. Now, are you going to cooperate . . . or do I have to take out your shield generators as well?"

Broj's mouth twisted with indignation. For a fraction of a second, he looked capable of anything. Then he seemed to settle down and consider his options—and come to the conclusion that he had none.

"All right," the Tellarite agreed with a snarl. He glanced at someone off-screen. "Lower the shields."

Shumar nodded approvingly. "That's better." He got to his feet. "Lieutenant Kelly, you're with me. Mr. Mullen, you've got the center seat. Keep our weapons trained on the Tellarite—just in case."

As Kelly slaved her weapons functions to the navigation console, the captain headed for the turbolift. To his surprise, his first officer insinuated himself in Shumar's path.

"Yes?" the captain asked, wondering what the man wanted.

"Begging your pardon, sir," said Mullen in a low, deferential voice, "but Earth Command regs called for commanding officers to remain on their ships. Generally, it was their subordinates who led the boarding parties."

"Subordinates like *you*, I suppose?"

The exec nodded. "That's correct, sir."

Shumar smiled at him. "This isn't Earth Command, Mr. Mullen. Starfleet has no regulations against captains leading boarding parties—at least, none that I'm aware of. Besides, I like to get my hands dirty."

By then, Kelly was ready to depart. Shumar clapped his exec on the shoulder and moved past him, then opened the lift doors with a tap on the bulkhead padd and went inside. After Kelly joined him, he closed the doors again and the compartment began to move.

The weapons officer glanced at him sideways. "So tell me," she said, "when was the last time you had occasion to use a laser pistol, Captain I-Like-To-Get-My-Hands-Dirty?"

Shumar patted the weapon on his hip. "Never, Lieutenant. That's why I brought you along."

Look for STAR TREK fiction from Pocket Books

Star Trek®: The Original Series

Enterprise: The First Adventure • Vonda N. McIntyre
Final Frontier • Diane Carey
Strangers from the Sky • Margaret Wander Bonanno
Spock's World • Diane Duane
The Lost Years • J.M. Dillard
Probe • Margaret Wander Bonanno
Prime Directive • Judith and Garfield Reeves-Stevens
Best Destiny • Diane Carey
Shadows on the Sun • Michael Jan Friedman
Sarek • A.C. Crispin
Federation • Judith and Garfield Reeves-Stevens
Vulcan's Forge • Josepha Sherman & Susan Shwartz
Mission to Horatius • Mack Reynolds
Vulcan's Heart • Josepha Sherman & Susan Shwartz
Novelizations
Star Trek: The Motion Picture • Gene Roddenberry
Star Trek II: The Wrath of Khan • Vonda N. McIntyre
Star Trek III: The Search for Spock • Vonda N. McIntyre
Star Trek IV: The Voyage Home • Vonda N. McIntyre
Star Trek V: The Final Frontier • J.M. Dillard
Star Trek VI: The Undiscovered Country • J.M. Dillard
Star Trek Generations • J.M. Dillard
Starfleet Academy • Diane Carey
Star Trek books by William Shatner with Judith and Garfield
    Reeves-Stevens
The Ashes of Eden
The Return
Avenger
Star Trek: Odyssey (contains *The Ashes of Eden*, *The Return*, and
    Avenger)
Spectre
Dark Victory

#1 • *Star Trek: The Motion Picture* • Gene Roddenberry
#2 • *The Entropy Effect* • Vonda N. McIntyre
#3 • *The Klingon Gambit* • Robert E. Vardeman
#4 • *The Covenant of the Crown* • Howard Weinstein
#5 • *The Prometheus Design* • Sondra Marshak & Myrna Culbreath

#6 • *The Abode of Life* • Lee Correy

#7 • *Star Trek II: The Wrath of Khan* • Vonda N. McIntyre

#8 • *Black Fire* • Sonni Cooper

#9 • *Triangle* • Sondra Marshak & Myrna Culbreath

#10 • *Web of the Romulans* • M.S. Murdock

#11 • *Yesterday's Son* • A.C. Crispin

#12 • *Mutiny on the Enterprise* • Robert E. Vardeman

#13 • *The Wounded Sky* • Diane Duane

#14 • *The Trellisane Confrontation* • David Dvorkin

#15 • *Corona* • Greg Bear

#16 • *The Final Reflection* • John M. Ford

#17 • *Star Trek III: The Search for Spock* • Vonda N. McIntyre

#18 • *My Enemy, My Ally* • Diane Duane

#19 • *The Tears of the Singers* • Melinda Snodgrass

#20 • *The Vulcan Academy Murders* • Jean Lorrah

#21 • *Uhura's Song* • Janet Kagan

#22 • *Shadow Land* • Laurence Yep

#23 • *Ishmael* • Barbara Hambly

#24 • *Killing Time* • Della Van Hise

#25 • *Dwellers in the Crucible* • Margaret Wander Bonanno

#26 • *Pawns and Symbols* • Majiliss Larson

#27 • *Mindshadow* • J.M. Dillard

#28 • *Crisis on Centaurus* • Brad Ferguson

#29 • *Dreadnought!* • Diane Carey

#30 • *Demons* • J.M. Dillard

#31 • *Battlestations!* • Diane Carey

#32 • *Chain of Attack* • Gene DeWeese

#33 • *Deep Domain* • Howard Weinstein

#34 • *Dreams of the Raven* • Carmen Carter

#35 • *The Romulan Way* • Diane Duane & Peter Morwood

#36 • *How Much for Just the Planet?* • John M. Ford

#37 • *Bloodthirst* • J.M. Dillard

#38 • *The IDIC Epidemic* • Jean Lorrah

#39 • *Time for Yesterday* • A.C. Crispin

#40 • *Timetrap* • David Dvorkin

#41 • *The Three-Minute Universe* • Barbara Paul

#42 • *Memory Prime* • Judith and Garfield Reeves-Stevens

#43 • *The Final Nexus* • Gene DeWeese

#44 • *Vulcan's Glory* • D.C. Fontana

#45 • *Double, Double* • Michael Jan Friedman

#46 • *The Cry of the Onlies* • Judy Klass

#47 • *The Kobayashi Maru* • Julia Ecklar

#48 • *Rules of Engagement* • Peter Morwood
#49 • *The Pandora Principle* • Carolyn Clowes
#50 • *Doctor's Orders* • Diane Duane
#51 • *Unseen Enemy* • V.E. Mitchell
#52 • *Home Is the Hunter* • Dana Kramer Rolls
#53 • *Ghost-Walker* • Barbara Hambly
#54 • *A Flag Full of Stars* • Brad Ferguson
#55 • *Renegade* • Gene DeWeese
#56 • *Legacy* • Michael Jan Friedman
#57 • *The Rift* • Peter David
#58 • *Face of Fire* • Michael Jan Friedman
#59 • *The Disinherited* • Peter David
#60 • *Ice Trap* • L.A. Graf
#61 • *Sanctuary* • John Vornholt
#62 • *Death Count* • L.A. Graf
#63 • *Shell Game* • Melissa Crandall
#64 • *The Starship Trap* • Mel Gilden
#65 • *Windows on a Lost World* • V.E. Mitchell
#66 • *From the Depths* • Victor Milan
#67 • *The Great Starship Race* • Diane Carey
#68 • *Firestorm* • L.A. Graf
#69 • *The Patrian Transgression* • Simon Hawke
#70 • *Traitor Winds* • L.A. Graf
#71 • *Crossroad* • Barbara Hambly
#72 • *The Better Man* • Howard Weinstein
#73 • *Recovery* • J.M. Dillard
#74 • *The Fearful Summons* • Denny Martin Flynn
#75 • *First Frontier* • Diane Carey & Dr. James I. Kirkland
#76 • *The Captain's Daughter* • Peter David
#77 • *Twilight's End* • Jerry Oltion
#78 • *The Rings of Tautee* • Dean Wesley Smith & Kristine Kathryn Rusch
#79 • *Invasion!* #1: *First Strike* • Diane Carey
#80 • *The Joy Machine* • James Gunn
#81 • *Mudd in Your Eye* • Jerry Oltion
#82 • *Mind Meld* • John Vornholt
#83 • *Heart of the Sun* • Pamela Sargent & George Zebrowski
#84 • *Assignment: Eternity* • Greg Cox
#85-87 • *My Brother's Keeper* • Michael Jan Friedman
   #85 • *Republic*
   #86 • *Constitution*
   #87 • *Enterprise*
#88 • *Across the Universe* • Pamela Sargent & George Zebrowski

Star Trek: The Next Generation®

Metamorphosis • Jean Lorrah
Vendetta • Peter David
Reunion • Michael Jan Friedman
Imzadi • Peter David
The Devil's Heart • Carmen Carter
Dark Mirror • Diane Duane
Q-Squared • Peter David
Crossover • Michael Jan Friedman
Kahless • Michael Jan Friedman
Ship of the Line • Diane Carey
The Best and the Brightest • Susan Wright
Planet X • Michael Jan Friedman
Imzadi II: Triangle • Peter David
I, Q • Peter David & John de Lancie

Novelizations

Encounter at Farpoint • David Gerrold
Unification • Jeri Taylor
Relics • Michael Jan Friedman
Descent • Diane Carey
All Good Things... • Michael Jan Friedman
Star Trek: Klingon • Dean Wesley Smith & Kristine Kathryn Rusch
Star Trek Generations • J.M. Dillard
Star Trek: First Contact • J.M. Dillard
Star Trek: Insurrection • J.M. Dillard

#1 • *Ghost Ship* • Diane Carey
#2 • *The Peacekeepers* • Gene DeWeese
#3 • *The Children of Hamlin* • Carmen Carter
#4 • *Survivors* • Jean Lorrah
#5 • *Strike Zone* • Peter David
#6 • *Power Hungry* • Howard Weinstein
#7 • *Masks* • John Vornholt
#8 • *The Captain's Honor* • David and Daniel Dvorkin
#9 • *A Call to Darkness* • Michael Jan Friedman
#10 • *A Rock and a Hard Place* • Peter David
#11 • *Gulliver's Fugitives* • Keith Sharee
#12 • *Doomsday World* • David, Carter, Friedman & Greenberger
#13 • *The Eyes of the Beholders* • A.C. Crispin
#14 • *Exiles* • Howard Weinstein
#15 • *Fortune's Light* • Michael Jan Friedman

#16 • *Contamination* • John Vornholt
#17 • *Boogeymen* • Mel Gilden
#18 • *Q-in-Law* • Peter David
#19 • *Perchance to Dream* • Howard Weinstein
#20 • *Spartacus* • T.L. Mancour
#21 • *Chains of Command* • W.A. McCoy & E.L. Flood
#22 • *Imbalance* • V.E. Mitchell
#23 • *War Drums* • John Vornholt
#24 • *Nightshade* • Laurell K. Hamilton
#25 • *Grounded* • David Bischoff
#26 • *The Romulan Prize* • Simon Hawke
#27 • *Guises of the Mind* • Rebecca Neason
#28 • *Here There Be Dragons* • John Peel
#29 • *Sins of Commission* • Susan Wright
#30 • *Debtor's Planet* • W.R. Thompson
#31 • *Foreign Foes* • Dave Galanter & Greg Brodeur
#32 • *Requiem* • Michael Jan Friedman & Kevin Ryan
#33 • *Balance of Power* • Dafydd ab Hugh
#34 • *Blaze of Glory* • Simon Hawke
#35 • *The Romulan Stratagem* • Robert Greenberger
#36 • *Into the Nebula* • Gene DeWeese
#37 • *The Last Stand* • Brad Ferguson
#38 • *Dragon's Honor* • Kij Johnson & Greg Cox
#39 • *Rogue Saucer* • John Vornholt
#40 • *Possession* • J.M. Dillard & Kathleen O'Malley
#41 • *Invasion! #2: The Soldiers of Fear* • Dean Wesley Smith & Kristine
     Kathryn Rusch
#42 • *Infiltrator* • W.R. Thompson
#43 • *A Fury Scorned* • Pamela Sargent & George Zebrowski
#44 • *The Death of Princes* • John Peel
#45 • *Intellivore* • Diane Duane
#46 • *To Storm Heaven* • Esther Friesner
#47-49 • *The Q Continuum* • Greg Cox
    #47 • *Q-Space*
    #48 • *Q-Zone*
    #49 • *Q-Strike*
#50 • *Dyson Sphere* • Charles Pellegrino & George Zebrowski
#51-56 • *Double Helix*
    #51 • *Infection* • John Gregory Betancourt
    #52 • *Vectors* • Dean Wesley Smith & Kristine Kathryn Rusch
    #53 • *Red Sector* • Diane Carey
    #54 • *Quarantine* • John Vornholt

 #55 • *Double or Nothing* • Peter David
 #56 • *The First Virtue* • Michael Jan Friedman & Christie Golden
#57 • *The Forgotten War* • William Fortschen
#58-59 • *Gemworld* • John Vornholt
 #58 • *Gemworld #1*
 #59 • *Gemworld #2*

Star Trek: Deep Space Nine®

 Warped • K.W. Jeter
 Legends of the Ferengi • Ira Steven Behr & Robert Hewitt Wolfe
 The Lives of Dax • Marco Palmieri, ed.
Novelizations
 Emissary • J.M. Dillard
 The Search • Diane Carey
 The Way of the Warrior • Diane Carey
 Star Trek: Klingon • Dean Wesley Smith & Kristine Kathryn Rusch
 Trials and Tribble-ations • Diane Carey
 Far Beyond the Stars • Steve Barnes
 What You Leave Behind • Diane Carey

#1 • *Emissary* • J.M. Dillard
#2 • *The Siege* • Peter David
#3 • *Bloodletter* • K.W. Jeter
#4 • *The Big Game* • Sandy Schofield
#5 • *Fallen Heroes* • Dafydd ab Hugh
#6 • *Betrayal* • Lois Tilton
#7 • *Warchild* • Esther Friesner
#8 • *Antimatter* • John Vornholt
#9 • *Proud Helios* • Melissa Scott
#10 • *Valhalla* • Nathan Archer
#11 • *Devil in the Sky* • Greg Cox & John Gregory Betancourt
#12 • *The Laertian Gamble* • Robert Sheckley
#13 • *Station Rage* • Diane Carey
#14 • *The Long Night* • Dean Wesley Smith & Kristine Kathryn Rusch
#15 • *Objective: Bajor* • John Peel
#16 • *Invasion! #3: Time's Enemy* • L.A. Graf
#17 • *The Heart of the Warrior* • John Gregory Betancourt
#18 • *Saratoga* • Michael Jan Friedman
#19 • *The Tempest* • Susan Wright
#20 • *Wrath of the Prophets* • David, Friedman & Greenberger
#21 • *Trial by Error* • Mark Garland

#22 • *Vengeance* • Dafydd ab Hugh
#23 • *The 34th Rule* • Armin Shimerman & David R. George III
#24-26 • *Rebels* • Dafydd ab Hugh
   #24 • *The Conquered*
   #25 • *The Courageous*
   #26 • *The Liberated*

Star Trek: Voyager®

   Mosaic • Jeri Taylor
   Pathways • Jeri Taylor
   Captain Proton! • Dean Wesley Smith
Novelizations
   Caretaker • L.A. Graf
   Flashback • Diane Carey
   Day of Honor • Michael Jan Friedman
   Equinox • Diane Carey

#1 • *Caretaker* • L.A. Graf
#2 • *The Escape* • Dean Wesley Smith & Kristine Kathryn Rusch
#3 • *Ragnarok* • Nathan Archer
#4 • *Violations* • Susan Wright
#5 • *Incident at Arbuk* • John Gregory Betancourt
#6 • *The Murdered Sun* • Christie Golden
#7 • *Ghost of a Chance* • Mark A. Garland & Charles G. McGraw
#8 • *Cybersong* • S.N. Lewitt
#9 • *Invasion!* #4: *Final Fury* • Dafydd ab Hugh
#10 • *Bless the Beasts* • Karen Haber
#11 • *The Garden* • Melissa Scott
#12 • *Chrysalis* • David Niall Wilson
#13 • *The Black Shore* • Greg Cox
#14 • *Marooned* • Christie Golden
#15 • *Echoes* • Dean Wesley Smith, Kristine Kathryn Rusch &
   Nina Kiriki Hoffman
#16 • *Seven of Nine* • Christie Golden
#17 • *Death of a Neutron Star* • Eric Kotani
#18 • *Battle Lines* • Dave Galanter & Greg Brodeur

Star Trek®: New Frontier

New Frontier #1-4 Collector's Edition • Peter David
   #1 • *House of Cards* • Peter David

      #2 • *Into the Void* • Peter David

      #3 • *The Two-Front War* • Peter David

      #4 • *End Game* • Peter David

#5 • *Martyr* • Peter David

#6 • *Fire on High* • Peter David

The Captain's Table #5 • *Once Burned* • Peter David

Double Helix #5 • *Double or Nothing* • Peter David

#7 • *The Quiet Place* • Peter David

#8 • *Dark Allies* • Peter David

Star Trek®: Invasion!

#1 • *First Strike* • Diane Carey

#2 • *The Soldiers of Fear* • Dean Wesley Smith & Kristine Kathryn Rusch

#3 • *Time's Enemy* • L.A. Graf

#4 • *Final Fury* • Dafydd ab Hugh

Invasion! Omnibus • various

Star Trek®: Day of Honor

#1 • *Ancient Blood* • Diane Carey

#2 • *Armageddon Sky* • L.A. Graf

#3 • *Her Klingon Soul* • Michael Jan Friedman

#4 • *Treaty's Law* • Dean Wesley Smith & Kristine Kathryn Rusch

The Television Episode • Michael Jan Friedman

Day of Honor Omnibus • various

Star Trek®: The Captain's Table

#1 • *War Dragons* • L.A. Graf

#2 • *Dujonian's Hoard* • Michael Jan Friedman

#3 • *The Mist* • Dean Wesley Smith & Kristine Kathryn Rusch

#4 • *Fire Ship* • Diane Carey

#5 • *Once Burned* • Peter David

#6 • *Where Sea Meets Sky* • Jerry Oltion

Star Trek®: The Dominion War

#1 • *Behind Enemy Lines* • John Vornholt

#2 • *Call to Arms...* • Diane Carey

#3 • *Tunnel Through the Stars* • John Vornholt

#4 • *...Sacrifice of Angels* • Diane Carey

Star Trek® Books available in Trade Paperback

Omnibus Editions
    Invasion! Omnibus • various
    Day of Honor Omnibus • various
    Star Trek: Odyssey • William Shatner with Judith and Garfield
        Reeves-Stevens
Other Books
    Legends of the Ferengi • Ira Steven Behr & Robert Hewitt Wolfe
    Strange New Worlds, vol. I and II • Dean Wesley Smith, ed.
    Adventures in Time and Space • Mary Taylor
    The Lives of Dax • Marco Palmieri, ed.
    Captain Proton! • Dean Wesley Smith

STAR TREK
THE EXPERIENCE
LAS VEGAS HILTON

Be a part of the most exciting deep space adventure in the galaxy as you beam aboard the U.S.S. Enterprise. Explore the evolution of Star Trek® from television to movies in the "History of the Future Museum," the planet's largest collection of authentic Star Trek memorabilia. Then, visit distant galaxies on the "Voyage Through Space." This 22-minute action packed adventure will capture your senses with the latest in motion simulator technology. After your mission, shop in the Deep Space Nine Promenade and enjoy 24th Century cuisine in Quark's Bar & Restaurant.

- -